T0369093

ALSO BY JOSEPH W. MICHELS

Outbound From Virginia
[A novel]

Bicycle Dreams
[A novel]

Deck Passage
[A memoir]

CHURCH

A NOVEL BY JOSEPH W. MICHELS

iUniverse, Inc.
New York Bloomington

Church

Copyright © 2009 Joseph W. Michels

All rights reserved. No part of this book may be used or reproduced by any means, graphic, electronic, or mechanical, including photocopying, recording, taping or by any information storage retrieval system without the written permission of the publisher except in the case of brief quotations embodied in critical articles and reviews.

This is a work of fiction. All of the characters, names, incidents, organizations, and dialogue in this novel are either the products of the author's imagination or are used fictitiously.

Credit for cover art photo:
Copyright © Stockphoto.com/Alex Nikada

iUniverse books may be ordered through booksellers or by contacting:

iUniverse
1663 Liberty Drive
Bloomington, IN 47403
www.iuniverse.com
1-800-Authors (1-800-288-4677)

Because of the dynamic nature of the Internet, any Web addresses or links contained in this book may have changed since publication and may no longer be valid. The views expressed in this work are solely those of the author and do not necessarily reflect the views of the publisher, and the publisher hereby disclaims any responsibility for them.

ISBN: 978-1-4401-7969-3 (pbk)
ISBN: 978-1-4401-7970-9 (ebook)

Printed in the United States of America

iUniverse rev. date: 10/13/09

DAY 1

I FELT THE VIBRATOR of my cell phone just as I was coming about in twenty-three knots of wind. White caps were everywhere, and the strong thrust of the Wester punching through the gap bridged by the Golden Gate was heeling my thirty-six foot sloop right down to the gunnels. No time to retrieve the phone from the front pocket of my jeans. I had locked the wheel and my hands were busy winching in the starboard sheet of the jib. By the time I'd trimmed the sails and taken control of the helm the phone signal had stopped. Whoever it was would leave a voice mail or wouldn't. I didn't care. I was screaming across the bay at close to seven knots, the sky a flawless blue, with the warm sun taking the edge off the cold spray coming off the swells. It was a fine spring day and I wanted to enjoy it.

Single-handed sailing on San Francisco Bay when the wind's up always makes my adrenaline flow and today was no different. But there'd be no white-knuckle moments on board owing to the lady-like way the grand old sloop cut through chop and absorbed the energy of erratic gusts. She sported a heavy displacement hull, elegant lines, and a well-balanced sail plan. We knew she'd be perfect for the kind of sailing Jack and I liked just as soon as we spotted her in a marina over in Richmond. She'd been given the name *Eagle* by her original owner and we didn't have the heart to rename her. Maybe it was out of respect for the way he'd taken such good care of her over the years. Or maybe it was just a matter of tradition. It didn't matter.

Sausalito was off to port and I steered closer to shore to take in the view. It was like a transplanted Mediterranean village—full of colorful homes scampering up the steep hills with a busy shoreline filled with street traffic. The masts of hundreds of sailing yachts berthed at the town's many marinas completed the picture. I guess I'd always preferred the image of Sausalito from the water and plotted a course that would take me there whenever I was out on the bay.

Once passed Sausalito I swung away from the shore and ramped up speed. I now had a following wind and deployed the sails to take maximum advantage. It was approaching noon and a number of sailboats were just heading out toward the open waters I'd just left. At cross-purposes, we weaved between one another; carefully managing a wide berth but relishing the proximity of so many fully engaged sailors.

I headed for Raccoon Strait, between Tiburon and Angel Island, to take a break from the strong winds. Cruising along at a sedate four knots, I kicked on the autopilot and headed down the companionway into the cabin to retrieve a cold beer and whatever Chelsea had packed in the way of a lunch. After bringing the items back up to the cockpit I brought the vessel into the lee of Angel Island and settled back to eat as the boat skimmed silently across the still waters. She'd obviously gone to my favorite deli for take out. The sandwich was one of their large, overstuffed creations she knew I was crazy about. I washed it down with an ice-cold beer.

Leaving the protection of Angel Island, Eagle's sails suddenly encountered the full force of the bay's wind and she heeled over as she dug her hull into the swells. The wind was on my starboard beam as I headed for home. Home was a marina in China Basin, next to the new baseball stadium.

I started the engine and kicked on the autopilot just past the Oakland-Bay Bridge, setting a course that would keep Eagle headed up into the wind as I furled the jib and mainsail. Motoring quietly around the marina breakwater, I ran up the main channel until I came to my turnoff. Eagle slipped easily into her berth and I jumped down to secure the lines. I knew Jack would be taking her out later that afternoon so I didn't button her all up—just hosed the salt off her deck and secured the cabin entryway.

* * *

The top was down in my convertible and I slid easily into the soft leather driver's seat. Before starting the car, I pulled out my cell phone to activate the ring function. All of a sudden I remembered the call I'd received earlier and punched in the code for voice mail access. It was the first of several messages that had accumulated while I was sailing and certainly the most important. Guy Sanderson of Mutual Insurance Company, headquartered in

New York, had left a message to call me in connection with a possible contract.

Guy worked in the claims division, heading up the department dealing with the loss of personal articles, particularly the theft of fine art and jewelry. I was a free-lance recovery specialist and Guy and others like him were my meal ticket. I rang his office.

"This is William Church, out in San Francisco. May I speak with Guy Sanderson?"

After a short pause the receptionist put me through. "Church, thanks for getting back to me. The reason I called is I think I might have something that would interest you. Listen, rather than going over it on the phone why don't you meet up with my associate, Emily Parsons. She's in the Bay Area on a home inspection and is staying at a hotel near Market Street. She can fill you in."

"I'll give her a call, what's the number?"

He gave me the number and the name of the hotel.

"Thanks, I know the place. Talk to you later."

I slipped the phone back into my pocket, started up the engine and pulled out of the parking lot. I live in one of the new luxury condominium buildings south of Market, and it took me only minutes to navigate the handful of blocks. I'm one of those guys that think this city has some of the most courteous drivers anywhere and is blessed with an absence of congestion…at least most of the time. Accordingly, I drive everywhere—regardless of the distance. I suppose it might also be that I get a kick out of driving…especially a car that performs like my German sports car. Anyway, my faith in the city's drivers didn't fail me and I was soon parking the car in its designated slot under the building.

I took the elevator up to my floor, headed down the hall and opened the door to my unit.

Chelsea had arranged for a maid service to give the place a cleaning while I was out on the water, and it showed. Not that I'm a slob or anything but even for a guy as neat as myself there's a point that comes after a couple of weeks of daily living when the attentions of a cleaning crew are unmistakably called for.

Chelsea is kind of my personal assistant. She's a part-time member of the concierge staff downstairs who needs the flexibility of part-time employment in order to pursue her real passion— modern dance. She's in her mid-twenties, dances like an angel, and for a few extra bucks gives my logistical needs a little extra attention. It helps she's as sharp as a tack and unbelievably efficient.

I hopped into the shower to wash off all the salt spray, threw on some fresh jeans and a navy blue polo shirt and headed for the kitchen. In a one-bedroom condo there's not much to a kitchen—just a glorified alcove off the living room/dining area. But it still had its new-construction luster since I don't cook, and most of the women I date would prefer to be taken out to one of the finer restaurants in town than to come back here and throw on an apron. That isn't to say I don't eat here. I do. But it has to be something that comes out of the fridge and directly into a dish. I'll condescend to work the toaster, the coffee maker and the microwave. That's it. Bottom line: I can prepare breakfast and lunch in the apartment, but almost invariably take my dinner out. Not that any of it happens with any great regularity since I'm often traveling.

I poured myself the remainder of the orange juice I'd freshly squeezed early that morning and took the glass over to the coffee table in front of the couch. The condo had floor to ceiling windows overlooking the Oakland-Bay Bridge and a fair slice of the surrounding bay. I watched the traffic on the upper deck of the bridge while I drank the juice. Relaxed and refreshed, I put a call through to Emily's hotel.

It was mid-afternoon and Emily Parsons had just returned to her room. I caught her on the second or third ring. After I identified myself she confirmed Guy's message and asked me to meet her for dinner that evening at the hotel. She'd be in the bar/cocktail lounge at about half past six. I agreed.

That gave me a good three hours to kick back, get in some reading and maybe a nap.

* * *

I recognized her by the way she was sizing me up. I could see her mentally running down the list of identifying markers Guy had given her: tall, athletic, blond, early thirties, well-dressed…

"Miss Parsons?" I said, coming up to her.

"Why, yes. And you must be William Church. Won't you join me?"

"Thanks," I said, taking the opportunity to study her as I settled into an upholstered leather chair. She was a tall, slender brunette tastefully outfitted in a red pleated-jersey halter dress. Her hair was done up in a ponytail that accentuated her youth— must be in her late twenties, I imagined. She was a knockout!

"Welcome back, Mr. Church," said the bar attendant who'd been nearby setting up a recently vacated table. "The usual?"

"Yes, thanks, Lisa."

"My, you must come here often. Guy mentioned you don't operate out of an office but I took it to mean you use your residence. Didn't think I'd discover that your base of operations is the cocktail lounge of this hotel."

"Hardly, Miss Parsons, or may I call you Emily?"

"Please do."

"The fact is, Emily, I do work out of my apartment, but being a bit small and out of the way it's hardly suitable as a venue for a professional meeting. Besides, this is San Francisco. I would be remiss if I didn't support the city's restaurants in the line of duty."

"Of course. How foolish of me."

"But seriously, as you can see it's a pleasant and quite convenient setting."

She just smiled.

"So, Guy says you're out here on business," I said, trying to change the subject.

"Guy should know. He sent me here. We've a new client with several museum-quality paintings. He wanted me to make sure the security arrangements are up to the task of protecting properties of such value."

"And?"

"There's work to be done. I'll stick around for a few days to see how it's progressing."

"Here you are Mr. Church," said Lisa as she set down a cocktail napkin, "high-end martini...straight up with a lemon twist... shaken. And a few more of those nuts I know you like."

"Thanks, Lisa."

"Can I bring you anything?" Lisa asked Emily.

"I'll have what Mr. Church is drinking, Lisa."

"Very well, ma'am."

"Please call me William...or just Church," I said after the bar attendant had left to fill Emily's order.

"William sounds a little too intimate. I'll call you Church. How's that?"

"That'll be fine," I said, raising my glass in acknowledgement.

"So how'd you get into the art recovery line of business?" asked Lisa, settling back in her chair, her legs comfortably crossed and her hands clasped loosely on her lap.

I could sense this was no idle question by her rhythmic patting of one hand on the other—almost as if she was timing my response. Had she been sitting in an office chair I do believe she'd be rocking back and forth...gently...expectantly.

"You want the short answer or the long one?"

"I haven't had my martini yet and you've hardly touched yours. I'm guessing we've got enough time for the long answer. Don't you?" she added with a smile.

"Okay. But it's not particularly interesting. About a year after college I joined the FBI as a Special Agent. After I'd completed my training at the FBI Academy in Quantico I was assigned to the art theft program at national headquarters. You've got to keep in mind I'd been a philosophy major in college so I didn't have much of a background in the arts. But that didn't seem to matter. They trained us. So, over the next two and a half years I worked with members of the agency's art crime team. These were guys who were deployed regionally and functioned as a kind of strike force in handling art thefts."

"It sounds exciting. Why didn't you stay with it?"

"I couldn't hack the bureaucratic mindset of the place or the chain-of-command straightjacket. As soon as my initial three-year contract was up I split."

'There must have been something about the job that appealed to you. After all, Church, you're still in the same business."

"I have to admit there were aspects of the job I did like, especially the opportunity to work on criminal investigations. And being sent overseas to work with Interpol on international crimes will always rank high on my list of great times."

"So, what did you do next?" she asked, sipping the martini Lisa had just placed on the table.

"I headed to graduate school where I hoped to pick up a little deeper knowledge of art and archaeology."

"How'd that work out?"

"I guess it worked out all right. I earned a Master's degree in the university's interdisciplinary program in archaeology and art history but the experience convinced me an academic career was not what I wanted. I realized I needed more action than what professorial infighting would bring."

"You seem to keep ruling out things," said Emily.

"I'd prefer to call it zeroing in on one's special talent," I said.

"And what's that?"

"Returning stolen objects to their rightful owners."

"You mean art objects."

"Any objects. But since most thefts of sufficient value to justify my involvement are thefts of artwork or cultural artifacts that's what I mostly deal with."

"You mean like the matter I'm to fill you in on this evening?"

"Yeah. Listen, why don't we get out of here and head into the dining room; you can brief me on the theft while we eat?" I said as I placed my credit card on the table and signaled for Lisa to retrieve it.

"As you wish Mr. Church," said Emily with exaggerated formality.

I took her hand and helped her up.

"Don't we have to wait for your credit card to be processed?"

"Lisa will bring it to us in the dining room, no need to worry."

* * *

"Good evening Mr. Church," said the dining room hostess, "would you and your guest like a table next to the window?"

"Please," I replied, gently prompting Emily to follow the hostess by a slight touch to the small of her back.

"This room is lovely," said Emily once we were seated. "And the view! It seems all of San Francisco lies beneath us."

"It does seem that way doesn't it."

"I must say, Church," she said, turning back towards me, "your city has a very special charm."

"I suppose it won't surprise you if I say I share your opinion. Most of us who've settled here can't imagine living anywhere else. What about you? Have you always lived in New York?"

"No, Church, I haven't. I grew up in a small town in central Pennsylvania and went to a state school. Didn't land in New York until it was time to go for graduate work."

"Excuse me, sir, would you like to order now?" asked the waiter, who had approached after having given us time to examine the menu.

Emily chose the striped bass and I the New York strip steak. "Would you care for some wine?" I asked.

"Yes, please, that would be very nice."

"My preference would be to order a bottle of Cabernet Sauvignon…that is, of course, unless you're one of those people who insist on white wine with seafood?"

Emily smiled. "No. I'm not that fussy. I'm sure I'll enjoy whatever wine you select."

"Wonderful! Why don't you bring us a bottle of your signature Napa Valley cabernet…the one highlighted on your bar menu?"

"As you wish," said the waiter.

"You were saying?" I said to Emily once the waiter had withdrawn.

"About what?"

"About how you came to be in New York…about pursuing your studies in the city."

"That's it, Church. With a couple of degrees in economics under my belt I managed to get hired at Mutual Insurance…

in the underwriting department. Moved to claims about a year ago."

"So what did Guy see in you that persuaded him to pull you out of underwriting and into the grubby world of theft protection and crime analysis?"

"Maybe you'll figure it out after we've worked together on a couple of cases."

"Oh, are we going to be working together?"

"Guy wants me to accompany you back to Chicago."

"Why is that? Is it because I'm in need of your analytical powers of police work, or could it be that Guy wants you to learn at the feet of a master?"

"I'll let you try to figure that out, Mr. Church," said Emily with an ingratiating smile. "In the meantime, why don't we eat this splendid food before it gets cold."

* * *

"So what do we know about this theft?" I asked once our waiter had poured us our after-dinner coffee.

"The police are classifying it as a home invasion."

"Where?"

"In a prosperous suburb of north Chicago. It's a wealthy couple...he made his fortune in real estate I gather. The couple—both in their late 60's—were home, along with a live-in housekeeper. It seems a gang—the police think some sort of street gang—pushed open the front door once the housekeeper was tricked into opening it a crack and barged in."

"Do we know how she was tricked?"

"She says all she could see on the doorstep was a young girl."

"Any count on how many were involved?"

"They're a little confused about that. Based upon what the old couple and the housekeeper reported, the police estimate somewhere between five and seven."

"Did they supply the cops with any identifying clues—gang colors, street names, tattoos, anything?"

"I take it they were too frightened. Anyway, the intruders wore hooded sweatshirts and almost immediately herded the old couple and the housekeeper into a downstairs bathroom and told them to shut up."

"They didn't ask them where their valuables were stashed?"

"No. And they didn't even bother to attempt to disconnect the alarm system. They seemed to feel they'd be in and out before any responding patrol would arrive."

"But the alarm system must have been deactivated if the housekeeper opened the front door."

"Yes, but there was a separate alarm system that would be triggered if the paintings were lifted off their wall mounts."

"That's all they took…just paintings?"

"No, they ransacked the house before touching the paintings. Took off with some cash, silver, jewelry…you know, the typical crash and grab stuff."

"So they must have known the paintings would be protected by a security device."

"Either that or they were just plumb lucky."

"They must have known a wealthy couple like that would have a safe somewhere in the house. You telling me they didn't try to force the old man to show them where it was and then get him to open it?"

"Apparently not."

"This doesn't make a lot of sense," I said, puzzling over the apparent inconsistencies in the behavior of the intruders.

"That's what the cops think also. They're scratching their heads over this one."

"Unless, of course, this was a commissioned robbery—targeting the paintings—and the crash and grab operation was either meant to conceal the true objective or was simply an opportunistic add-on."

Emily just shrugged.

"Tell me about the paintings."

"It's a group of French Impressionist paintings of the late 19th and early 20th Centuries: a Bonnard café scene, a Boudin rural landscape, a Dufy seashore view, a Matisse beach scene, together with a Vuillard still life and a Renoir portrait."

"Were they stripped from their frames or taken in their frames?"

"The latter. They weren't large, Church...all six were in the two by three foot size range, and the frames might have added a few inches."

"Tell me about the frames. Were they modern or the antique kind with gold-gilded plaster over a wooden base?"

"Again, the latter. You trying to gauge their weight?"

"Yeah, and their fragility. Each would have needed to be handled carefully, not stacked. I'm thinking it would have taken at least three of the guys to bring out the paintings once they'd triggered the alarm."

"You thinking the size of the home invasion team might be connected to the number of paintings seized and the desire to take them in their frames?"

"It's a possibility. Were their any other museum-quality paintings or other fine art in the house?"

"There were—several large oils of considerable value, together with a fairly impressive collection of antique porcelain figurines."

"So the crew ignored those items…just stuck to the Impressionist collection and what they could grab and fence easily."

"That seems to be the case. What are you thinking, Church?"

"The street gang, if that's what they are, clearly felt more comfortable grabbing stuff they knew they could fence. Stealing the paintings probably wouldn't have occurred to them unless someone instructed them to. I've got to believe this was a commissioned job, Emily. Do you happen to know if these paintings were loaned out for exhibit anytime in the past several months?"

"That's the thing, Church, these people were careful not to loan their paintings out—even anonymously—for fear something like this could happen."

"That being the case, I'd say it narrows the list of likely perpetrators to serious collectors—collectors who are in a position to pick up rumors of who owns what from well-placed art dealers or auction houses."

"But those kind of people can't possibly rub shoulders with street gangs back in Chicago!"

"I'm sure you're right, Emily. That's why I've got to go to Chicago and attempt to locate the gang that pulled off the heist."

"Can you wait until I've finished with my job here? Guy did want me to accompany you."

"No problem. I'll do some checking around at a distance, so to speak. Day after tomorrow work for you?"

"I'll just have to make it work," said Emily, getting up from the table.

"Before you go upstairs to your room, tell me, what's your company's claims liability for the six paintings?"

"Guy says we've an exposure well into the millions."

I nodded, and followed her out of the dining room.

DAY 2

"GUY SANDERSON, PLEASE."

"Guy? It's Church. Listen, I met your associate, Emily Parsons, yesterday."

"Yeah, she's cute, but that's not why I called. What's this business about her tagging along on my investigation of the Chicago theft?"

"Don't sweat it, Church. She's new to the game and I thought it'd help her come up to speed. If she's in the way we'll pull her out. But give her a chance. She's pretty sharp. Did she fill you in regarding the details of the theft?"

"Yeah, she did…over dinner. Speaking of that, I take it I'm on full expenses, including picking up the tab whenever she and I incur joint expenses?"

"You mean like cocktails and fine dining?"

"You read my mind."

"Yeah, you're covered. Just charge everything to your credit card and forward me an annotated printout whenever you need a new infusion of cash."

"Will do. Talk to you later."

It was seven o'clock in the morning. I'd hung around until Guy could be reached at his office back in New York City but now I was free to head to Crissy Field for my morning run. Dressed in cotton shorts, a polo shirt and sweatshirt, with a good pair of running shoes on my feet, I headed out the door of my tiny flat. Unlike most people, I like to eat breakfast before a run. A good-sized bowl of cereal, a large glass of freshly squeezed orange juice and a slice of coffee cake generally does the trick.

I rolled out of the garage, the top down, and headed over to the Embarcadero. Traffic was still light at this hour and I made good time down the palm-lined avenue—past the Ferry Building, past Fishermen's Wharf and on to Bay Street. One of the local classical music stations was playing a nice Beethoven piano concerto. I turned up the volume and gave it my full attention. Bay curved around the grounds of Fort Mason and connected to Marina Boulevard. No fog obscured the bay, and with the sun low on the horizon the Golden Gate Bridge picked up brilliant highlights of reddish gold. But I had plenty of time to enjoy the bridge once I'd begun my run so as I drove along I let my attention be drawn to the string of marinas off to my right—each with an eye-catching collection of recreational boats, both sail and power.

I pulled into the parking lot of Crissy Field and parked. Crissy Field's been a lot of things during its history—a seasonal home of the Ohlone Indians, an anchorage for Spanish and Mexican ships, a World War I army airfield, a Coast Guard Station—but now it's a beautifully restored park and bird sanctuary with a fine running path parallel to the bay. Despite the early hour, dozens of runners, walkers and folks out to exercise their dogs gave the place a festive air. I pulled my sunglasses from the armrest compartment and slid out of the car. Starting with an easy jog, I headed west down the path—towards Fort Point at the base of the Golden Gate Bridge, a distance of about two miles. The air was crisp and clear, the tide in ebb phase. Shore birds hungrily searched freshly exposed tidal flats for food. About the time I'd gone a mile or so a large container ship passed under the bridge and into the bay. It was piled high with metal shipping containers— probably headed for the docks over in Oakland. I began to ramp up my speed.

The guys in a Bridge Security Patrol cruiser parked at the base of the bridge watched me as I ran through the Fort Point parking lot and over to the chain link fence where a wooden board with two hands painted on it was hanging. It's customary to touch the hands before turning and heading back—one of those quirky habits San Franciscans love to indulge in. The run back to the car offered a different kind of view. Instead of windswept headlands and the bridge one caught sight of the skyline of the city.

A westerly breeze had picked up, giving me an added push. The sun, still at a low angle, threw its glare directly into my face, forcing me to pull the bill of my baseball cap further down over my forehead. I was building up a fair amount of body heat now that I was three-quarters through my run. Without cutting my stride I pulled off the sweatshirt and bunched it up, gripping it in my left hand. Beads of sweat dried quickly as the wind cut through the thin material of the polo shirt. God, it felt good! I reached the car minutes later, jumped in and headed for the closest coffee bar.

* * *

I drove back downtown, intermittently sipping coffee and thinking about how my day was shaping up when the car radio switched from classical music to the ring of a telephone. The Bluetooth link between my cell phone and the car had just kicked in. I fingered the talk button on the steering wheel and called out: "Church here."

"Church, it's Chelsea."

"Hey, Chelsea, what's up?"

"Just wanted to touch base with you. You be needing me today?"

"Yeah. I'll need you to book two seats, first class, on a flight out of SFO midday tomorrow for Chicago…and get me a reservation at that hotel on the north side I usually use—make it an executive suite with two bedrooms."

"You got a new job?"

"Yeah, an art theft in the Chicago area…be working for Guy Sanderson on this one."

"Who's the mystery party?"

"A gal named Emily Parsons. Works for Guy."

"She cute?"

"Absolutely."

"So what do we have here—a second girl-Friday or a love interest?"

"Neither. Guy wants her to tag along to pick up pointers. She's new to the game."

"She know she'll be sharing a suite with you?"

"Not yet, but I'm a gentleman, right?"

"Right, Church. But you're still a man…and a very attractive one. You may be putting her in harms way."

"She's a big girl, Chelsea. Anyway, I've got loads of self-control."

"In some areas, sure, but when it comes to attractive women I wouldn't bet the house on your purported self-control!"

"Now, now, Chelsea, have a little faith."

"Okay, Church. I'll take care of the travel arrangements. Anything else?"

"Yeah, get me reservation at that restaurant I like—the one over on California Street. Make it for seven o'clock this evening… party of two. See if you can get my favorite table."

"Will do, but I'm telling you, Church, she might get the impression you're interest in her is not just professional."

"I'll risk it. Talk to you later." With that, I broke our connection.

By this time I was cruising down Howard Street heading for my gym. The gym was located in a non-descript two-story industrial building on Folsom, between Eighth and Ninth Streets. It took up all of the ground floor. Boris, the owner, had converted the second floor into a sculpture studio, with a small section set aside as a hideaway. The hideaway portion amounted to a bed, a bathroom alcove, and the transplanted remains of what was once a stainless steel kitchen from out of some greasy spoon joint. His actual residence was in Hayes Valley where he lived with his wife, Gloria. It was Boris whom I wanted to see. The workout could wait.

I parked in front of the gym. Unlike most of the city this part of town didn't attract a clientele with cars. Curb space was always available. I put the top up and locked the doors.

"Boris upstairs?" I asked the young trainer manning the reception desk.

"Yeah. There's a whole lot of banging going on so I guess he's doing his sculpture thing."

Boris was a middle-aged Russian Jew who'd immigrated to Israel after the collapse of the Soviet Union. He was quickly recruited by the Israeli Army and assigned to special ops. They wanted to capitalize on the formidable skills in personal combat he'd learned during an earlier stint in the Soviet military. About a half-dozen years ago he showed up in San Francisco, set up this mixed martial arts gym and began to pursue his real love: metal sculpture. But not ordinary, that is to say academic, sculpture. No. Boris loved to retrieve odd pieces of scrap metal from junkyards and cut, hammer, weld or forge them into abstract works of art. It seemed today was one of those days where hammering was to be the handmaiden of art.

"Hey, Boris!" I shouted as I reached the top of the stairs.

"Hey, Church!" he replied, putting down his hammer and removing his plastic face shield. "What's up?"

"You got a guy works out here…used to be connected in Chicago?"

"You mean, Jerry?"

"Yeah, that's the guy. He going to be in today?"

"Don't know for sure but it's likely. Why? What's your interest?"

"Need to get a line on a crew who've just committed a home invasion out in the northern suburbs of Chicago. Thought maybe he'd have some thoughts on the matter."

"Something tells me you've got a recovery job linked to that caper. Am I right?"

"Yeah. So tell me, what the hell are you making?" I said pointing to the rat's nest of copper belting he'd been pounding rivets in.

"Come on, Church, you know the symbol for the mathematical concept of infinity. These loops in the belt depict a three-dimensional expression of that concept...anyone can see it."

"If you say so, Boris. You going to hang it or will it simply lie in a corner somewhere accumulating dust?"

"It's a mobile, smart guy!"

"You making it on commission?"

"Naw, just something to keep the juices flowing."

"Well, when it's done let me take another look at it. Maybe I can find a place to hang it in my flat."

"You'd do that?"

"Boris, you're a buddy AND an artist. Why the hell wouldn't I?"

"Love ya, man!" said Boris as he wrapped his big arms around me.

"I'll let you get back to work," I said, breaking free and giving him a gentle punch to the shoulder. "Right now I need to get into a little action with some of your regulars downstairs."

"You do that," said Boris as he turned back to the bench on which the sculpture was lying.

I headed downstairs and over to the locker where I kept a pair of sweatpants. After removing my running shoes and putting the sweatpants on over my shorts I walked out onto the large cushioned mat at the center of the floor and called out: "Any of you ready to partner in some moves?"

"I'll join you," said a big beefy guy with a solid display of tattoos up and down his right arm.

"Great! Name's Church," I said, extending my arm to shake his hand.

"Name's Frank," he said, shaking my hand. "What's your pleasure?"

"Thought we'd practice takedowns to begin with," I said.

"Let's do it," he said as he executed a sudden sweep aimed at my legs, intending to catch me unawares.

I countered with a defensive move backward then pivoted and shot my right leg up to his chest. He was still off-balance from the sweep and collapsed under the force of my strike. I was on him instantly and put a lock on his upper torso until he signaled for a release.

"Christ, you're fast," he said, staggering to his feet.

"You're not so slow yourself," I replied with a smile. Why don't we run through a series of grappling maneuvers and submissions?"

"He nodded, still catching his breath."

"This time, let's pace ourselves, shall we?"

Frank and I went at it for close to an hour, testing each other on takedowns, strikes, escapes and reversals. We were about the same weight but I was a couple of inches taller. At six foot, four inches in height and two hundred and ten pounds in weight I often had difficulty finding martial arts partners my own size. Frank was the exception and worked out well as a partner, dirty tricks and all.

We were sitting on a bench just off the mat drinking bottled water when the guy Boris called 'Jerry' came through the front door. He sauntered over to the reception desk like he owned the place, smacking his hand down on the counter for emphasis as he made some sort of point in his conversation with the trainer, then laughed. The trainer pointed to me and Jerry turned his attention my way. I got up and walked over.

"Hear you want to talk to me," said Jerry, eyeing me curiously. Jerry was middle-aged and carrying a little extra weight but hard where it counted. He wore well-pressed gabardine slacks, a white sport shirt and black leather jacket. He ran a hand nervously through the thick but closely cropped hair on his head.

"Boris mentioned you might be in today," I said, smiling. "I'm William Church. Been wanting to ask you a few questions about Chicago."

"What makes you think I know anything about Chicago?"

"Humor me. I'm working on that home invasion heist north of the city. Cops seem to think it's the work of a street gang. You got any ideas who they might be?"

"Whoa there fella! You come on pretty strong. Who the hell are you?"

"I'm not a cop if that's what you're asking. I'm private...been retained by an insurance company to get back some of the items that were taken."

"Yeah, I read about it. Sounds like a bunch of jerks—you ask me."

"I need to get a handle on who those jerks might be. You got any ideas?"

"Why come to me? Hell, I haven't lived there in years."

"The word is you're connected. I figure a caper like that's bound to get tongues wagging. Thought you might be willing to share some gossip you might've heard from some of your Chicago pals."

"Help him out, Jerry," said Boris who'd just come down the stairs and seemed to have caught the tail end of our conversation.

"You know this guy?"

"He's a good friend...maybe even a patron of the arts, that is if he buys a piece of my work."

"You'd buy some of his crap?"

"Boris's got potential, Jerry, don't write him off."

"Christ! A regular Good Samaritan!

"Hey! You're disrespect'n me!" said Boris, putting an arm around Jerry's neck and theatrically waving a fist in his face.

"Hell, you're too thick-skinned to take notice," said Jerry. "Get the hell out of my face!"

"Okay. But you'd be smart to level with Church. He's a good friend to have."

"You mean he's got muscle as well as brains?"

"Yeah, you better believe it. Ask Frank over there. Hey, Frank! How'd Church do this morning?"

"He put me on my butt more times than I care to remember."

"Well, I don't hear much. The thinking is that these guys wouldn't have gone so far out of their hood unless they were in desperate need of serious cash."

"That make sense to you?" I asked.

"Yeah, it does…especially if they're in the drug trade big time."

"You thinking they've got a big buy coming down and were strapped for cash?"

"That's the only way I can figure it. Hell, these punks are generally happy with enough ready cash to eat, treat their women nice and get high. That kind of bread they can boost in the hood. No sense taking the risk of doing something stupid in a part of the city they don't know."

"So who d'you know's been pushing for a bigger slice of the drug market in the city?"

"Among the gangs? Hell, it could be any of them."

"Well, thanks, Jerry. You've been a help," I said, shaking his hand.

"I didn't tell you squat!"

"The drug buy angle is a good one. You led me there."

"If you say so…Boris, tell this joker to get lost so I can get a workout in."

"I'll be seeing you around, Jerry," I said as I headed to the locker area.

* * *

I drove back to my apartment very much in need of a shower and a fresh set of clothes. Chelsea was manning the concierge desk as I entered the lobby.

"Hey, Church, the airline and hotel reservations came through and I managed to get you a table for this evening."

"Great, Chelsea!" I said, walking over to the desk. "Listen, I don't know how long I'll be out of town on this new job. Take care of the place for me, Okay?"

"Will do. So, Church, you going to tell me a little more about this new woman in your life?"

"She's not 'a new woman in my life', Chelsea. She's an associate…just someone I'll be working with for a few days. But to assuage your curiosity here's what I know about her: she's in her late twenties, grew up in central Pennsylvania, finished her college work in New York, and to the best of my knowledge is unmarried."

"You forgot about the pretty part."

"Yeah, she's very pretty. You happy now?"

"It'll do for now but if it drags on for more than a few days I'll be after you for more details."

"A deal!" I said with a smile. Now let me go so I can clean up and head out."

"Where you off to?"

"Lunch with Jack, I hope, then over to the range for a little firing practice...which reminds me, give the range a call and reserve two lanes for right after lunch."

"Can do, boss," said Chelsea with a bright smile as she reached for the telephone.

I took the elevator up to my floor, thinking I need to get to Chelsea's next dance performance. Don't want her thinking I'm taking her for granted...especially now that she's ruminating about the so-called 'new woman in my life'.

The shower felt good after a morning of strenuous workouts. I toweled off, shaved, and applied a brush to the thick tousle of blond hair on my head, hoping to force it into a shape my hair stylist would recognize—one he'd worked hard to achieve. I pulled on a fresh pair of jeans, white sports shirt and a cotton navy blue blazer. Once I slipped on my black leather loafers I was ready to go.

I took the elevator down to the parking garage and jumped into my car. I raised the security grill on the entrance with the remote and accelerated into the street.

* * *

"Special Agent Barker here."

"Jack, it's Church. How'd the sail go yesterday?"

"Took it easy. Had a few novices with me. How was yours?"

"Memorable! Listen, I'm heading towards the Presidio. Any chance you can meet up with me for lunch...maybe get a little time in at the range afterwards?"

"Can do. See you at that joint near the gate…ETA twenty-five minutes."

That 'joint', as Jack referred to it, was one of my favorite watering holes. Located near the Lombard Gate of the Presidio, its dark interior decorated with framed old photographs commemorating special moments in the city's past, and serving up affordable drinks and excellent bar food, the place had a regular following most days of the week. I was part of the Sunday brunch crowd. But I'd stop in at other times as well if I was in the neighborhood…like today.

I found a slot at the curb about a half block from the entrance, parked and walked towards the entrance to the establishment. The tables out front were packed and one of the regular waitresses busing dishes waved as she saw me approach.

"You got a free table inside?" I asked.

"Yeah, Church. Grab whichever one you want."

"Hey, Sam!" I said, waving to the bartender as I made my way towards the larger seating area at the rear.

"Hey, Church. You going to have a martini?"

"Not today, Sam. I'll need to stick with coffee."

I headed for my favorite corner table and slid onto the upholstered banquette that ran along the wall.

"I'm waiting for Jack," I said to the waitress who'd come over with menus.

"Yeah, I thought as much when I saw him hurrying down the block."

"Bring us a couple of coffees, Alice…make mine decaf."

"You guys working today, huh?"

"Yeah, Alice, we are…and listen, I'll have the bar burger with everything on it."

"And I'll have the same, Alice," said Jack as he slid in behind the table.

"Hi, Mr. Barker," said Alice.

"What's up?" asked Jack once the waitress had left us alone.

"Got a new assignment. An art heist in a suburb north of Chicago."

"Yeah, I read something about it…seems it was some sort of home invasion."

"That's what the cops are going with. I think there's more to it than that."

"You think the gang will try to ransom the art?"

"Not likely. I doubt they even still have the art in their possession."

"What are you saying?"

"I think this street gang was commissioned to do the job. Hell, they were way off their turf…seemed more interested in what they could smash and grab. The art heist was the reason they were there but once inside their instincts had them searching the place for cash, jewelry, silver…stuff they could fence downtown."

"You don't think that was a ruse…something to confuse the cops?"

"Possibly, but I've a feeling they didn't really believe those paintings had all that much value despite what they'd been told. Wanted to make sure they left with something they knew they could convert to cash."

"You got a theory?"

"Word on the street in Chicago has it connected to a major drug buy. That's what I'm going with."

"Here are your burgers, gentlemen," said Alice, making room on the small table for the two large plates. "You want some more coffee?"

"Please, Alice. And some more water too."

"Will do!"

Conversation came to a halt as Jack and I gave our attention to the food.

"When you planning to head east?" asked Jack as we finished our coffee.

"Tomorrow."

"That why we're going to spend a little time on the firing range?"

"Well, you've got to get in some range time each month anyway and, yes, it won't hurt for me to be at the top of my game heading into the streets of Chicago."

"Don't you sometimes wish you still had Special Agent status… and all the backup us feds can supply?"

"Won't be surprised if I have exactly those thoughts when cornered in some dark alley a few days from now," I said with a laugh.

We left the restaurant and headed for our cars. The indoor firing range was located in one of the single-story warehouse buildings in the old hangar complex across from Crissy Field. I made it just moments before Jack pulled up in his government issued sedan.

"You call ahead for range time?" asked Jack as we walked towards the entrance.

"Yeah, they're expecting us."

The security guard at the door checked our federal concealed weapon permits and waved us through. We headed for the sales counter to check in and to purchase additional ammo and some paper targets. Before entering the range, we stopped to put on the ear and eye protectors handed us by a skinny guy in a t-shirt with the name of the range spelled out in bold black letters.

Upon entering the firing area the Range Master had us remove our weapon from its waistband holster, extract the magazine and lock open the slide action. Once he'd satisfied himself the weapons were cleared, in good operating condition and that the ammo we'd chosen to use was of the approved kind, he motioned for us to take lanes five and six.

"You want to push the targets the whole eighteen yards?" asked Jack as he reloaded his government-issue semi-automatic.

"Yeah, why not," I replied, checking the action on my 38-caliber piece. It was also a semi-automatic and held an eight-round clip.

After getting permission from the Range Master, Jack and I toggled the electric switch on our respective target frame and watched the frame advance towards us. We quickly attached head-and-torso paper targets to the frames and toggled the motor to take the frames out the full eighteen-yard distance from the firing line.

We worked through several clips at that distance then brought the targets closer for tactical firing. After running through our range ammo we cleared the weapons and headed for the gun-cleaning tables just off the hall from the range proper.

"You going to be in touch with your old buddies in the art theft squad at FBI headquarters?" asked Jack as he ran a wire brush through the barrel of his weapon.

"Only under duress, that I can assure you," I replied as I inserted my standard ammo into the clip.

"You may be out of your league on this one, Church, especially if it's drug related. It's not just some guy or couple of guys looking for an easy, non-confrontational and non-violent heist. This time, you're up against a street gang with lots of firepower. You'll need backup."

"I'll be careful. Besides, I've got the feeling all I'll need from the gang is some information. Don't think it'll come down to my having to strong arm a bunch of thugs into turning the paintings over to me."

"I hope you're right," said Jack with a sigh. "But don't be pigheaded, if it looks like you'll need a posse give your old buddies a call."

"I'd sooner put a call through to the Chicago Police Department. It's their turf after all."

"Whatever. Just don't get yourself in a fix you can't handle."

I gave Jack a pat on the back. "Love it when you act like we're married."

"Go to hell!" said Jack with a laugh.

With our weapons cleaned and operational and back in their respective waistband holsters we headed for the front counter to check out.

"You headed back to the office?" I asked as we walked to our cars.

"No. I've got a couple of people to see in connection with an investigation I'm running. Won't be back in the office until later. You?"

"Thought I'd head back to the apartment…pack, maybe catch some shuteye. Got a dinner engagement later on."

"Do I know her?"

"No. She's an associate of Sanderson. He asked me to let her tag along on this job."

"Pretty?"

"A knockout!"

"Lucky man!"

"Maybe. But her presence could really crimp my style. Don't relish having to look after her safety while trying to squeeze a bunch of street toughs."

"I see your point. Good luck in any case…talk to you later."

I watched as Jack drove off then headed for my car. I paused before climbing in, my mind going over the facts of the case that had prompted Jack's concerns. I was used to working alone…liked it that way. But this deal was way more unpredictable—possibly more violent—than what I was usually called in to handle. To hell with it! I thought. It'll be what it'll be!

* * *

As I headed back to my flat it occurred to me I hadn't touched base with Emily since early yesterday evening. Waiting for the light to turn green at Marina, I hurriedly pulled my cell phone from out of the breast pocket of my blazer and punched in the numbers to her mobile. Bluetooth kicked in and the radio on my dashboard lit up with the call. After several rings she picked up.

"Hello, Emily?"

"That you, Church?"

"Yeah. Wanted to check in with you…see if you're free this evening for dinner."

"Why? Are you asking me out on a date?"

"Let's just say we've got a lot to talk about in connection with our trip to Chicago and I'm guessing we're both in the mood for some good food served in a terrific setting."

"I take it you have some place in mind other than the usual suspects."

"That I do." I gave her the name of the restaurant. "You can look it up on the internet," I added.

"I'm still north of the city on that security job but I think I can wrap up my end of things by five o'clock this evening."

"That'd put you back at your hotel a little before six. Can you be ready to be picked up by quarter to seven?"

"Boy, Church, you don't give a girl much time to primp, do you!"

"When she's as beautiful as you I've got to figure there's not much need for primping. Am I right?"

"No you're not! But, yes, I can make it."

"Great! See you then."

I fingered the off switch to the car phone and smiled. She may turn out to be a real headache once we're in Chicago, I thought to myself, but right now she has the makings of a pleasant companion.

Still, if I were honest I'd have to admit I'm approaching this evening's affair with more in mind than just business. I'll have to watch out, this could get out of hand real fast!

I was almost at the end of Marina Boulevard and anticipated the right-turn on to Laguna for the connection to Bay Street. Gradually I worked my way over to the Embarcadero and, eventually, to that rapidly gentrifying neighborhood where my apartment complex was located.

Before going up to my flat I grabbed a tall decaf at the local coffee bar. Chelsea was nowhere to be seen as I entered the lobby so I headed directly for the elevators. It was late afternoon: too early for business types to be heading back and too late for the home-based crowd to be running errands, leaving me in the solitary possession of the elevator as I hit the floor button. I sipped the coffee as the elevator made its ascent, thinking how I'd spend the next couple of hours. There was a good novel, only half read, lying on the coffee table and an extensive music library on my computer. Both prospects suited my mood.

* * *

"I like it," I said, taking in the black knit turtleneck dress Emily had on.

"You don't think it's too dressy?"

"Not at all. This is San Francisco; we dress as we please. Anyway, the dress suits you perfectly…brings out the east coast glamour in you."

"Now you're teasing me!"

"No, not at all," I hastened to assure her as we took the elevator down from the hotel lobby to where my car was parked.

"Well, you look very sharp yourself," she said, smiling.

I nodded in acknowledgement of her compliment. I had on black jeans and a well-tailored tweed sports jacket over a black cotton shirt.

"You want the top up?" I asked as I opened the passenger side door for her.

"If you wouldn't mind. I'd hate to have the first item on the menu be the brushing out of windblown hair."

"Gotcha."

Once the top was secured, I rolled out of the hotel turnaround and headed for California Street. "I take it you finished up that assignment you'd come out here to handle."

"Enough of it I suppose. Probably could have justified spending a few more days on it but with you dragging me off to Chicago in the morning there wasn't much chance for that."

"You could stay here for a while longer and catch up with me in Chicago a little later…"

"Not on your life, Church! You don't get rid of me that easily."

"Didn't think so," I said, laughing.

"So what's the story about tomorrow?"

"Our flight leaves around noon. I'll pick you up in a limo at ten o'clock. Be out at the hotel's turnaround."

"This'll be a non-stop flight I hope."

"Non-stop and first class."

"My, you're lavish with the company's money, aren't you?"

"All for a good cause—keeping you happy and in a good mood."

"Is that what you told Guy? That's terrible!"

"Just a joke, relax."

"And what arrangements have you made for us in Chicago… dare I ask?"

"I've booked the two of us into a suite at a high-end hotel."

"You've done what? Aren't you taking just a few too many liberties?"

"Please, give me the benefit of the doubt. The suite comes with two bedrooms, each with its own bath. You'll be as safe as novitiate in a remote nunnery. I'm really a perfect gentleman… despite appearances to the contrary."

"I'll bet!" she said, looking out the window as we sped down the street.

I pulled up in front of the restaurant and handed the car over to the valet. "Truce, Okay? No more arguing," I said as I put my arm around her waist and gave her a squeeze. "Let's just enjoy our meal and talk of inconsequential things…all right?"

"All right…but can we at least talk about what you plan to do when we get to Chicago?"

"Only if you promise not to turn the conversation into an argument."

"How can I promise that? What if I find your proposed actions to be unacceptable…maybe even illegal?"

"See, that's why I think we should hold off that discussion until we reach Chicago…let tonight be just a time for us to be a couple out on a romantic evening."

"You're teasing me again."

"You won't think so once you've tasted the wine and sampled the cuisine."

* * *

Two hours later we left the restaurant and waited outside for the valet to bring around the car. The evening was clear and the air a balmy fifty-five degrees. I had my arm around Emily. She looked up at me and smiled.

"You were right, Church, the place didn't lend itself to shop talk. God! The artwork in there…and the interior design! I can see why you like it so much."

"So you've no complaints about the food either?"

"You know I don't."

"Here it is," I said as the valet brought the car to a halt right in front of us. As I helped her into the car she pointed to the convertible roof and gestured for me to put it down.

"You sure?" I asked, once I'd slipped into the driver's seat.

"This is my last night in San Francisco and I want to savor it, especially after that great meal."

"Okay," I said, triggering the mechanism that retracted the top.

"But you mustn't go too fast. There are lots of glorious Victorian houses to admire and a full moon overhead. I don't want to miss anything."

"As you wish."

I drove leisurely down Bush Street, offering her brief glances of some of the more distinctive neighborhoods of the city. The evening was still young and pedestrians filled the sidewalks.

"I could get used to this," she said, stretching and stifling a yawn.

"You talking about me or the city?"

"The city, silly. Though I have to say you've proven to be an adept host."

"Glad to be of service," I said with a smile.

A half an hour later I pulled into the turnaround in front of the hotel. I waved off the attendants and turned to Emily. "Look, I know it's customary to invite myself in for a nightcap at the bar upstairs, or at least offer such a prospect, but tomorrow's a busy day and I'd just as soon head straight home. You mind?"

"Of course not. I've got packing to do and some phone calls to make. But it's been a lovely evening, Church."

"Good." I signaled to the attendant who opened the passenger door and helped Emily out. "Tomorrow, ten o'clock on the dot!"

She nodded, smiling, and headed towards the open doors of the reception area.

DAY 3

OUR FLIGHT TOOK OFF on time, around noon of the following day. Emily had the window seat while I managed to stretch out comfortably on the aisle. Little was said about the previous evening. Emily seemed intent upon reestablishing the more formal, business-like relationship we'd started off with. As for myself, I welcomed the opportunity it provided me to concentrate on the business at hand, namely how to make contact with members of the street gang who had pulled off the art theft.

There seemed to be a few options. The most obvious was to try and persuade the Chicago Police to share with me their thoughts as to who might be involved. Or better yet, locate a newspaper reporter working the story who might already have been given a lead by a police insider. Maybe I should have Boris get Jerry to supply me with a name of one of his connections—see if the scuttlebutt around town can point me in the right direction. And of course there was always the direct approach—hitting the streets and chatting up the kids hanging out...see if something materializes. None of these approaches were likely to succeed with Emily hanging on my arm. I would need to find something for her to do—to keep her busy enough that tagging along with me wasn't a real option. With this thought in mind I turned to her.

"Listen, Emily, you've got special expertise on home security. Why don't you take the lead in checking out the scene of the crime, following up with the police...maybe undertaking further interviews with the victims if you think it helpful?"

"And what would you be doing while I was so engaged, pray tell?"

"I thought I'd check around a bit—maybe get a line on the street gang."

"You know something you're not telling me."

"Not really. I've got a source who tells me the word out on the street has it that the break-in was most likely connected to a big drug buy—the gang needing serious cash. I thought I'd check it out."

"You mean a ransom angle?"

"Not likely. If it were, your office would have been contacted by now...or the victims would have been given that message. No, more than likely the gang had a buyer in mind before they even went in."

"That doesn't make sense. How would a street gang know anything about moving stolen paintings...or casing out a mansion miles out of their neighborhood?"

"Both good questions, and why I think it would be helpful for you to pursue those questions with the police and with the victims."

"You've got some other theory in mind, don't you?"

"You remember my suggesting to you this might have been a commissioned job…during dinner that first evening."

"Yes."

"What if we're dealing with an intermediary—a criminal outfit that persuades a local street gang to consider getting into the drug trade in a big way, offers to bankroll the buy in exchange for the gang's assistance in getting their hands on the paintings in question."

"Isn't that pretty far-fetched? Why wouldn't your so-called intermediaries just do the heist themselves…you know, a quiet break-in when the house was unoccupied, or when the old couple was asleep? Hell, they could have saved whatever money they'd promised to the gang. No, Church, it doesn't fly as a theory. It makes more sense to consider the art theft just a last minute grab after rifling the house for more easily fenced goods."

"All good points, Emily, and why I think we should be checking out these more obvious scenarios. Maybe it wasn't a street gang after all, or maybe—as you say—it was a gang but the art theft component was not initially on the agenda."

"And that's my job—to work these angles?"

"Somebody's got to do it and you're now part of the team."

"So let's get back to what you'll be doing, Church."

"As I said, I'll be checking out the least plausible theory."

"The drug angle?"

"Yeah."

"And you're not about to tell me how you'll proceed in your investigation, are you?"

"Frankly, Emily, I don't know. I've got a few options but until I'm on the ground and have had little time to make a few enquiries I couldn't honestly tell you."

"Sure," she muttered, snapping open the magazine she'd put aside earlier and reinserting the earphones of her audio player, making it clear the conversation was over.

The remainder of the flight was passed in silence, my thoughts taken up with the best way to gain a connection to the gang.

* * *

It was early evening by the time we reached the hotel. Chicago weather didn't seem much different from that of San Francisco, at least today: somewhere in the low 50's I imagined. It was cloudy but there was no sign of rain. And the wind off the lake seemed about the same as the wind off the Pacific that kicks up around late afternoon. A bellhop collected our luggage and pointed us in the direction of the reception desk.

"Your room is ready Mr. Church," said the young woman handling registration as she handed me the key cards. "Have a pleasant stay."

"We're on one of the higher floors," I murmured to Emily as we followed the bellhop to the elevators. "Wait! You go ahead. I've got to stop off and pick up a couple of the Chicago newspapers. I won't be more than a minute," I added, handing her one of the card keys, together with the little key envelope on which our room number was listed.

"You sure? We can wait," said Emily.

"It's all right. You go ahead—the bellhop is waiting."

"Here, give him this," I said, handing her a ten dollar bill.

She pocketed the bill and hurried after the bellhop, who'd continued on towards the elevators.

I headed for the hotel gift shop where I hoped to find a few remaining papers despite the lateness of the day. Several of the racks were empty but there were still a few copies of the leading metropolitan papers. I collected a copy of each and paid the cashier. By the time I reached our room Emily had taken care of the bellhop—who passed me in the hall—and was checking out the suite.

"It's gorgeous!" she said to me as I followed her into the second bedroom, "but don't you think it's rather extravagant?"

"It's what we need," I said, coming up alongside her as she looked down on the city from the large bedroom window.

"We wouldn't need even half the amount of space if we were in a relationship," she teased.

"Is that a proposition?" I asked.

"Certainly not! Just an observation."

"Well, why don't you choose which of the two bedrooms you'd prefer? I'll take the other."

"This one will do nicely," she said, turning and facing the room. "Would you be sweet and bring in my luggage?"

"By all means, Miss Parsons," I said, bowing slightly.

By the time I'd retrieved her luggage and brought it into the bedroom she was in the bathroom with the door shut. "I think it's best we book a table for dinner in the hotel's restaurant," I shouted through the door. "How much time do you need?"

"I want to grab a quick shower," she said through the door. "Give me an hour."

"Will do!"

I called down to the hotel dining room and made a reservation for 7:30, then collected my luggage and carried it into the second bedroom. I decided to grab a shower as well. A half hour later, I put on my black double-knit sports jacket, gray slacks, a white shirt and suitable tie. Emily was still not out of her room yet so I took a seat in the central parlor area of the suite and began to scan the newspapers.

The metro section of the first paper had a brief 'breaking news' story about a major drug bust on the Westside. There weren't too many details but the thrust of the story was that the cops had been tipped off about a drug buy and had caught several members of a local street gang taking possession of a large shipment of illegal drugs. The suppliers were alleged to be an out of state outfit with ties to the Caribbean area. Further details were to be announced soon, according to a police department spokeswoman.

The story grabbed my attention. I put down the newspaper, got up from the chair and absently walked over to the window, speculating on what the drug bust might mean to the case.

"Okay, I'm ready," said Emily as she walked briskly into the parlor area wearing the same black knit turtleneck dress she wore at the restaurant the previous evening.

"You look lovely," I said, turning away from the window.

"Thank you. But I really do need to pick up a few outfits, especially if we're anticipating a long stay here in Chicago. Are we?"

"Can't say. But anything you buy will be in the line of duty... at least that'll be my claim when I submit my expenses to Guy."

"What a guy! So, let's go."

We left the suite and took the elevator to the hotel's restaurant. Once we were seated I brought up the topic of the newspaper article.

"You think this might be the same gang that pulled off the home invasion?"

"There's a good chance. Anyway, that's an angle maybe you can work when you contact the police."

"Okay, but it'll have to wait until I've done a bit of shopping."

I smiled. There was none of that resistance to being shunted into routine investigative work she'd exhibited earlier in the day. Picking up the tab (albeit indirectly) for a few outfits was proving to be a good investment—whether Guy would concur or not. We settled into our evening meal, letting the strains of air travel dissipate as we shared a fine bottle of Napa Cabernet and explored the restaurant's imaginative menu options.

Two hours later, we returned to the suite. There was some awkwardness at first as we danced around the question of whether we should share a nightcap from the courtesy bar before retiring to our respective bedrooms. The presence of two small bottles of brandy in the small fridge decided the issue. Emily collected two brandy snifters from the shelf holding an assortment of glassware and placed them on the coffee table. I brought over the bottles and opened them.

"You're going to hit the streets, aren't you?" she asked as she sat down on the comfortable couch, tucking her legs under her.

"Yes, Emily, I am," I replied, handing her a snifter.

"And you don't want me along, isn't that true?"

"You've got important things to do and, yes, it's better you not accompany me."

"You think I'll be in the way…maybe even spook a possible informant who'd not relish having any witness around—seeing him talking with you."

"You make my case wonderfully. But there's also the matter of your personal safety."

She smiled. "Don't worry, Church, I'm just teasing. All I wanted was a straight answer and you gave it. You will take care, William, won't you?"

The concern reflected in her expression moved me, as did her use of my first name. I leaned over and kissed her lightly on the lips. She interrogated me with her eyes once we drew apart, questioning my intentions…and possibly her own.

I thought it best to bring the matter to a close. "Well, I'm off to bed," I said, emptying my glass with one final swallow and getting up from the couch.

"Good night then," she said, continuing to remain seated and still toying with her drink.

I gave her a final wave and opened the door to my bedroom, closing it once I was inside. Some minutes later, as I went about the task of preparing for bed, I heard the door to her bedroom open and close as well.

As I lay in bed I began to review the day's events, particularly that final bit of drama over snifters of brandy. I wasn't sure where we were going in this relationship but it seemed clear we best put it on a shelf until after the job was done. But I was only one-half of the equation—how Emily was going to play it remained to be seen.

DAY 4

I ROLLED OUT OF bed at 6:00 AM the following morning, called room service and ordered breakfast for two for 8:00 AM, pulled on a pair of black workout pants and matching polo shirt and headed for the hotel gym.

When I returned forty minutes later there was still no sign of movement in the other bedroom. I knocked on her door and shouted "breakfast will be here in a little over one hour, rise and shine!" I smiled when I heard a muffled epithet and headed for the shower.

I caught the weather report as I dressed. It was to be another San Francisco kind of day: breezy, cool, somewhat overcast but no rain. I pulled on a pair of blue jeans, a dark blue canvas shirt, running shoes, and a hooded sweatshirt long enough to conceal the gun holstered at my waist.

A knock on the door signaled the arrival of breakfast. I opened it and ushered in a kitchen attendant who rolled in a breakfast cart. He laid everything out on the dining table—located off to the edge of the living room area—and left. I was just in the process of pouring Emily a cup of coffee when she opened her bedroom door and walked sleepily into the room. She had slipped into a hotel robe to cover her nightgown but otherwise one could see she was fresh from a deep sleep.

"God! Church! You running a boot camp or something?" she said, stifling a yawn.

"Good morning to you too," I said cheerfully. "Here's some coffee," I added as I handed her the cup.

"Why do we have to be we up so early?" she asked after taking a sip.

"We don't. It's just the way I like to begin the day."

"Well, tomorrow morning just order breakfast for yourself. What did you order by the way?"

"I didn't know how hungry you'd be so I ordered juice, eggs, bacon and toast, but also a basket of breakfast rolls, bagels and Danish pastries."

"All I need is some toast and jam, a little juice and lots of coffee," she said, sitting down at the table and picking up a cloth napkin.

"I'll keep that in mind," I said with a smile, returning my attention to the eggs and bacon.

"So, where are you off to?" she asked as she applied strawberry preserve onto a piece of whole wheat toast.

"I need to pick up a rental car…do a little reconnoitering."

"When will I see you?"

"Let's meet up for cocktails…say about 5:30?"

She nodded affirmatively and turned her attention to the morning newspaper that had been left at the door to our suite.

During a quick visit to my bedroom/bath unit to freshen up I grabbed a baseball cap from my luggage and headed out.

"Please be careful, Church," she said, putting aside the newspaper.

"Always am," I replied, blowing her a kiss.

* * *

I headed down Ogden Avenue until I reached Roosevelt Road, then turned right and began to cruise, systematically checking out the streets of two of the three neighborhoods on the Westside rumored to be a possible location of the bust, at least as speculated upon by the guy who wrote the newspaper article. It was still early and I really didn't think I'd run into a lot of young men loitering in front of small neighborhood mom and pop stores or lounging on front porches. I just wanted to get a feel for the neighborhoods.

There seemed to me to be an unrelenting sameness about the area: a lot of two and three-story brick town houses positioned right up against the sidewalk, a few trees, a scattering of empty lots, and a fair number of cars parked along the curb. It was definitely a residential area but one lacking the well-cared-for appearance of Westside neighborhoods further to the north.

It was getting close to noon and no obvious gang hangouts had yet caught my attention. I began to think that whichever gangs were operating in the area probably advertised themselves in the form of a duded up car filled with young men cruising slowly through their respective territory. I didn't imagine I'd run into any until sometime that evening. I'd have to come back, I thought as I headed back to the Near Northside for lunch.

I handed the rental car off to a valet at the hotel and went up to the suite. I'd need to change into something a little more elegant if I planned on enjoying some Paella and a good Priorat wine at that highly regarded Spanish restaurant one block from the hotel I'd been reading about in one of those glossy city magazines left casually in the suite.

The suite had already been attended to, with the beds freshly made, the bathrooms cleaned and all signs of our early morning breakfast removed. I went into the bedroom and stripped off the street outfit, replacing it with charcoal slacks, a white sport shirt and a lightweight blue blazer. I put my gun with its holster into the room safe and locked it. As I was finishing up, I could hear the door to the suite opening. I stepped out of the bathroom and glanced through the open door into the central parlor area. It was Emily, laden with department store bags.

"Oh! You're back," she said, catching sight of me.

"Just returned, and just about to head out to a nearby Spanish restaurant for lunch. Have you eaten?"

"Goodness sakes, no! I've been shopping nonstop ever since the stores opened."

"Will you join me?"

"Let me get these things unwrapped and hung up first. Can you wait a minute?"

"Take your time. It looks like the shopping expedition was a success."

"I found three new outfits and a pair of shoes," she called out from her bedroom. "Don't have a fit when you see the bill."

"All I'll do is pass it on to Guy…let him have the fit."

"Thanks a lot."

"Don't worry, I'll attach it to all the other items being expensed during our stay in Chicago…with a note explaining the critical role you've played in the investigation."

"You're teasing again."

"Perhaps just a little…but all in good fun," I replied loudly, taking a seat on the couch.

"Give me a few more minutes…I want to freshen up."

"No problem."

While I waited for Emily I gave some thought to the tasks I'd set for her—checking out the scene of the crime, interviewing the victims and getting up to speed on the police investigation. No reason I shouldn't come along with her now that I had the afternoon and early evening free. The more I thought about it the more I liked the idea.

"Okay, I'm ready," she said as she appeared at the door to her bedroom wearing a nicely cut light wool blazer in black with matching boot-cut trousers.

"That's quite a classic look," I said, admiringly.

"You like it? It's one of the outfits I bought this morning."

"Very much!"

"I also bought another outfit for serious work—a black sleeve-jacket, with a white knit top and a gray pencil skirt."

"And for play?"

"I thought you'd never ask. For the evening, I bought a gorgeous sequined short-sleeved top in a blend of cashmere and silk together with a pair of elegant black slacks…also a pair of shoes tailor-made for the outfit."

"I can't wait to see it…but our next evening out will have to be put off until tomorrow at the earliest I'm afraid."

"What are you up to, Church?"

"I've got to hit the streets this evening…see if I can't shake loose some information on the identity of the street gang."

"Perhaps my work this afternoon will make that unnecessary."

"Perhaps, particularly since I've decided to accompany you on your rounds."

"But I still retain the lead in any inquiries, right?"

"Right. Now let's go have some lunch. I'm starving."

We left the suite and headed for the elevator.

"I take it we're going out to the victim's house straight from the restaurant," said Emily as we waited.

"Not exactly, we'll need to come back here first to pick up the car."

The elevator arrived and brought us swiftly down to the lobby. We walked out the main entrance and turned left. The restaurant was just down the block. It was a starkly modern, upscale kind of place, with lots of leather and chrome and large mirrors behind the bar. Only the flamenco music whispering quietly out discreetly placed loudspeakers gave a hint at the ethnic signature of the owner's culinary pretensions. We were shown to a lushly upholstered banquette and handed menus together with the wine list.

As I'd hoped, several excellent Priorat wines were listed. I selected one and asked the waiter to bring it around straight away.

"What kind of wine is that?" she asked once the waiter had left.

"It's a delicious blended red…mostly Grenache, but with Carignan and Cabernet Sauvignon as well. I'm sure you'll like it."

"I'm sure I will," she said absently as she turned her attention to the menu.

"Listen, Emily, I've got a favor to ask you."

"What's that?"

"I really have my heart set on having a traditional Spanish Paella. It's basically a rice dish but laden with chicken, sausage, and all sorts of shellfish. The trouble is the restaurant prefers to prepare it for no less than two persons—given the lengthy preparation and cooking time involved. So do you think you'd be okay sharing such an entrée?"

"How well does it go with the wine?" she asked in a teasing manner.

"Great!" The wine comes from the Catalonia Region of Spain—it's a match made in heaven!"

"So, how could I refuse?"

"You're an angel!" I said, taking her hand and giving it a squeeze.

The waiter returned with the wine and poured each of us a glass. When I told him of our choice he seemed delighted but warned it would be close to a half hour before our food arrived. I thanked him for the information but indicated it would not be a problem.

The time passed swiftly as I gave her a rundown on my morning cruise through the streets of the Westside while she in turn offered up a blow-by-blow of her search for outfits among the many boutique-like enclaves of the city's department stores.

"It looks marvelous!" exclaimed Emily as the waiter placed the plate of steaming Paella in front of her.

"Taste it, then take a sip of the wine. You'll see what I mean about a match made in heaven."

"Mmm! It is good!" she said. "I have to say, Church, hanging around you has its advantages. You do enjoy living well!"

"Let's hope Guy doesn't view it as an extravagance…and I suppose the best way to guarantee that is to make some progress on the case. So, my lovely young lady, once we've finished this marvelous food let's make haste on our appointed rounds."

"By all means, Sir William, but let us tarry a while on the task at hand."

* * *

We drove north on Lake Shore Drive, heading for a wealthy neighborhood some eight or so miles from the hotel. The wind coming off the lake gently buffeted the car, forcing me to give all my attention to the handling of the vehicle. Emily, seated beside me, had her head turned towards the lake. She seemed absorbed by the view: as far as one could see whitecaps dusted the surface of the wind-whipped water, and periodically dramatic eruptions of spray could be glimpsed—triggered by the collision of surging water against some immovable barrier. We turned left on to Ridge Avenue at the upper end of Lake Shore Drive and worked our way through the neighborhoods north of Edgewater.

"I think we must be getting close," said Emily as she took note of the up-scale homes coming into view. "According to the map we'll probably want to turn at one of the next intersections. We may have to jockey around a bit since the house might be on a one way street."

"Got it," I said, reducing my speed and positioning myself for a turn.

The intersection came up fast and I made the turn. We were in a neighborhood dominated by stately homes set back from the road. Emily monitored the house numbers as we cruised slowly up the street, motioning for me to pull over when she spotted the house. It was a grand structure in red brick with a fully covered front porch running the entire length of the building. Large French windows facing the street bracketed the elaborate front doorway. Brick columns supported the porch and a peaked roof crowned the two-story building.

I parked the car and came around to open the side door for Emily. We stood there for a moment getting our bearings. The house was set back a good distance and perched on a gentle rise. Freshly manicured lawns enveloped the house, along with stately, old growth trees.

"There's got to be an alley out back that provides access to the garage and to the rear entrance," I said. "We'll check it out later. Let's go in."

A red brick walkway extended from the sidewalk to the porch, with a set of stairs compensating for the rise, and another set of stairs, this time of wood, leading up to the porch.

"It's your show," I said as we reached the porch.

Emily nodded and pushed the doorbell.

The door was opened by a middle-aged woman whom I took to be the housekeeper. She was an Hispanic woman of short stature dressed in a white tailored shirt and black trousers.

"I'm Emily Parsons of the Mutual Insurance Company," said Emily, "and this is Mr. William Church, my associate. "We're here in connection with the home invasion that took place recently. I believe your employers are expecting us."

"Yes, they are expecting you. Please come in," said the housekeeper, opening the door wide enough for us to gain entry.

She led us to a large living room off to the right of the entrance hall. "I will call them. Please make yourself comfortable."

I settled into an armchair while Emily prowled the room, examining the large paintings on either side of the fireplace as well as the many small decorative pieces of table art distributed strategically on all available surfaces.

I could hear voices coming from the hallway and a moment later the housekeeper was back, along with a rather overweight couple in their sixties who were dressed casually. She had on a pair of shapeless gray trousers and a loose-fitting navy blue blouse. On her feet she wore a pair of house slippers. The man had on a pair of blue jeans and a white dress shirt open at the collar with the sleeves rolled up, British style. On his feet he wore a pair of gray athletic shoes.

"You'll have to forgive us, we're not accustomed to visitors, especially this time of day," said the lady of the house. "But of course you're not visitors, really, rather more like contractors or some other sort of professionals. But do sit down won't you?"

"Thank you," said Emily, taking a seat on the small straight-back chair located at the far end of the coffee table. "I'm Emily Parsons of the Mutual Insurance Company and this is my associate, Mr. William Church. As I mentioned on the phone, we're here in connection with the art theft."

"Yes, I remember. How can we help you?"

"Well, if you wouldn't mind we'd like to have you go over the events of that evening one more time."

"Where would like us to begin? I'm sure everything we could tell you should be in the police report."

"Yes, I'm familiar with the report but it's always helpful to hear the facts directly. Perhaps if your housekeeper wouldn't mind we might begin with her account of what transpired at the front door...at the start of the whole affair."

"It was rather late...at least for this household...around eight o'clock in the evening when I heard the front door bell ring. As you may have noticed, there are large clear glass windows on either side of the door so I could look out without having to unlock the door. I turned the front porch light on and peered out. Standing there all by herself was a slightly built young girl— she couldn't have been more than twelve or thirteen. She wasn't dressed shabbily but then again she wasn't wearing the kind of clothes one generally sees kids wearing in this part of town. I called out to her, asking her what she wanted. She didn't reply, just kept standing there...looking a little dejected. I didn't know what to do but felt compelled to do something. The missus and her husband were already upstairs and I didn't want to trouble them so I turned off the exterior alarm system and unlocked the front door. Before I had a chance to ask her once more what she wanted I was pushed aside and a bunch of young men rushed into the front hallway. They'd apparently been hiding up against the front of the house but far enough away from the doorway windows to avoid detection. Anyway, the girl herself never came in. I didn't see her again.

"What happened after that?" I asked.

"Well, it's hard for me to say. They demanded I tell them who else was in the house and where, then shoved me into the guest bathroom and told me not to make a sound."

"Did you attempt to call out, or seek to escape...maybe through the bathroom window?" asked Emily.

"Heavens no! One of them remained with me...just stood there staring at me. I was so frightened I didn't know what to do.

"Could you describe him or any of the others?" I asked.

"They were young men, I could see that, but all of them wore hooded sweatshirts and gloves. I couldn't make out anything special about them—not even what race they were, though if I had to guess I suppose they were blacks or Hispanics."

"What about the way they talked, did you detect an accent or anything special about their form of expression?" I asked.

"They talked street slang, that I could hear, but I was too nervous to pay any attention. I just wanted them to go away and to not hurt me."

"Perhaps you might pick up the story madam. Were you and your husband at all aware of what was going on downstairs?" asked Emily.

"Gracious no! Arnold and I were just about to change into our bedclothes when the bedroom door crashed open and a bunch of hooded thugs barged into the room."

"What happen next?" I asked.

"One of them rushed over and hit Arnold in the face. Arnold tried to defend himself but one of the others kicked him in the stomach and he fell. Then the two of them helped Arnold up and marched him out of the room."

"Did they ask your husband anything…like whether he had a gun or if there was a safe in the house?"

"They didn't ask me a goddamned thing!" said Arnold. "Just dragged me down the stairs and pushed me into the bathroom where they were holding Marina."

"Did one of them continue to remain in the bathroom… keeping an eye on the two of you?" I asked.

"Yeah, and this one had a gun…made sure we saw it. I heard my wife scream but couldn't do anything…not with that gun in my face."

"What happened next?" asked Emily, directing her question to the woman of the house.

"They didn't hurt me or anything…just told me to shut up—threatened to kill my husband if I didn't."

"Did they ask you any questions…about your jewelry or about any cash kept in the house?"

"No, nothing like that…just forced me to come downstairs where they put me into the guest bathroom along with Marina and my husband."

"How many of these guys were left in your bedroom after the two of them had taken your husband downstairs?" I asked.

"Just the two that made me shut up and who escorted me downstairs."

"So we've accounted for five men. As you went down the stairs—either of you—did you happen to notice any other men standing about?" I asked.

"I can't say for sure, but there might have been another guy standing next to the front door…the porch light was out and all I saw were shadows."

"What about the men themselves? Could either of you offer the police any identifying descriptions?"

"They were all hooded like Marina said and everything happened so fast," said Arnold. "And once we were stuffed into the bathroom the guy with the gun made it clear he would shoot if any of us tried anything stupid. After a few minutes he backed out the door, pointing the gun at us as he did so, then shut the door, leaving us all alone. We never laid eyes on any of them again."

"So I gather the answer is no, none of you could give the police any helpful identifications—is that right?" asked Emily.

"Some were dark skinned, some were lighter skinned. They didn't talk much, and what they said to one another was in some sort of street slang that none of us understood. We didn't see any hair, faces were in the shadow of the hoods they wore and all had on gloves. So, yeah, we can't give you anything to go on...wish we could," said Arnold.

"What happened next," I asked.

"Well, we could hear them rummaging through the house looking for things, sometimes a couple of them would walk past...like they were heading for the front door—probably taking things out to their car," said the wife.

"Any idea how long they were in the house?" I asked.

"Hell, it seemed forever!" said Arnold.

"Marina, here, reports that the girl rang the front doorbell at about eight o'clock. Did any of you happen to check the time when you finally figured out the men were gone?" asked Emily.

"It was about eight-thirty, I think," said the housekeeper.

"But we didn't actually leave the bathroom until the police showed up," said Arnold.

"How did they happen to arrive...was it because of the alarms on the paintings?" I asked.

"That's what they said. They estimated they were at the front door—which was slightly ajar—within ten minutes of the security company's phone call to them," said Arnold.

"So the whole thing lasted somewhere between twenty minutes and a half an hour...that right?" I asked.

"That would be our sense of it," said Arnold.

"And when you had time to look around and assess your losses what did you find?" asked Emily.

"The place was a real mess!" said Arnold. "They did a real number on our bedroom and on my study…took the cash I had in my desk and my wife's jewelry."

"And my silver…don't forget that, Arnold!"

"But the real loss were the paintings," said Arnold. "It took us years to put together that set of French Impressionist masterpieces…they were kind of the centerpiece of our collection. You've got to get them back for us."

"We'll certainly make every effort to," I said. "Can you tell us where, precisely, in the house they were located?"

"Let me show you," said his wife as she got up from the sofa and walked towards a pair of French doors at the back of the room. Emily and I got up and followed her, with Arnold and the housekeeper bringing up the rear.

She opened wide both doors revealing a room almost as large as the room we were in. "Originally this was the dining room—and still serves that purpose from time to time—but in recent years we've been using it principally as an art gallery. As you can see, the walls are mostly bare. All six of the stolen paintings were hung in this room."

The fastening hooks that once held the paintings were still in place, as were remnants of the wiring that used to be attached to alarm sensors mounted at the back of each frame. They revealed a pleasingly symmetrical layout: a painting on each side of the large fireplace and two paintings on each of the two end walls of the rectangularly shaped room. The wall opposite the one where the fireplace was located still contained two quite large Nineteenth Century oils. The center of the room was taken up by a large mahogany dining table, but the chairs had been set up against the walls—leaving the table accessible as a surface upon which a number of reference books on art had been placed. Several stunning porcelain figurines sat on the fireplace mantel.

"They don't seem to have trashed this room or the living room," observed Emily.

"Probably didn't think we'd have anything of value—leastwise what they thought of as valuable—in these rooms," said Arnold.

"They did take the silver from the buffet over there," said his wife, pointing to a heavyset and highly ornamented piece of furniture just to the left of the French doors, "but not a piece of our porcelain collection was taken or maliciously damaged."

"I think we've seen enough," said Emily quietly, "why don't we return to the living room. Perhaps we can all sit down. Mr. Church and I have only a few more questions if that's all right, then we'll be on our way."

Emily led us back into the living room and prompted us to take a seat. She went back to the straight-back chair she'd sat on originally. I returned to the same chair I'd been in earlier and the couple took their place on the sofa. The housekeeper remained standing.

"What we need your help on is the question of what motivated this gang to choose your home for the break in," said Emily, looking directly at the owners of the house.

"Heavens! I certainly don't know," said the lady of the house. "The police seemed equally in the dark."

"Let's assume for the moment that the answer to the question raised by Miss Parsons is that they were after the paintings," I said. "It's a reasonable assumption given the extraordinary value of the six paintings—particularly as a set—compared with the aggregate value of all the other items taken from the house, wouldn't you agree?"

"That can't be," protested the husband, "nobody even knew we had those paintings. They were never loaned out for exhibition and we seldom had guests over, and then only our very closest friends. How in the devil would a bunch of thugs off the streets of Chicago manage to secure such information…and why would they want to?"

"Precisely, so let's forget the gang for a moment and concentrate on the question of how it could have become known that you and your wife possessed such valuable art?"

"From whom did you buy them?" asked Emily.

"They came under auction over the years…and at different auction houses—all perfectly respectable," said the wife.

"Did either of you personally do the bidding or did you engage an agent to represent you?" I asked.

"Hell no! We wouldn't dream of doing the bidding ourselves— that's a job for professionals. We always used one or another of the agents affiliated with the firm of Knightwood & Stone," said Arnold.

"And where are they based?" asked Emily.

"Why…in New York City…on Madison Avenue, near east Forty-Ninth Street. You don't suppose they would've been behind it, do you?"

"We're just trying to get a picture of who might have had special knowledge of your art collection…and perhaps some appreciation for how much it would be worth in today's market," said Emily, trying to calm him down.

"Once the six paintings were in your possession did you have an occasion to have any of them—or their frames—restored or cleaned?" I asked.

"From time to time we would have a restorer come to the house to examine the paintings…see if any of them needed attending to," said Arnold. "I think in all this time only two frames and one painting required work. They were all in excellent condition when we took possession of them. Paintings of this caliber are not left to deteriorate by their owners, I can assure you."

"I'm sure you're right," said Emily, "but you must admit it does provide a third party an opportunity to become acquainted with your collection."

"Ernst Betteldorf is a kind and trusted old man! He came to us with the highest professional and personal references. Indeed, most serious collectors here in the Chicago area use him…or wish they could," said the wife.

"I take it from what you've just said that on occasion you or your husband do socialize with other serious art collectors here in the Chicago area. In that context would it have been possible— perhaps inadvertently—for you to have mentioned the fact that you and your husband were in possession of one or more of the paintings belonging to the set that has now been stolen?" I asked.

"Yes, of course. In fact, that's how it came to be that on occasion we would be asked by one or another of the area's art museums to loan them paintings, especially when the theme was French Impressionism—but we never agreed. None or our paintings have been publicly exhibited…at least not while we've owned them."

"But would you say that none of your collector acquaintances, or the museum curators who approached you, had a firm idea about the full identity of the six paintings: the artists involved, the themes, the techniques used?"

"Yes, I believe I can say that with full assurance. We were careful to talk of our paintings in only the most general terms. Certainly, we mentioned the names of various artists and alluded to the fact our collection contained landscapes, portraits and such, but not in any detail or in a way that would permit one to deduce the specific identity of any one of the paintings."

"And your housekeeper, could she have shared information regarding the art collection with any of her acquaintances?" asked Emily, looking directly at the woman standing off to the side of the couch.

"I most certainly did not!" said the housekeeper, not giving Arnold or his wife time to reply. "I have few acquaintances and none who would have any interest in the furnishings of the house of my employers."

"But you must have been aware of the extraordinary value your employers attached to these paintings and the other art objects scattered around the house—after all, you were familiar with the elaborate electronic security systems protecting the house were you not?" inquired Emily softly.

"Indeed I was," said the housekeeper. "But of what possible interest would such things be to people in my circle—most of whom are employed in other wealthy homes…homes most likely also secured by elaborate electronic systems. As for my sisters, believe me when I say our conversations are for the most part taken up with family matters or with the mundane things of everyday life."

"Yes of course," said Arnold's wife, "the idea is absolutely ludicrous! Marina has been with us for years and in all that time we have never had a reason to question her honesty or her discretion."

"That's very reassuring," said Emily. "I apologize if my questions seemed to insinuate any suspicion on my part regarding Marina's integrity. They were simply meant to explore all logical possibilities regarding the source of the information the criminals put to use so effectively."

"Well, this has been most helpful," I said as I got up from the chair. "Unless Miss Parsons has further questions I imagine we might bring this part of our enquiry to a close and leave you good people to attend to more important matters."

"I only have one final question which perhaps might be impossible for any of you to answer with any degree of confidence but I'll ask it anyway: 'Is it your sense the getaway vehicle was parked out front, or would you be inclined to believe it was hidden in the back alley?"

"I imagine you're interested in knowing the likelihood of one of our neighbors or a passerby noticing what was going on," said Arnold.

"Yes, that's precisely what I'm driving at," said Emily.

"The only thing I sensed was movement towards the front door," said the housekeeper. "I don't think any of us could have heard them using the rear entrance—locked up in the guest bathroom the way we were."

"They could've had two vehicles—one out front and one in the alley; using the one in the alley to transport their loot," said Arnold.

"Or none out front," said his wife. "We just don't know…and the police did say they checked with our neighbors and none of them reported seeing anything."

"Well, we'll check out back on our way out and see if there's any indication they might have used the rear entrance," I said, signaling to Emily to hasten our departure.

"You think there's a chance we'll get our paintings back?" asked Arnold as he walked us to the front door.

"The insurance company must think so," replied Emily. "Otherwise it would not have engaged Mr. Church. He's a highly regarded art recovery specialist."

"Oh, I see," said Arnold, turning towards me.

We made our goodbyes and walked to the car.

"Are we really going to check out the alley behind the house?" asked Emily as I opened the passenger-side door for her.

"Might as well. I'm curious whether their information on the residence was thorough enough to include the concealment potential of parking in the alley."

I pulled out into traffic but took a quick right turn at the next intersection. The alley was not well marked and heavy tree growth along the side street prevented one from spotting the entrance until the very last moment. I slowed down and turned in. The alley was narrow but appeared well maintained. It was lined with garages, utility areas where refuse containers were kept, and fenced-in backyards accessible by latched gates.

"There's the house," said Emily, pointing to a white stucco structure with a large screened-in porch facing the backyard.

I rolled to a stop at what I imagined would have been the place the gang parked their car if they'd chosen this option for concealment. The detached garage was flush to the street so I pulled as close as I could to the recessed utility area, allowing me to get halfway off the street. Cars could easily have passed through the alley even with me parked there, though having a car parked here sometime after dark might have seemed suspicious to nearby neighbors heading down the alley towards their garages. We sat there with the engine idling for some minutes, imagining various scenarios the night of the break-in.

"Let's get out and approach the house through the back gate," I said. "See if it's an easy access point."

The gate's latch was not padlocked and the gate swung open easily, with no noticeable screech from rusty hinges. A cement walkway led from the gate to the rear porch, with a spur leading off to the side door of the garage. The walkway cut across the back lawn and was unencumbered by close vegetation, making the movement of people and goods to the garage or to the alley uneventful except for the distance involved—it being a good hundred feet or so by my reckoning. We walked the distance and approached the rear porch.

"It doesn't matter if the porch was locked," said Emily. "We know they entered through the front door. The only question is how difficult would it have been to maneuver around the side of the house and climb on to the front porch without making too much of a racket."

"Let's find out," I said, stepping off the walkway and heading for the shrubbery off to my right. The house had a relatively square footprint and the lot was broad as well as deep, allowing for sufficient landscaping space to permit a narrow strip of side lawn to link the front lawn with the back. I circled wide of the shrubbery hugging the house and kept to the lawn. Emily followed. Once we'd reached the front of the house we had two choices: we could access the front porch by the front steps or we could work our way through the shrubbery and climb up and over the low fencing at the side of the porch.

"I'm betting the girl approached from the front steps and the guys climbed over the side," said Emily.

I nodded in agreement and signaled for her to follow me back to the car.

"Christ! The yards of these old houses are sure full of big trees and overgrown shrubs. You could sunbathe naked out here and no one would even know," said Emily once we'd climbed back into the car.

"Just what I was thinking; concealment is good, access is easy. The only worry would have been some inquisitive neighbor troubled by the sight of an unfamiliar car parked part way into the alley. But I'm thinking it was late enough commuters would already have arrived home, and those stepping out for the evening would not have returned yet."

"So you're going with the idea the gang parked out back, not in the street out front?" asked Emily.

"Yeah, which give credence to the theory the gang had plenty of advance information on the layout of the house—that someone set this up pretty professionally and just recruited the gang to pull off the job."

"So where to now?" asked Emily.

"Let's head over to the local precinct station…let you exercise your charm and flaunt your good looks in pursuit of whatever new they've come up with regarding the home invasion."

"But not fill them in on our thinking I take it?"

"You've got it!"

* * *

The station was on Clark Street, not far from where we were located. I drove down one of the connecting streets and turned right on to Clark. The precinct station was some distance to the south. You couldn't miss it: a large modern red brick monolith on the corner of Clark and Schreiber. We pulled into the parking lot at the rear of the building and went in. We followed directions to the detective division office and announced ourselves to the person at the desk just inside the reception area.

"You want to see Detective Jablonski. He's heading up the home invasion case," we were told.

"Is he here?" asked Emily.

"Yeah, just a minute, I'll get him."

It took a little more than a minute but eventually a tall, angular-looking guy in his forties walked up to us. "You the folks covering the insurance investigation of the home invasion that occurred in our precinct?"

"Yes. I'm Emily Parsons of the Mutual Insurance Company and this is Mr. William Church, a special consultant retained by the claims department to assist us in our enquiries."

"Well, how can I be of help," he said somewhat skeptically.

"I've read the original police report that was faxed to our claims department last week and was wondering what additional progress has been made on the case."

"You came all the way to Chicago to get an update?"

"No, of course not, Detective Jablonski, Mr. Church and I are here to interview the victims and to examine the premises. We've just come from the residence, and since your office was nearby I felt it only proper to introduce myself and my colleague and to volunteer our services should that prove helpful."

"Appreciate the offer but we've got all the expertise we need now that we're hooked up with the FBI's art crime team."

"Yes, they're an extremely competent outfit—one we often depend upon to assist in the recovery of missing art—but does that mean you're treating this as an art theft burglary rather than a simple home invasion?"

"I didn't say that. We're still treating it as a home invasion, but since some valuable artworks were taken along with other stuff we wanted to put the word out through the FBI to galleries, auction houses, and private collectors that might be approached locally by these kids…or to fences—get them to know the heat is on."

"Any line on which gang was responsible?" I asked.

"Not yet. The bitch of it is we've no reliable descriptions of the perps…that housekeeper and the old couple are nearly worthless as witnesses, and the guys who pulled the thing off didn't leave any clues. We've got the word out and are following up leads, but in a case like this all sorts of crackpot citizens call in with one theory or another—keeps us hopping but doesn't get us very far."

"But surely the local gang network in this part of the city must be fairly put out by this brazen intrusion on to their turf," said Emily. "Are they being helpful?"

"Hell no! Soon as they figure out who did the deed they'll do a drive-by shooting over in that gang's hood—pop off a few as a lesson to stay the hell away from this neighborhood."

"So your best bet is to locate some of the loot once it's been fenced and follow the trail back to the sellers?"

"That's about it. But that'll take time. These guys—if they're smart—will hold on to the easily identifiable stuff for a while."

"And you think included in the stuff they'll hold on to are the paintings?"

"That'd be my guess. So I don't think either you or the FBI will come up with anything solid on the artwork for a while yet."

"Why do you think they took those paintings?"

"Beats the hell out of me; they'll be a bitch to unload. The only thing I've come around to believing is that the crash and grab booty wasn't as much as they'd hoped for and just grabbed the smaller paintings at the last minute to top off their take."

"Well, you've been very patient with us, Detective Jablonski. We'll not take up anymore of your time. But please, if there's anything the Mutual Insurance Company's claim division can do that you think might be helpful to you in your investigation don't hesitate to contact us," said Emily handing the detective her card.

Jablonski grunted in acknowledgement and pocketed her card then opened the door to the outer hall and escorted us out.

* * *

I headed down Schreiber and turned left on to Ravenswood Avenue, staying on it until it merged with Ridge. In minutes we were back on Lake Shore Drive.

"Are we going to talk about it?" She asked.

"Absolutely," I replied, "but first, let's get to the hotel and settle into a couple of those comfortable chairs I noticed in the bar off the lobby. I'm in need of a good martini and I imagine you could use something equally refreshing."

We drove in silence, again with me concentrating on the traffic and Emily gazing out on the lake. It was rush hour and progress was slow. But we finally managed to reach the hotel and hand the car over to the valet. We entered the building and headed for the bank of elevators that would take us to the hotel bar on the mezzanine floor. The bar was busy but we were able to grab a couple of armchairs off to the side of the room. When the waiter came over Emily ordered a glass of Chardonnay and I a martini. While we waited for the drinks to arrive, Emily started in.

"Okay, Church, what do you think we learned today?"

"Well, I think we're both agreed the home invasion was a planned event, targeting this residence in particular and most likely motivated by a desire to steal those six paintings."

"And?"

"And the cops seemed to be bent on treating the case as an unpremeditated home invasion, or at least that's what they want us and the rest of the world to believe."

"So where do we go from here?"

"We've got two lines of enquiry to pursue based upon what we currently know. First one is to trace the leakage of information relating to the existence of the paintings to whoever commissioned the crime."

"And the second?"

"Follow up on the drug angle."

Our drinks arrived, along with a bowl of nuts and other items to nibble, and we paused long enough for the server to lay everything out on the low table in front of us.

"Let's focus on the first. You think it's the old art restorer don't you?"

I took a leisurely sip of my martini, set the exquisitely thin and beautifully shaped glass gently down on to the table and nodded approvingly. "Let's look at the options. The bidding agents employed by Knightwood & Stone would have had to have formed a conspiracy since no single one of them handled all auction bids, and there's the problem of a time lapse: not all acquisitions occurred in the same year. Similarly, it's hard to believe the leakage occurred at the auction houses themselves. They've far too much to lose should it ever get out they could not be trusted to be discreet. And of course there's the problem that more than one auction house was involved. Indiscreet gossip within the Chicago art collector community, or among local museum curators, can't be ruled out as the source but I tend to be convinced Arnold and his wife were sincere when they insisted they took special care not to reveal the precise identity of any of the paintings. And without such information it's unlikely a risky venture like this one would have been commissioned. As for the possibility that it all came down to the loose tongue of the housekeeper seems somewhat farfetched. Who would she have talked with? As she said herself, her acquaintances for the most part were other domestics in other wealthy homes—persons accustomed to being around valuable articles and therefore not inclined to pay undue attention to such details."

"But what is it about the restorer that makes him your primary suspect?"

"The time element to begin with. Whoever supplied the information was in possession of pertinent and timely facts regarding the location, condition, and security provisions attending to this particular set of paintings. Secondly, the authoritative nature of the information presumably revealed. Whoever purchased this information must have had considerable confidence in its accuracy. A professional restorer had both the requisite knowledge to accurately appraise the value of the works but also to be certain the paintings were what he believed them to be. And finally, his age: we are informed he's an elderly man—an immigrant one would suppose—who might understandably be interested in securing a hefty sum just before stepping into retirement."

"Why do you bring up the possibility that he's an immigrant?"

"Let's assume he is, and let's assume his retirement plans involve returning to his country of origin, might not part of the payoff be facilitation of such a move?"

"Are you suggesting there may be a link between our restorer and the nationality of his buyer?"

"It's still all very speculative, Emily, but such thoughts give us some direction in our enquiries. Tomorrow we'll look up this Mr. Ernst Betteldorf and feel him out."

"And tonight?"

"Ah, you're on your own for dinner this evening I'm afraid. I've got to do a little business relating to our other line of enquiry."

"Suit yourself," she said, rising from her chair. I'll probably just order something from room service and call it an early night. You coming?"

"Be up in a moment…need to make a phone call or two."

As Emily left the bar I signaled the server to come over. "Can the kitchen fix me up a club sandwich, some chips, and a tall glass of tap water?"

"Certainly Mr. Church."

"Oh, also could you bring me another martini?"

"Of course."

"Thanks."

Once the server had gone I settled back and began to think through the problem of getting more information about the drug bust without revealing my interest to the cops. The last thing I wanted were the Chicago police connecting the home invasion with the drug bust—they'd be all over it in a second and it'd make my job of prying information out of the gang that much more difficult.

As I saw it, there were several possibilities. I could give Boris at the gym a call—get him to have Jerry put me in touch with one of his pals here in the city who knows what's happening on the streets. Or I could call my buddy Jack—have him contact the police saying the FBI has an interest in the case. Or maybe I should have Emily or Chelsea call pretending to be a reporter for a local paper in some nearby town looking to write a front-page story. Hell, I could just contact the reporter whose article in the metropolitan paper caught my eye and talk him into sharing whatever new he has on the story, but I'd need to be careful—not get him thinking I'd make a better story than the drug bust itself.

As I ruminated over these various alternatives my club sandwich and a second martini showed up. I took a sip of the freshly chilled beverage and took a bite of the sandwich. As I worked through the problem it occurred to me all I really needed to know was the precise location of the drug bust. There would be no way I could interrogate the members of the gang already picked up in the bust but if I knew where they hung out I could probably connect with one or more who were still out on the street. Also I needed to get the information right away if I was to use it this evening. With these thoughts in mind I began to favor the option of having Emily try to call the cops handling the case and make the reporter pitch. I hurriedly munched down the rest of the sandwich, finished off the martini and signaled for the check.

Emily was sitting in the living room area of our suite reading a magazine when I came in. She looked up. "You make your calls all right?"

"Turns out you're the one who needs to make a call."

"What do you mean?"

"I've got to learn the location of the drug bust and I need to learn it right now. And I can't do it in a way that lets the cops connect the home invasion with the bust so neither you nor I can approach the precinct directly."

"So what's the deal?"

"I want you to call the Chicago police department posing as a cub reporter for the Oak Park Chronicle and ask to speak to someone in public affairs—tell them you've heard a rumor the drug bust occurred in a neighborhood right next to Oak Park and the citizens of this community are anxious."

"They'll buy that?"

"I think so...anyway it's a gambit worth trying," I said, handing her my cell phone.

"Okay, I'll give it a try," she said as she keyed 411 for information. "Yes, please give me the number of the Chicago Police Department...the Public Affairs Office. Thank you," she added as she wrote down the number.

While I took a seat across from her she keyed the number and waited. "This is Penelope Freter of the Oak Park Chronicle...

yes, I'm a reporter. My boss asked me to contact you people—we've a rumor going around about that drug bust that made the news yesterday…yes, that one. Rumor has it the bust occurred in a Chicago neighborhood bordering our community and our residents are worried. Is that rumor true? Yes, I'll wait." While she was on hold she whispered: "He's forwarding my call to the precinct handling the case".

"Hello, whom am I speaking with? Oh, Officer Reynolds… yes, this is Penelope Freter. I'm a reporter for the Oak Park Chronicle trying to nail down a rumor about the location of that drug bust your office is handling. We've heard it occurred in a neighborhood right next to Oak Park…is that correct? Oh, I see. Well, I'm sure the citizens will be relieved but I think my boss will need something more specific. Can you tell me the nearest intersection to where the bust occurred? Thank you, that'll help. I'll let my boss know." She closed the connection and handed me back my phone.

"What did you learn?" I asked.

"Officer Reynolds is a detective attached to the police station on Ogden Avenue—the Area Four precinct. He assures me the bust occurred far from Oak Park."

"Did he say where?"

"Yes, near the corner of Whitehall and Atherton. Is that where you'll head this evening?"

"Just as soon as I change into something more suitable," I said, coming over to where she was sitting. "You were great!" I whispered, then leaned over and gave her a light kiss on the lips.

"My, my, William. Does this mean we're an item?"

"It means you deserve a reward…let's say dinner tomorrow evening at one of the city's swankiest restaurants."

"It's a date. Now why don't you get changed while I head for the shower. I'll want to freshen up before room service brings me dinner. Just think, while you're prowling that Westside neighborhood on an empty stomach I'll be nibbling on delicacies fresh from the hotel's gourmet kitchen."

"Sorry to disappoint old girl but I've already eaten…had a club sandwich in the bar after you left, but I do appreciate the sentiment."

"That figures. Can't imagine a guy as big as you not provisioning himself before sauntering out to do battle with the underworld."

I laughed and headed into the bedroom.

* * *

I changed into the outfit I'd worn early that morning: blue jeans, a dark blue canvas shirt, running shoes and a hooded sweatshirt. The thirty-eight was holstered at my waist, concealed under the sweatshirt. I slipped out of the hotel suite while Emily was still in the shower and made my way down to street level where I had the valet bring around my rental car. Thanks to the early morning reconnaissance I knew exactly where the intersection of Whitehall and Atherton was located. That was helpful since street signs were hard to read in the vanishing light of evening. The intersection itself showed me nothing—just a non-descript quadrant of old houses with unkempt yards. I cruised the streets, making an ever-widening orbit around the intersection. There weren't many pedestrians out and about so I focused my attention on street traffic, looking for customized cars with a brace or more of young men. I cruised slowly, hoping some member of the local gang would spot me and think maybe I was either a buyer or had something to sell.

The strategy worked. After only fifteen minutes of cruising a low-riding muscle car pulled up alongside me. Four young men with hooded sweatshirts—the hoods up—sat bolt upright, looking straight ahead—their eyes concealed under heavily rimmed sunglasses. The driver, his side window open, gestured for me to pull over. I complied. The muscle car also came to a stop. The driver motioned for me to put down the window on the passenger side of the car. I fingered the toggle switch and powered the window all the way down.

"You got business here?" he asked, still not turning in my direction. The other three, however, were giving me their best threatening stares.

"That depends…you the man?"

He nodded then pulled over and parked. All four got out of the car. I did the same. I stood beside my car—close enough that nobody could position himself behind me but far enough away I had room to maneuver. The four of them approached, the leader in front. Once they reached me they fanned out, covering all avenues of escape.

"I asked you a question," said the leader menacingly.

"And I answered."

"You some kind of wise guy or something?" said the biggest guy in the group as he took a couple of steps closer to me.

The leader motioned for big guy to stand fast. "What you want?" he asked me.

"First, I gotta know who I'm talking to. You guys part of that gang that got busted last week during a drug buy?"

"That be none of your business…less'n you're a cop."

"I'm no cop but I still gotta know the answer to my question… can't see how we can do business without it."

"Yeah? Well maybe we'll first see how much bread you got… that'll tell us if doing business with you be worth our while."

"Or maybe we just take the bread and split," said the tall, skinny one.

"You guys hard of hearing! Why should I tell you my business if you're just a bunch of punks looking for an easy score."

"I'm through putting up with your smart ass attitude…you hear me?" said the leader as he pulled a wicked-looking knife from out of his back pocket. Now you gonna tell me what I want to know or we're gonna take care of business another way."

I shrugged, feigning a passiveness meant to put them off guard then swung my right leg through a powerful arc that ended with my foot colliding with his hand, sending the knife flying.

"Jesus! I think you broke my wrist you bastard! Get him!"

The big guy, who was closest, lunged for me—intent on getting me into a bear hug. I walked into it, kneeing him in the groin then grabbing him by the hood and smashing his face down on my rising knee. I hardly had time to extricate myself from the collapsing body of the big guy when the tall, skinny kid advanced—a knife in hand. I stepped aside, grabbed the arm holding the knife, broke his grip then punched him in the stomach. As he bent over I stepped behind and placed him in a hammerlock. It was a good move since the small guy had pulled a gun and was about to shoot. He hesitated, not having a target. I took advantage of it, shoving the tall, skinny kid and propelling him violently into the other guy. The impact knocked both off-balance giving me time to wrest the gun from the small guy's hand and toss it into the adjacent yard. But just as I was about to turn and face the leader the big guy grabbed me, intending to turn me around so he could land some heavy blows. I got a leg between his legs and tripped him up, then arched backward, throwing all my considerable weight on to his unstable body—causing both of us to crash to the ground, me on top. I rolled clear and kicked him in the head. This time he lost consciousness.

Before the others could recover their weapons I grabbed the leader—now standing with an incredulous look on his face holding his wrist—and shoved him into my car. "Don't make a move, asshole, or I'll break the other wrist—you hear me!" He nodded and slumped to the far corner of the passenger side of the front seat. I started the engine and hit the accelerator. We shot down the street, heading for the Kennedy Expressway where I figured I could lose anyone trying to tail me. It took a while to locate the expressway and more time to locate an onramp but finally I had us moving south, away from the city. I pulled off at an exit that seemed to lead to a quiet bedroom community and came to a stop at the first darkened street I could find.

I turned off the ignition and turned to him. "Now, we don't have a lot of time. You've got a choice: either answer my questions satisfactorily and have me get you to an emergency room so your wrist can be looked after or I shoot you in the gut and leave you out here to die." As he tried to make sense of what I'd just said I pulled out my gun and pointed it at him.

"Okay, man! Ask your questions!"

"First off, you a member of the gang that got busted last week?"

"Yeah."

"You take part in that home invasion out north of the city?"

"What you talking about?"

"Don't screw around, asshole, your life's on the line!"

"Yeah, okay, me and some of the others did the thing."

"Who put you up to it?"

"Man, I don't know! All I know is some outfit recruited us to snatch some paintings off the old couple's walls—said we get a bundle of loot in exchange for the paintings."

"How? By fencing them?"

"Hell no, they'd give us the money themselves…said they had a buyer for the stuff."

"Did they give you the money?"

"Yeah. That's how we planned to score big with a drug buy."

"So what happened?"

"Somebody tipped off the cops…knew all about it: where, when—the whole Goddamn business!"

"You think it was the guys who put you up to the snatch that sold you out?"

"Hell if I know but, yeah, they could have."

"But you don't know who they were?"

"Like I told you, they just showed up flashing a lot of money... there were three of them—all armed, I guess so we wouldn't get any funny ideas about ripping them off."

I sat there thinking about the information the guy had given me.

"Jesus, man! This wrist hurts all to hell! Get me to a doctor!"

I nodded, turned on the ignition, put the car in gear and pulled away from the curb. I got back on the expressway and made for the medical clinic I'd spotted while cruising in the gang's neighborhood. "I'm going to let you off back in your own hood so cool it!"

"Yeah, thanks, man."

"And another thing, you don't know me...you and those other clowns never saw me—you got that?"

"Sure, man, but I'd kinda like to know where you fit into all of this?"

"I'm sure you would, friend, but it's not going to happen. The less you know about me the healthier it is for you."

"You going to dump this stuff on the cops?"

"Not a word. This conversation was just between you and me."

We rode in silence the rest of the way. I dropped him off at the emergency entrance to the clinic and watched long enough to make sure he actually went in. God knows what story he'd tell the attending physician.

* * *

Emily was still up when I returned to the room, sitting on the couch in one of the hotel's bathrobes—her laptop open on the coffee table.

"Thought you'd be in bed by now," I said.

"Should be, but wanted to get a progress report ready for my boss. How'd it go?"

"Made some progress. Hooked up with members of the gang that pulled off the home invasion."

"They confirm your suspicions?"

"Yeah. Some guys put them up to snatching those paintings. The rest of the home invasion stuff was purely improvisational."

"You don't look any worse for wear—what happened? You just charm the information out of them?"

"Hardly. But nobody got shot, nobody's dead…only one guy needed medical attention."

"And nobody can link you to the deed, eh?"

"That's about it. Got any of that brandy left in the minibar?"

"Of course! What did you think, Church—that I'd have drunk both bottles by the time you came back?"

"Whoa! Just a conversational gambit, hoping you'd suggest I open one for you too."

"Sorry. I guess the lateness of the hour and my own nervousness about how you'd manage to stay healthy prowling the streets after dark has kind of put me on edge. Yeah, go ahead and open one for me."

"Will do," I said, going over to the minibar and extracting two small bottles of premium brandy. "I appreciate the concern, old girl, but you've got to understand I do this kind of stuff for a living," I added as I poured the amber liquor into snifter glasses.

"And I'm sure you're very good at it but that doesn't get us worrying types off the hook."

"No, I suppose not. Anyway, let's toast to safe harbors after a storm."

She smiled as I raised my glass and touched it to hers. "You're a charmer—that's all I can say."

I settled down on the couch alongside her. We didn't speak again for a while—just sipped our drinks and let the alcohol do its job relieving much of the tension both of us had built up over the evening. Finally, Emily broke the silence.

"Does what you learned tonight affect how we'll play it tomorrow...you know, with the art restorer?"

"It gives us a little more clarity. We now know for a fact the paintings were the objective and that means our focus on Herr Betteldorf is right on target. It also gives us a little more leverage—chances are we can come down on him a little harder knowing he's either our man or somebody who can probably make an educated guess who else it could be."

"Are we going to make an appointment with him?"

"Nope. We're just going to drop in on him at his studio—hopefully use the element of surprise to our advantage."

"Well, we both better get some rest if that's our strategy."

"Good point," I said, getting up from the couch. "Toast and coffee at 0900 sharp! See you then."

"Good night, Church."

DAY 5

BETTELDORF'S STUDIO WAS JUST off South Halsted Street, a low rent neighborhood on the lower Westside now known as the Chicago Arts District owing to the fact that more than thirty art galleries cluster there among countless lofts and artist workshops.

"I wonder if it's simply a coincidence that Betteldorf's studio is in the same general neighborhood as the street gang used in the heist?" mused Emily as we drove along the Kennedy Expressway.

"Interesting thought," I said.

It was mid-morning and the weather promised to be a bit more rainy and blustery than the previous two days. I found I had to use my windshield wipers to clear away the intermittent scatter of raindrops just so I could keep an eye on the crowded and fast moving traffic around us. The Interstate ran parallel with Halted Street for much of the way, helping me maintain my bearings in a fairly straightforward manner. Once we saw signs for the Eighteenth Street exit I knew we'd arrived. I pulled over to the right lane, slowed down and made the turnoff. There didn't seem to be much traffic on the surface streets—maybe because of what part of town we were in, or perhaps because of the time of day. In any case we made it with no difficulty. We cruised along until we spotted the building, but couldn't find parking at the curb on our side of the street, obliging me to make a U-turn at the next intersection and come back up. Here, there were plenty of available parking slots and I pulled into one about half way down the block. The two of us climbed out.

"It's that large building across the street," said Emily, checking the number out front.

"Yeah, but which entrance?"

"I'm not sure. Let's see if there's some sort of directory."

We finally found an entrance containing a small brass plate affixed above a letter slot with the name *Betteldorf Restorations* on it. "This is it," she said.

We were both dressed more casually this morning. Emily had on a blue Batik peasant blouse and stretch jeans. I had on a pair of black jeans, a white shirt and a black/brown tweed sports jacket. We climbed the stairs to the second floor. The small, somewhat gloomy landing contained entrances to two units. The one on the left sported a brass plate identical to the Betteldorf plate downstairs. There was a doorbell just below it. Emily looked at me questioningly. I nodded. She rang the bell.

After what seemed an inordinate amount of time I could hear someone shuffling towards the door. There was a pause, then the door was opened cautiously revealing a bald, gnomish-looking man dressed haphazardly in a worn, out-of-fashion dark suit. What appeared to be chemical stains were present in liberal quantities across the front of the jacket and on the upper portion of the slacks.

"Mr. Ernst Betteldorf?" asked Emily.

"Yes, I am Ernst Betteldorf. How can I help you?"

"We're very sorry to disturb you and would have called for an appointment but we're in the city for only a short time and hoped dropping by like this would be all right."

"And your business would be...what?"

"I'm Emily Parsons of the Mutual Insurance Company of New York. This is my associate, Mr. William Church. We're investigating that theft of French Impressionist paintings from the home north of the city. You're familiar with the case I presume."

"Yes, please come in," he said, opening the door fully so we could step inside.

The unit was clearly a loft—a large space with wooden flooring, unfinished walls, large windows, and theatrical lighting of the sort intended to allow maximum control over the illumination of selected areas of the room. Several large tables covered with white butcher's paper were positioned below the lighting arrays. Next to them were easels, some holding paintings. A slight stench of chemicals greeted us as we moved further into the room.

"We can talk more comfortably over here," he said, guiding us to a small sitting area with couch and chairs around a coffee table—all resting on a large, well-worn but expensive-looking Persian carpet.

As he talked, I took note of his accent. It was thick and unmistakably German.

"Now what is it that brings you to me in regard to this case," he said.

"We were informed you had occasion to examine the paintings in question. It would be helpful to gain your professional assessment of their condition and value…perhaps also some sense of who might covet their possession," said Emily.

"Ah, but of course. You are suggesting I am one of the few art experts to have some familiarity with these paintings. In this you are correct. The owners of these paintings were not inclined to display them publicly nor, I might add, to allow them to be subjects of journalistic or academic review. A pity since they formed an exquisite grouping."

"So what can you tell us about them?" asked Emily.

"The Renoir portrait of Madame Girard is my favorite. It has all the warmth of color and light we have come to expect from him. Perhaps most playful in an artistic sense is the Dufy. This canvas with its depiction of the seashore full of sparkling blues and reds brings a smile to one's countenance. The same can perhaps be said of the Matisse, especially with respect to his use of color and his somewhat frivolous treatment of life at the beach. The Boudin landscape is far different. It has a seriousness about it—a kind of existential reality that invites the viewer to think of life in all its somber aspects."

"And the Vuillard still life?"

"A masterpiece really—faithful representation of the form of the objects but executed with a sensuousness of color and technique that few artists can achieve. And of course we cannot forget the Bonnard with its extravagant use of the full palette of color in the café scene—a canvas one would be wise to contemplate pleasurably at some length."

"I take it you approve of the collection," said Emily.

"Of course I approve. All the facets of style dominant in French Impressionist painting of the late Nineteenth and early Twentieth Centuries are to be found in these six modest-sized paintings. To have them displayed as a set on one's wall would be as if one held—almost as a still life—the epochal currents of art flowing across the threshold of the Twentieth Century!"

"Who else would share your enthusiasm for this particular collection of paintings?" asked Emily.

"Any serious collector of Impressionist art most certainly, and were they to be put up for auction as a set I would imagine art museums around the world would be eager to bid on them.'

"But could they be marketed—either singly or as a set—given that they are stolen property?" I asked.

"It's not likely. We are speaking of very well known artists of historic significance. To avoid the possibility they were fakes an auction house or private collector would demand an exhaustive examination of their pedigree which would immediately reveal their illicit history."

"I see…not to change the subject but I couldn't help noticing you have a pronounced German accent, Mr. Betteldorf. Have you been in this country long?"

"For more years than I care to contemplate…but why do you ask?"

"I don't mean to be inquisitive, Mr. Betteldorf, but it seems to me, based upon what you've told us, whoever commissioned the theft received critical information regarding these paintings from someone well-placed to secure it. You seem to be the one person—other than the owners—who uniquely qualifies."

"Are you insinuating I had something to do with this theft?"

"What I'm trying to ascertain, Mr. Betteldorf, is whether—and with whom among your acquaintances either here or abroad—you might have shared such privileged information?"

"Absolutely no one, Mr. Church! I have a reputation for being discreet as well as exceptionally competent…you can ask any of my clients. There is simply no circumstance I can imagine where I would endanger that reputation for the sake of the momentary pleasure of some idle gossip!"

"Perhaps not for the pleasure of some idle gossip, but surely one can imagine other more compelling incentives that might tempt even the most honorable of men?"

"What are you getting at?"

"Humor me a bit, Mr. Betteldorf, would it be fair to say—given your age—that contemplation of retirement sometime in the very near future would not be out of the question?"

"If and when I choose to retire is none of your business, Mr. Church, and I'm inclined to regard your line of questioning as insulting. I would appreciate it if you both would go; I have work to do."

"Look, Mr. Betteldorf, you've got two choices: either cooperate with me or deal with the Chicago police, the FBI's art theft squad and possibly also Interpol. I'm not interested in seeing you go to jail or in screwing up your retirement plans but I'll make damn sure the authorities put a spotlight on you if you don't play ball with me. Is that understood?"

"You've got no evidence I had anything to do with it. You're just bluffing to see if you can get me to admit something... something I am innocent of. I have half a mind to call the police myself and tell them you are trying to blackmail me!"

"By all means call them better yet call Detective Jablonski who's heading up the case. He'd be real interested in knowing the true object of the home invasion was the removal of those six paintings from the house. I have witnesses that can testify to that—members of the street gang that pulled it off. Right now, he thinks the theft of the paintings was a last minute impulse on the part of some naïve kids who think they can fence the damn things. You're way off his radar. I can change that with a simple phone call you want me to?"

Betteldorf seemed to shrink even smaller as he absorbed the message. After a moment or two he raised his eyes and looked desperately into mine. "I meant no harm...at least at the very beginning," he said in a quiet voice.

"Why don't you start there," I said, softly.

"It began with a visit from Herr Reichwein some months ago."

"Who is this Herr Reichwein," asked Emily.

"An old and dear friend of mine...a man active in the acquisition and sale of European artworks."

"You say he was visiting...from where?" I asked.

"He now lives in Berlin though when I first met him we were both living in Frankfurt."

"Why do you say it all began with his visit?"

"We were talking one evening about the scarcity of fine French Impressionist artworks, especially ones suitable for private collectors. He asked whether such paintings were to be found among the collections of my clients here in the Chicago area. I of course immediately thought of the Arnold Walker collection—the one you are currently interested in."

"What did you tell him about the collection?"

"I described it in some detail but was very careful to omit any information that would reveal the identity of the owner."

"But something happened that changed your thinking."

"Yes. Yes, regrettably that is so. Herr Reichwein speculated that a collection of that sort would be worth a great deal to certain parties...parties he failed to name. "Perhaps the owners would be flattered to be approached," he said to me. I of course would receive a generous finders fee if a purchase could be effected, and did I not aspire to live out my retirement in Berlin...comfortably and securely?"

"So it all started out innocently—you were simply helping out an old friend while at the same time possibly benefiting your client."

"Yes, exactly so. And the prospect of enriching myself in the process and what that would mean for my retirement served as an irresistible added inducement."

"So you disclosed the identity of the owner?"

"Yes. But then Herr Reichwein insisted I describe precisely the location of the residence, where in the house the paintings were displayed, how they were hung, what security was in place, and details of the comings and goings of Arnold and his wife as well as that of their live-in help. When I resisted he threatened to make public my indiscretion in a manner that would effectively ruin my business. While I tried to get over my shock at the extent of his betrayal he calmly wrote me a check for ten thousand dollars—a kind of down payment on the so-called finder's fee, he said."

Betteldorf rose from his chair and stood before us, absently picking at the chemical stains on his coat. After a moment or so, he looked up—a penitent expression on his face—and continued: "It was calculated blackmail…I can see that…but I thought to myself what does it matter? Either way, my practice would be shut down…better to take the money and return to Germany where this disagreeable business could be forgotten."

"So you complied with all his demands?"

"Yes."

"And what did you think when you learned of the home invasion and the theft of the six paintings?"

"I was shocked…and ashamed."

"But you must have had some suspicion something of the sort was in the works once your friend, Mr. Reichwein, pressed you for details. Did you give any thought to alerting the authorities… or the Walkers for that matter?"

"Yes, I suppose I did have some suspicion his demand for information was connected to something illegal but I had no idea what it might be or even if it would actually occur so I felt no pressure to contact the authorities or the Walkers. And he reassured me no knowledge of my indiscretion would ever come to light as long as I remained quiet concerning his enquiries."

"You've been very helpful Mr. Betteldorf," I said, getting up from the couch. We won't take up any more of your time. However, before we leave we'll need you to supply us with contact information on Mr. Reichwein: where he lives, his business address, his phone number—things like that. Will you do that for us?"

"Yes, yes, of course. I have his card here someplace," he said as he stepped over to one of the tables that seemed to serve as his desk and began to rifle through a pile of papers. "Here it is...I believe it has all the information you require."

I examined the business card Betteldorf handed me. "May I keep it?"

"Please. I have another."

"One last question, Mr. Betteldorf, were you not surprised your friend had such unlikely connections here in the city: street gangs and armed thugs for example?"

"There is no way he would have had such connections; I am absolutely certain of this. He is a man much like myself—a man who lives in a world of great art, moneyed patrons and grand estates. No, this terrible thing is the work of someone else... someone who has used Herr Reichwein as an intermediary—a conduit, if you will, of vital information."

"And you have no idea who this other person might be?"

"No, but whoever it is cannot be regarded lightly. He or they have proven to be capable of violence. I worry for my own safety."

"I'll keep your name out of it as I pursue my enquiries, I promise you that, but equally important is for you to go about your business in a normal manner so as not to raise questions in the minds of those who might be watching."

"You think somebody is watching me?"

"Let's just say the sooner you wrap up your affairs here and move to Berlin the better off you'll be."

"Yes, I…I understand."

"Good. We'll be going then." I signaled to Emily who rose from her chair and followed me to the door. Betteldorf trailed behind, hunched over, with his eyes to the ground—seemingly diminished by the full weight of his shame, knowing his complicity in this crime was beyond denial and quite likely to become publicly known should events spin wildly out of control.

* * *

"My God, Church, you got him to divulge everything!" said Emily as we walked to the car.

"We were lucky. We had some leverage. It's doesn't always work out as successfully."

"But you figured out it had to be him."

"It was an educated guess…helped in no small part by the reluctance of the Walker family to make public their ownership of such valuable paintings. We'd still be floundering around if the press had been given access to the collection."

I opened the car door for Emily, made sure she was comfortably seated then came around and climbed behind the wheel. But before I could key the ignition both doors were jerked open and a gun was pressed up against the side of my head. Emily let out a stifled scream as she was being dragged out of the car.

"Slide out nice and easy," said the guy holding the gun.

I did as instructed but exaggerated the awkwardness of trying to unravel my six-foot-four-inch frame out from under the steering wheel, using the maneuver to conceal my removal of the thirty-eight from its holster. The guy holding the gun had to back off to give me room to stand up. I gripped the top edge of the car door for support with my left hand as I tried to stand—my back to the guy—and smoothly swung the gun level with my waist—releasing the safety catch in the process. As I turned towards him his eyes were on my face, his pistol pointed menacingly in the same direction. "Take it easy." I said softly as I shot him twice in quick succession. He got off one shot but the force of the impact of my initial round knocked him off balance, causing his aim to shift slightly to the right with the result that the bullet passed several inches wide of my head.

"Church!" screamed Emily.

I dropped down into a squat and grabbed the dying shooter's gun from his hand.

"Drop your gun, asshole, or this lady gets a bullet through the head!" said the other guy.

"All right," I said, "I'm coming around…just don't hurt her!" I stood up slowly so the second shooter could see me, holding in my left hand the first shooter's gun held high over my head.

"Come around nice and slow…keep that gun up where I can see it!" he said.

I did, but the thirty-eight was still in my right hand—still concealed by the car.

"Toss the gun over here," he commanded, "and let me see your other hand!"

"I think I'm gut shot!" I moaned, bunching over as if trying to relieve the pain to my right side...Jesus, it hurts!"

"Serves you right, asshole!"

As I came around the back of the car my right hand was concealed in the folds of my sports jacket, as if trying to stanch the wound, allowing my own gun to remain out of sight.

"Let her go," I said feebly. "Whatever you want she's not part of it."

"No dice. Now drop that gun in the gutter and stay where you are!"

Just then a late model black sedan accelerated from a parking space someplace down the street and screeched to a stop just feet from where I was standing. The driver—a heavy-set guy—climbed out of the car. "Christ, Arni, Ted's all shot up!" he said, looking down at the body of the first shooter.

"I said drop the gun!" yelled the guy holding Emily, whom he pushed aside so he could point his gun directly at me. "Drag this bastard into the car!" he shouted.

Seeing his gaze shift to the driver of the sedan, I freed my gun from the folds of my jacket and squeezed off two shots. We were only about ten feet apart so the shots hit their mark. The guy didn't have time to refocus on me and line up a shot before crumpling to the ground. I leaped over to where Emily stood—frozen in horror—and pulled her down against the curbside of our car. "Stay here!" I whispered.

Meanwhile, the third guy hesitated for a moment then jumped back into the black sedan and sped off. I caught a good look at the license plate and memorized the number. "Quick, get in!" I said to Emily as I helped her up and opened the car door for her. She offered no resistance—just slumped down in the seat, her hands over her eyes. I turned back to the second shooter. If he wasn't dead he soon would be. I made sure his gun was in plain view so the cops would recover it quickly. My prints were all over the first shooter's gun so I wiped it down with the pulled-out tail of my shirt then walked over to the body and placed the weapon back in the grip of the dead man's hand, reestablishing his ownership of the piece.

All this time the street was empty; people around here smart enough to get indoors when they hear shooting. But the sound of approaching sirens meant the cops would be on the scene in minutes. I stood next to the car, my hands held high—the right hand holding my federal concealed weapons permit, the left my California private investigator license.

Two squad cars rolled in simultaneously and both cops stepped out, their guns leveled at me. "Place those documents on the hood of the car and turn around—your hands on the roof, legs spread!" said the one cop.

I did as instructed. As the cop approached, I called out: "I'm armed—handgun in a holster on my belt."

The first cop removed my semi-automatic then cuffed me. A crowd began to assemble now that the cops had arrived and the shooting was at an end.

Meanwhile, the second cop had turned his attention to Emily. "Step out of the car, miss!" he said, opening the car door. Still somewhat in shock she climbed out slowly and stood before him.

Once he'd reassured himself Emily was not armed and posed no threat he put through a call to get more back up.

"Get them to send a medical examiner and some homicide detectives," shouted the first cop.

While they waited for others to arrive they placed Emily in the rear of one of the squad cars, myself in the rear of the other. I could tell it was going to be a long afternoon.

A half-dozen more cars showed up within minutes, as well as a coroner's vehicle and an ambulance. Several of the uniformed cops were tasked with crowd control while the others watched as the paramedics checked out the two guys I'd shot. Once it was confirmed they were dead the medical examiner team began its work documenting the crime scene.

One of the homicide detectives came over to the car I was in carrying my two documents. He took a long look at me then opened the door and motioned for me to climb out.

"You want to tell me what happened?" he asked as he removed the cuffs.

"The two guys jumped us as we were about to drive away. The guy lying on the street put a gun to my head and ordered me to climb out. I was able to put a couple of rounds in him, the impact of the first one threw off his aim just enough for his shot to miss my head. The second shooter—the guy lying on the sidewalk—had pulled my companion out of the car and was holding her as a shield. I faked a gut shot wound to conceal my gun and dropped him when his attention was deflected by the arrival of the escape vehicle."

"What d'you know about these guys?"

"Not a hell of a lot. Never saw them before. The guy lying on the street was called 'Ted' by the driver of the escape car. He also referred to the guy lying on the sidewalk as 'Arni'. The escape vehicle was a black four-door sedan, Illinois license plate."

"You get the plate number?"

"Yeah. You want to write it down?"

"Yeah, later. Right now I'd like to know what their beef with you was?"

"So would I, detective. The only other thing I know is they were intending to kidnap us—the guy now lying on the sidewalk yelled to the driver of the car to get me into the back seat. So whatever they had in mind killing us right here was not on the agenda."

"So they wanted a chance to get some information out of you?"

"That'd be my guess."

"You working on a case here in the city?"

"Miss Parsons is with the claims department of a New York insurance company. I'd been retained as a consultant to assist her in evaluating insured losses arising from a home invasion north of the city. We were down in this part of town just to check out the art scene—kind of a special interest for both of us."

"You telling me three hoods tried to pull you and your girlfriend off the streets in broad daylight for no apparent reason?"

"You know these guys?"

"Yeah, Arni Siracusa and Teddi Kladnov. They're freelance muscle. The guy driving the car was probably Benny Small—the three of them hire out to whoever don't want to get their hands dirty, you know what I mean?"

"Yeah."

"So what I've got to believe is that some outfit or person unknown hired these guys to either lean on you or your girlfriend in order to shut down whatever you're working on or they were interested in extracting some information...maybe snuff you afterwards—that make sense to you?"

"I'll buy that, but you'll need to give me time to try and work out who might be behind it all. Right now, detective, I can't give you anything...nothing that immediately comes to mind makes any sense."

"Okay, have it your way, but you and the lady need to follow me down to police headquarters where we'll get a steno to take your statements. Ballistics will want to verify the gun that shot these two guys was yours. After they're through you can have the thirty-eight back."

"Thanks," I said as I headed for our car. I could see they'd already permitted Emily to return to the car: she was sitting quietly on the passenger side. I jumped into the car, keyed the ignition and pulled swiftly away from the curb. Keeping within the speed limit, I maneuvered back up to Eighteenth Street and over to the expressway, following the detective's car all the way.

As we drove, Emily seemed to come out of her hysteria-fueled trance. "Oh Jesus!" she moaned—still not fully free of the demons released by the violence she'd just experienced.

I put my hand on her shoulder and gently rubbed it. "You'll be okay, Emily, just give it some more time."

"Who were they, Church?"

"The cops I.D.'d them as freelance hoods. The detectives are curious about what it is about our work that would trigger a visit by such heavys but I gave them nothing...told them I'll need some time to try and figure out who we might have annoyed."

"But won't witnesses tell them about our visit to Betteldorf... won't Betteldorf identify us?"

"I don't think Betteldorf will get involved...he's got to be thinking their attempt to grab us is connected to him. No, he'll be heading straight for Europe just as fast as he can. As for others who might have watched, they'll focus on the gunplay...won't give much thought to what we might have been doing before then."

"I was so scared," she said.

"As soon as we finish up at police headquarters we'll go back to the hotel and have a nice lunch...maybe get you a stiff drink to help you unwind...that sound okay?"

"I guess...but I can't help thinking we could have been killed!"

"It's true. And even if there hadn't been any gunplay we'd probably now be strapped to a couple of chairs in some brownstone basement with the same goons using unthinkable techniques to get us to answer a lot of questions."

"So you think Betteldorf would not be far from the truth thinking it was our investigation that triggered this attack?"

"No doubt about it."

Emily just shivered and wrapped her arms tightly around herself.

"Hold on, we're almost there," I said.

* * *

I pulled up to the hotel and gave the car to the valet. As the elevator took us up to the mezzanine floor I pulled Emily close and gave her a long hug. The elevator door opened and we headed—hand in hand—for the Café. Only a few tables were occupied—not surprising given the lateness of the hour. The hostess seated us at a table close to the far wall. Both of us admired the elegant but cheerfully homey interior before quickly turning our attention to the menu—it had been many hours since we'd last eaten. I ordered the day's steak entrée, Emily a salad. Hoping to unwind a little before our food arrived, I asked our server to bring the drink order right away: Emily had chosen a single malt scotch, myself—a martini—straight up.

I'd been given back my documents and my gun after we'd finished dictating our statements, and after the cops had put through a series of phone calls checking up on us. I'd mentioned my buddy Jack's name as a personal reference. Emily had referred them to her boss, Guy Sanderson. Once they learned I was ex-FBI and still in good standing with the agency a lot of the tension seemed to be lifted. The cops could see it was a righteous shoot but that didn't mean they liked it. Knowing I was one of the good guys helped a lot. The question running through my mind as I sipped my martini was whether to revisit the street gang and see if I could confirm the three guys who made the money-for-paintings deal were the same as the guys who tried to take us down, or to simply assume it and head directly for Berlin.

My thoughts were diverted by the arrival of our food. We both ate quietly.

"I don't think I can take any more of this," said Emily as we sipped our coffee.

"Any more of what?" I asked.

"All this violence. Oh, I know it's not anything out of the ordinary for someone like yourself, Church, but I'm not like you…I can't just keep working the case knowing there are people out there who wish us harm."

"You plan to return to New York?"

"I think I ought to…don't you? I'm just a bundle of nerves at this point…there's no way I can be of any use to you."

I nodded in agreement and sipped my coffee.

As we got up from the table and headed for the elevator, Emily turned to me.

"I think I'll lie down for a while," she said.

"Good idea. I've got to make some phone calls but I'll try not to disturb you."

It had begun to rain steadily by the time we reached the room and the pale light of the late afternoon sun—struggling to penetrate the passing clouds—barely illuminated the living room area. Emily started to switch on the lights but I gently restrained her hand.

"Leave the lights off for now," I said, taking her in my arms. "I just want to say how much I've enjoyed this crazy time we've had together…you've been amazing."

"Oh, William, you're a hard guy not to like…even when you pull stunts that almost get us killed."

I didn't want to let her go…just kept my hands loosely at her waist. She made no attempt to break free—just smiled, her eyes gazing up at mine as our lips inched closer. The kiss was full and sensuous, and I found myself stroking the small of her back as I pulled her closer and closer. Before I knew it her hands were caressing my neck. As I started to move my hands underneath her peasant blouse she whispered for me to wait…wait until we were in her bedroom.

She took my hand and led me across the room and over to the doorway leading to her side of the suite. The drapes were only partially open, casting an even darker light. I took her in my arms once again—this time unhesitatingly exploring her body as I kissed her hard. She broke free momentarily—just enough to slip out of her blouse and jeans. When she returned to my arms the full impact of her womanly figure triggered a sharp jolt of excitement. She could sense it and hurriedly removed my jacket and began unbuttoning my shirt. I stepped back, removed the holstered weapon from my belt, kicked off my shoes and stepped out of my slacks. Again she took my hand, drawing me back towards the bed, then laying down and pulling me down on top of her.

The lovemaking was intense—all those days of pent up animal attraction seemed to demand an instantaneous resolution. It was early evening before we finally climbed out of bed—Emily heading for the shower and myself for the minibar.

Sitting there in the darkened room draped in one of the hotel's courtesy robes and sipping a snifter of brandy I revisited the question of my next move. Emily would be leaving early the following morning, having expressed a desire to book a flight for New York on one of the many non-stops between O'Hare and La Guardia. This left me free to press my luck in pursuit of the paintings. The more I thought about it the more I was convinced the attempted take down earlier in the day was connected to the case. Probably the guy I braced yesterday evening warned his paymasters of my interest. They needed to know who the hell I was and what I was planning to do with whatever information their client's informant—Betteldorf—supplied me during our morning visit to his studio. I'm guessing they'd have neutralized Emily and myself, and then Betteldorf, had I not turned the tables. I didn't worry about the third guy. The cops would have picked him up by now. And I didn't think whoever was handling the Chicago operation would risk engaging a new team—especially if the paintings had already left the country and if they had a suspicion Betteldorf was soon to be much more accessible—upon his arrival on their home turf of Berlin.

The bottom line, I concluded, was that my interest in the Chicago phase of the operation had come to an end. I put down the snifter, turned on the side table light and pulled my cell phone from out of the deep pocket of the robe. It would still be late afternoon in California and I thought I could still catch Chelsea before she went off shift at my condo complex.

"Hello, Chelsea?"

"Yeah, Church, what's up?"

"Book me on a non-stop flight from SFO to Frankfurt for the day after tomorrow with a connecting flight to Berlin, you got that?"

"Okay, but what about your lady sidekick—she going too?"

"No, she'll be heading for New York."

"So what gives? You and she have a falling out?"

"I'll fill you in when I get back."

"And when will that be...seeing as you've asked me to book you out of SFO in less than forty-eight hours?"

"I'm grabbing a red-eye flight as soon as I can pack and get over to O'Hare."

"My! You two sure must have had some wing-dinger of a fight."

"Nothing so dramatic my dear Chelsea; in fact, just the contrary. But if it pleases you to think so far be it for me to set you straight."

"Ah, come on, Church, let a girl enjoy a few moments of delicious imaginings."

"Well, while you're enjoying those moments could you also reserve a room for me at the hotel I like near the Pariser Platz, in Berlin's Mitte District?"

"Will do, boss. Any idea of how long a stay you've got in mind?"

"No, but give them a tentative estimate of about three days."

"You want to know what's been happening with your other clients while you've been away?"

"Tell me tomorrow morning...make it late morning, I'll probably need some sleep and a good run before being ready for your million-dollar smile and all your youthful exuberance and athletic beauty!"

"Flattery? My goodness, Church, she must have been a good influence on you despite the brevity of her presence."

"Good night, Chelsea."

"Okay, I can take a hint. See you tomorrow."

I put down the cell phone and headed for Emily's room to retrieve my clothing and the gun. She was still in the bathroom and didn't hear me. After dumping the items on the bed I headed for the shower. By the time I'd cleaned up and dressed I could hear Emily moving about the central living area of the suite. She showed up at the doorway to my bedroom wearing one of the hotel's robes and holding a glass of wine.

"What are you doing?" she asked as she noticed my luggage open on the bed and piles of clothing stacked nearby.

"Got to leave…catching a red-eye to San Francisco just as soon as I finish packing."

"Why? What's happened?"

"Nothing special, just thought I'd get a jump on the guys pulling the strings on this art theft matter. The trail seems to lead to Berlin and that's where I'll be going…just as soon as I touch base back in San Francisco."

"Were you going to leave before saying goodbye?"

"Of course not, Emily," I said as I stopped packing and turned towards her. "There's probably a lot we need to say to one another…about our feelings…about everything that's happened today, but I'm thinking we should let a little time pass before we get into all that. In the meantime maybe just a simple goodbye is exactly what's called for. What do you think?"

"Works for me," she said with a smile. "I'm not one of those girls that hang an emotional price tag on every bedding…although I've got to admit I'm tempted in your case."

"Thanks for the warning," I said as I took her into my arms. "But the temptation is mutual."

"What do you mean by that, sir?" she playfully enquired as she kissed me lightly.

"I mean you're the kind of woman that's hard to turn away from."

"But here you are running breathlessly away from my warm and inviting bed. How should I feel about that?"

"Ah! A good question my fair damsel," I said as I returned the kiss. "How, indeed! Let's just say neither of us is in a good position to answer such a question in the heat of the moment—at least not in a way that stands a decent chance of serving us well."

"So when, then?" she asked coyly.

"You don't give a guy much room for maneuver do you? But let me propose the following: you meet the plane I'll be returning on after retrieving the paintings. Then, once we're back in that warm and inviting bed of yours we can revisit all those delicious boy/girl questions to our heart's content. What d'you say?"

"I've got a feeling I've just been handed a line," she said, giving me a punch on the shoulder. "But what the hell, you've got a deal!"

I quickly finished up with the packing and brought my bags into the central living room area where Emily was now seated, wine glass in hand, toying with a plate of munchies she'd discovered in the minibar.

"I'll take care of the hotel bill on my way out," I said, coming over to give her a goodbye kiss.

"Will I hear from you during your stay in Europe?" she asked, leaning forward to accommodate my farewell kiss.

"I'll keep Guy posted. I'm sure he'll keep you in the loop. If he doesn't, ring up Chelsea and let her know. She'll fill you in on all the gory tidbits."

"Let's hope there won't be any gory tidbits! But thanks, I'll do that."

I gave her a final wave then headed out the door.

DAY 6

IT WAS ABOUT ELEVEN o'clock in the evening, California time, when the plane on which I'd managed to secure a first class seat finally arrived at SFO. After picking up my one piece of checked luggage I headed for the taxi queue outside the terminal. I gave the cabbie the address of my building south of Market and nodded off.

I came back to life once we pulled onto Interstate 280 and came in sight of the city's skyline. The brilliant lights of the tight cluster of downtown buildings shimmering in the crystal clear air always gave me a lift—maybe even more than the lit-up Golden Gate Bridge. I tracked the image as we neared the King Street terminus of the Interstate, savoring the inherent beauty of my adopted city. Minutes later, the cab pulled up in front of my building. I paid the cabbie, retrieved my two pieces of luggage from the cab's trunk and headed for the front entrance. The security attendant manning the lobby gave me a welcoming wave as I made a beeline for the elevators. It was close to three o'clock in the morning

Chicago time and I was dog-tired. Somehow I managed to punch the right floor button, extricate myself from the elevator and put my key in the right door. Once inside, I dropped the luggage on the couch and headed for the bedroom. Sleep was a top priority and I meant to get to it without any undue delay.

* * *

I woke up to the drumming sound of my cell phone as it vibrated on the wooden surface of the night table. I had a brief memory of having turned off the ring function so as not to be disturbed during the night. I hadn't counted on the amount of racket a vibrating phone could make when placed on a solid surface. Reluctantly, I grabbed the phone and looked to see who was calling me. Chelsea's lovely young face filled the screen.

"What's up?" I asked after having finally succeeded in sliding the "unlock" icon to the right.

"You, I hope," she said.

"Why, what time is it?"

"Jesus, Church, you must have really been out of it last night. Usually you've been up for hours by this time of the morning."

As she spoke, I turned to the digital alarm clock that also stood on the night table and learned it was after eight o'clock. "Okay, I'm running a little late but hell, Chelsea, I thought we agreed to meet up later on this morning."

"We did. And I'm sorry to have disturbed your sleep, boss, but Emily just called and asked me to let you know she arrived safely in New York. I gathered she felt you'd want to know right away…you know, the way lovebirds do when they're parted for the first time."

"None of your snide comments, sweetheart, but thanks for waking me up. You get the bookings all right?"

"Yup. You're scheduled to fly out of SFO on tomorrow's six o'clock flight, getting into Frankfurt early the following morning. You'll have a layover of about two hours that'll put you in Berlin in plenty of time to check into the hotel before lunch. And just to make sure they've got a room ready for you I booked you in for the previous night. You happy now?"

"You're an angel. Let's meet for lunch—you in the mood for that organic food place on the docks outside the Ferry Building?"

"You read my mind. See you there at noon—I'll make a reservation for one of the outdoor tables."

I returned the phone to the night table, leaned back against the pillows—my hands clasped behind my neck—and tried to map out my day. I needed to touch base with Jack, do a run and maybe lift a few weights. But most of all I felt an urge to refresh my take on Impressionist art—see what it is that drives some people to commit a crime, including attempted murder, just to possess it. That called for a visit to the Legion of Honor Fine Arts Museum in Lincoln Park.

I climbed out of bed, carried out my morning ablutions and threw on a pair of shorts, a polo shirt and a pair of running shoes. Chelsea, bless her heart, had restocked my supply of Valencia oranges so I pulled several from the fridge and cranked up the juicer. Glass in hand, I walked over to the wall of window glass that offered a panoramic view of the Oakland-Bay Bridge and studied the traffic on the upper deck. It was one of the perks of what otherwise would be a depressingly tiny condo unit. Traffic seemed to be moving fairly well despite being rush hour, and the glistening waters of the bay—bathed in sunlight—gave the promise of another of the city's unheralded but quite common days of spectacular weather. I returned to the kitchen alcove and poured a generous portion of cereal into a bowl, splashed some milk into it and stood next to the counter reading the previous week's news magazine while I ate.

Reenergized, I grabbed a sweatshirt and headed out. The sports convertible started right up and before long I was motoring down the Embarcadero on my way to Crissy Field. I'd put the top down and the fresh morning air blew away any remaining fatigue from last night's red eye special. I couldn't help thinking it would be a great day to be out on the Bay sailing but realized that pleasure would have to wait until I got this business taken care of. I made it over to Crissy in record time and pulled into the large parking lot at the east end. The thermometer in the car registered in the mid-fifties: warm enough especially with the sun well above the horizon to do without the sweatshirt. I left it in the trunk and headed at a brisk clip down the track towards the base of the Golden Gate Bridge a mile and a half away.

I'd worked up a good sweat by the time I got back to the car but kept a towel in the trunk for just such occasions. After wiping myself down I climbed back into the car and headed for the indoor firing range just across the way. My semi-automatic needed cleaning after the fracas in Chicago and the range had all the gun cleaning supplies and equipment I'd need. The drive took only a couple of minutes given that the distance was less than a mile. I removed the weapon and its holster from the trunk where I'd stashed it earlier that morning and secured it at my waist, concealed under the sweatshirt I now was wearing. The security guard at the entrance recognized me but I still flashed my federal concealed weapons permit as I entered. The gun cleaning tables were in a room just off to the left of the range proper. At this time of day there wasn't much action so I had plenty of area in which to work.

By the time I made it back to my flat after stopping to pick up a coffee it was close to eleven o'clock, giving me less than an hour to clean up and meet Chelsea for lunch.

* * *

The sun had warmed considerably by the time I reached the Ferry Building and the prospect of an alfresco lunch among the crowds drawn to the waterfront filled me with pleasure. I pulled into the lot just to the left of the building, parked and headed inside. Built at the turn of the century, the Ferry Building and its distinctive clock tower continue to serve as the defining landmark of the city's waterfront, especially now with all the food shops and restaurants that line the interior. I walked down the length of the sunlit nave, taking in the aromas of artisan cheeses and breads, fresh produce and roasting coffee, only turning towards a bayside exit once I reached the approximate location of Chelsea's favorite outdoor dining destination. I don't know if it has a name; if it does it's one that escapes me. I think of it as that outdoor café featuring organic foods that's precariously situated somewhere out on the vast esplanade behind the Ferry Building. But the food is terrific and dining there always puts Chelsea in a good mood.

As I pushed through the crowds I spotted the tiny cluster of tables off to my right. Chelsea was already seated. She waved to me as I approached. She was dressed in a stylish t-shirt/shorts combination that tastefully revealed her absolutely perfect dancer's figure: long and slender but entirely sensuous. Her blond hair was done up in a ponytail that accentuated her youthfulness and on her feet she wore a pair of delicate strap sandals in natural leather.

"Hey, Church," she said as I pulled out a chair and sat down. "See you're still alive and kicking."

"That I am," I said. "What are we having?"

"Linguini and scallops, white wine, and a very delicate arugula salad with feta cheese topped with a vinaigrette dressing...you up for it?"

"Why not! So, how's the dancing coming?"

"You can't put me off that easy, boss, give me the lowdown on Chicago."

"You interested in the case or in my relationship with Emily?"

"Gee, what a choice! Emily, of course!"

"Okay, here's what I can tell you. We work well together as a team, she's almost as gorgeous as you, but she's not a real fan of physical violence."

"Let's start with the physical violence part. What happened?"

"We got caught up in an attempted abduction. I had to shoot a couple of bad guys."

"And she was there?"

"Yeah, one of them was holding her when I shot him."

"Jesus! I can see where that could put a damper on a budding relationship."

"Actually it didn't, but it did motivate her to put some distance between us…at least until this case is resolved."

"So that's why she's now in New York City and you're here."

"Yeah."

"I'll take a pass on the question of which of us is the fairest since you being a gentleman all I'd get is a typical male line. Let's get to the case. Where's it stand?"

Before I could answer the young woman waiting tables came over to get our order. Chelsea ordered for both of us but let me have some input on the choice of wine. I selected a bottle of Russian River Chardonnay by a winery I'd come to respect.

"Okay, give me a blow by blow," she said once the young woman left. I did so, starting with the tip I'd received regarding the possibility the home invasion might be connected to a major drug buy then moving on to our interview with the home owners, the police and ultimately with the painting restorer, Betteldorf. I skimmed lightly over my altercation with members of the street gang but gave her enough so she could see I'd been able to confirm the link.

"So you're going to follow up on Betteldorf's contact in Berlin?"

"That's it. That's why you've made all those travel arrangements."

"Wow!"

Just then, our server came with our first course and the bottle of wine. We turned our attention to her, patiently monitoring her effort at uncorking of the wine and offering me the opportunity of sampling it. It was delicious: dry, but with a pleasant fruity taste and with just enough oak to satisfy my need for a solid finish. I acknowledged my approval and let her fill our glasses.

"So what else is happening with William Church Recoveries Ltd.?" I asked once she'd left out table.

"That new art gallery on the peninsula is ready for you to do a security walk through. I keep putting them off but they're getting anxious: their opening date is only a few weeks away and they want to make sure they've made sufficient provisions for the safety of their artists' installations."

"What else?"

"That insurance company based in Dallas you do work for called. It seems a valuable coin collection was stolen from a home in Houston and they want you to recover it."

"Tell them I'll get right to it once I've finished up this job… tell them it shouldn't be more than a week or so."

"Will do. There's another job waiting as well. Seems an elderly and quite obviously wealthy set of grandparents are troubled by the prospect of their daughter and her husband taking their two grandchildren on a tour of Latin America. They're worried about kidnappers and want you to vet the itinerary—advise the parents on what parts of what countries should be avoided."

"Why'd they come to me?"

"Seems they learned of your safe recovery of that eleven year old boy from Miami that got kidnapped in Mexico City last year."

"Have them fax the itinerary. I'll take a look at it tomorrow morning. Anything else?"

"Nope, that's it."

"Okay, but if you get a chance either some time today or early tomorrow I'd appreciate it if you'd drop by that international currency exchange place on Market and pick up some Euros for me."

"Will do. So how do you like the salad?"

"Except for the fact I prefer romaine to arugula it's great!"

The rest of the luncheon was devoted to culinary conversation, with Chelsea arguing for an Alice Waters kind of cuisine while I tried to defend my dedication to martinis and steak.

* * *

A sailboat race off the marina breakwater caught my eye as I drove towards the Presidio. I was tempted to turn off and head down there but knew if I did I'd never make it to the Legion of Honor. So I kept going, entering the Presidio at the Lombard Gate and sticking to Lincoln Avenue as it wound its way through the sprawling Civil War Era military base that now serves as a scenic refuge for urban weary residents and tourists alike. I drove slowly, capitalizing on the absence of traffic to get more than just a momentary glimpse of the Golden Gate Bridge and of the narrow passage of water leading out from it towards the Pacific Ocean. No freighters were in view but dollops of white on the deep blue canvas of the water signaled the presence of sailboats cautiously venturing beyond the safety of the bay.

I picked up a little speed as I passed through the residential zone known as Sea Cliff that begins where the Presidio leaves off, finally making my way up into that part of Lincoln Park known as Lands End—a piece of heavily forested high ground overlooking the Pacific Ocean. There on a landscaped piece of land sits the monumental Beaux Arts building known as the Legion of Honor. I pulled into a parking spot at the edge of the circular fountain located across the road from the museum. An almost thread-like jet of water rose steadily from the center of the fountain, reaching some ten feet or so into the air. I paused for a moment to take in the setting. Gardeners kept a steady supply of blossoming flowers growing along the wide concrete walkway leading up to the entrance and tourists were taking photos of their handiwork. I joined them, equally drawn by the profusion of vivid colors assembled for our enjoyment.

But finally I turned away from the scenery and entered the museum. A portion of the west wing was dedicated to Impressionist paintings belonging to the museum's permanent collection and it was those paintings I wished to see. There is seldom a time of day when the museum does not have a goodly crowd of visitors and today was no exception. But I made my way through the galleries without much difficulty—not stopping to take in paintings of other periods—and finally reached my destination. The place was filled with visitors so my desire to give attention to each painting required patience as one or another person momentarily blocked my view while pausing to give the painting a quick study.

I was especially interested in the French Impressionists as it was from among these painters that the couple in Chicago had assembled their representative collection—the one stolen during the home invasion. Fortunately, the museum had examples of the paintings of all six of the artists involved, as well as several of the works of one of the more definitive of French Impressionists, Claude Monet. I began with Monet, taking careful note of his style as reflected in the three works on display: *The Grand Canal, Venice; Sailboats on the Seine; Waves Breaking*. I'd sat in on a few lectures on the Impressionist Movement while at the university but had trouble recalling much in the way of technical attributes beyond the more obvious: vibrancy of color, bold brush strokes, a playfulness with natural light, outdoor themes of 'everyday' import. More subtle considerations involving the application of paint to canvas escaped me. So I occupied myself with studying the more general aesthetic effect each painting tended to elicit— which came down to asking myself "would I want to live with it?" On that basis, only *Sailboats on the Seine* made the cut.

I moved on to the lithographs of Pierre Bonnard, one of the six artists included in the stolen set. Two of his works were on display: *La partie de cartes* and *Femme assise sa bagnoire*. The first was a scene of a card game done in charcoal and the second a woman in a bathtub. Both were surprisingly understated in their execution, offering minimal strokes to convey the scene and leaving the viewer to fill out the detail, but I kind of liked the effect.

A single painting by Henri Matisse caught my eye as I moved across the gallery. It was entitled *Girl in a Hat and Veil* and done in color aquatint. What I liked about it was the two-dimensional effect where the woman, the table she leans against, and the backdrop of flowering shrubs all seem to compete for prominence. This one really connected with me. I'd hang it in my flat in a minute!

A Raoul Dufy wood cut entitled *La Danse* was hanging nearby. Done in black ink on white paper, it depicted a sailor dancing with a local maiden on some tropical island with a sailing ship at anchor just beyond the foliage. I was struck by the energy and movement Dufy conveyed through his use of bold cuts and was instantly reminded how critical these two attributes were to this artistic movement.

The two oil paintings on display by Eugene Louis Boudin, *Harbor at Bordeaux* and *Figures on the Beach*, gave one the feeling of looking at scenes through some sort of old fashioned hand-made window glass where the images were faintly blurry due to the ripple effect often encountered in such glass. What surprised me was how effective it was in giving the scenes an almost dream-like quality that I found rather charming.

At the far end of the gallery I spotted the works of the final two artists represented in the set stolen in Chicago: Edouard Vuillard and Pierre Auguste Renoir. Vuillard's *La Patisserie* hung on the wall to the right of an opening leading to the next gallery. Next to it was his *Le Jardin devant L'Atelier*. Both were color lithographs. In the former, bold panels of brown, gray and black, with touches of green and red, are transformed into a delicate image of a café scene when viewed at a distance. In the latter, the same effect is produced but this time it's through the clever use of gray and green daubs that one recognizes the garden outside the artist's studio.

I've always been a fan of Renoir's paintings, especially his use of vibrant colors and his voluptuous rendering of females and children—themes well illustrated in his *Mother and Child*, an oil on canvas painted in about 1895 hanging to the left of the opening. I can't say I'd rank it among my favorites but it drives home why art of the Impressionist movement seems to attract such ardent collectors.

I turned and retraced my steps back through the gallery, through the interconnecting rooms leading to the front lobby and out into the sunshine. It was late afternoon and the number of tourists idling in front of the flowerbeds had diminished considerably. As I walked to the car my thoughts were still focused on the artworks and I kept thinking whoever was behind the art theft couldn't be accused of harboring eccentric taste—an insight not conducive to simplifying the task before me.

* * *

"Hey Jack, it's me, Church," I shouted once the radio indicator on the car dashboard signaled I'd made the connection.

"Church! It's good to hear from you. Where are you?"

"On Lincoln, on my way back to the flat. What're the chances of us getting together for drinks?"

"Any time, buddy."

"Let's say about six…at the hotel bar."

"Will do, see you then…and be ready to give your old sailing partner a full debriefing on that shoot up in Chicago!"

I pressed the disconnect button on the steering wheel and refocused my attention on the curving roadway ahead of me as I navigated the Presidio grounds. I stayed off the principal roadways that cut through the city in order to avoid rush hour traffic and made it back to my building in less than a half hour. Chelsea was on duty when I entered the lobby. She motioned for me to join her at the front desk.

"That was a nice lunch, Church," she said once I'd approached.

"Always is when I'm out with you, gorgeous. What's up?"

"Picked up the Euros you requested. They're sitting on the coffee table in your condo, along with the airplane tickets and a confirmation sheet on the hotel reservation in Berlin…oh, and also, that Latin American itinerary I was telling you about arrived about an hour ago. I put it up in your flat along with the other stuff."

"Great! I'll take a look at it tomorrow morning. Right now, I need a hot shower and a change of clothes. I'm meeting Jack for drinks at six."

"Well have fun…though it's hard to see how two grown men can enjoy themselves without the presence of at least one charming lady seated across from them."

"Are you angling for an invite?"

"Perish the thought! Anyway, I'm on duty until 7:30."

I blew her a kiss and headed for the elevator. Once inside the flat I headed for the bedroom, stripped off the jeans, white sports shirt and lightweight cotton sports coat I'd been wearing and headed for the shower. Properly refreshed, I changed into a pair of black jeans, black cotton shirt and a black and tan tweed sports jacket. I had some time before heading over to our favorite hotel bar so I powered up my lap top and caught up with the day's news.

* * *

Jack arrived before I did and chose seating off to the far side of the lounge where we could talk quietly. He was wearing the typical FBI uniform: non-descript suit, white shirt and tie. But his athletic build, his healthy shock of dark hair and the bright expression on his face gave credence to the real Jack underlying that bureaucratic guise. I pulled up a chair across from him and reached for the martini he'd already ordered.

"So give me the lowdown on that shooting the cops called me about," he said, settling back in his chair, his right hand gently holding a glass of single malted scotch.

I described in detail the sequence of events that began with my bracing one of the leaders of the street gang who admitted pulling off the home invasion. "Clearly, the guy fingered me to the wise guys who handled the cash-for-paintings deal. I imagine we picked up a tail as soon as we left the hotel the next morning. Once they saw we'd made the connection between Betteldorf and the heist they must have panicked and thought to take us out."

"Why not just shoot you right there and then rather than attempt a snatch?"

"My best guess is they needed to find out how far the whole thing had unraveled so they could let their paymaster know."

"From what you've told me it seems they made a real bad judgement call, seeing as how nobody but you and that insurance woman had tied Betteldorf to the case. If they'd just taken the two of you out the cops would still be clueless."

"That's right, and they're still clueless. I haven't shared what I've learned with the authorities, nor has the insurance company."

"Well buddy that means you and the girl are still in danger. Don't think it'll take the bad guys much time to figure out the cops are still working the case as a simple home invasion."

"I'm counting on it. Once I show up in Berlin they'll be real interested in having a conversation…should bring them out into the open."

"Yeah, but they won't be so easy to get the drop on next time, not after the way those two heavies ended up dead. Which brings up the question as to why you chose to go for your gun with a gun pointed right at your head?"

"Probably not the smartest move I've ever made, but Jack, you know me, there's no way I'm going to let some clown subdue me…even if it means risking death. Anyway, I thought it was a gamble I could take. They didn't know enough about me to worry I might be armed, they had me outnumbered, had the drop on me, had Emily as a hostage—so I'm thinking they'd be a little slow on the uptake and I was right…just barely."

"You going armed to Berlin?"

"Yeah, I've still got a valid concealed weapon permit issued by Interpol—one of the perks of having helped solve several big ticket crimes over there while with the FBI."

"True as that might be you'll do well to remember the Europeans don't take kindly to a shooting no matter how righteous. It'll take more than a phone call to me to get the authorities off your back."

"I figured that'd be the case but it works both ways, the bad guys will want to avoid gunplay just as much. That gives me something of an advantage since they'll worry I'm some sort of Wild West cowboy who'll come out shooting if they threaten me."

"Interesting logic. Hope it plays out that way."

Well, let's turn to a more pleasant topic: how's the sailing been?"

We spent the rest of the time together catching up on Jack's outings on the Bay, the condition of the boat, the cases he was working on and the ups and downs of his relationship with Lisa, his current girlfriend. After a couple of drinks we moved on to a new Italian restaurant just off Market where we had the restaurant's signature seafood pasta dish and washed it down with some Chianti Reserva.

DAY 7

Sunshine threw an eye-opening glare across the bedroom prompting me to climb out of bed despite the early hour—a consequence of a fog-free morning and my negligence last evening at failing to close the window drapes. Actually, it was a good thing, I told myself, because I needed much of the shortened workday to tie up a few loose ends before heading to the airport around three o'clock that afternoon. I sat at the kitchen counter spooning my cereal while I read over the itinerary Chelsea had left for me to examine. All in all, the grandparents' concern about the travel plans of their daughter and her husband seemed a little overblown. True, the newspapers have had a field day reporting on drug violence in Mexico and elsewhere in Latin America but most of the violence affects only those involved in the drug trafficking business itself, not tourists. Still, a family of wealth needed to take the risk of kidnapping seriously, as did senior executives of prominent corporations. But in this case the grandparents had been able to avoid undue publicity regarding their wealth, making it less likely members of the family would show up on the radar of gangs responsible for abductions. In any case, I dutifully vetted the itinerary, deleting those stops where the risks were unacceptably high and adding alternative destinations that would please the grandchildren but for some reason had been left off the original itinerary. I printed out my comments, attached them to the itinerary sheets and stuffed the whole batch of papers in a large manila envelope with "Chelsea" scrawled prominently across the sealed flap.

By the time I'd finished it was too late for an early morning run at Crissy and anyway I needed a gym workout a lot more than a run so I threw on some street clothes, grabbed my gym bag and headed out.

"Make sure Chelsea gets this," I said to the attendant at the desk in the lobby as I handed her the manila envelope.

"Will do Mr. Church."

I acknowledged his reply and walked towards the elevator that would take me to the underground parking garage. Minutes later, I was cruising down Howard on my way to the gym on Folsom Street. I turned left at Dore Street then left again on to Folsom, crossed Ninth and parked. Boris the sculptor greeted me at the front desk.

"Been a while since you last showed up…been out of town or what?" he said as we shook hands.

"Christ, it's been only a week," I said. "You'd think you were my manager getting me ready for some sort of prize fight."

"Naw, just an old worrywart with too little to do and a hankering for some company. What'll you say to lunch…today, after your workout?"

"It's a deal but it'll have to be a quick one. I've got a plane to catch later today and I haven't yet packed."

"So, you gonna be gone long this time also?"

"No, Boris, I'm not…leastwise not more than a week if I can help it, and whatever you think for most people a week is not a long time!"

"You'd get an argument on that I'd wager," said Boris with a laugh. "So what's your pleasure: weights or martial arts?"

"Weights today, so there's no need to scrounge up a partner for me," I replied as I headed for the changing room.

Boris had sunk a lot of money in good quality weight machines, free weights and benches. It was a pleasure to build up a sweat working through set after set of repetitions on such equipment. Frank, my workout partner the previous week, was toweling off after a shower as I came in.

"Hey, Church, you're too late for another roll on the mat."

"Not to worry, Frank, all I've come for is some time with the weights."

He laughed and returned his attention to the business at hand while I sought out my locker. I changed into gym shorts, a T-shirt and a pair of cross-trainers and headed for the weight room. I started out with some stretches, turned next to abdominals then began a more lengthy set of upper body strength exercises—some with free weights and others with Nautilus-style machines. I rounded out the set with leg curls, leg presses and adduction/

abduction routines. By the time I'd run through the circuit a couple of times I'd built up a healthy sweat. Pausing to wipe the sweat off my face and neck I began to think about heading for the showers. I glanced up at the clock on the wall and realized it was getting late. If I was to have lunch with Boris I had better hustle.

This part of the city has lots of small lunch places, most run by immigrants from one part of the world or another and catering to workers in the light industrial shops that comprise the bulk of neighborhood businesses. Boris and I walked to the one at the corner nearest his place. It was run by an eastern European couple in their fifties who prepare fresh sandwiches each morning and stock a goodly range of ice-cold beverages. We took our sandwiches and drinks to one of the small tables on the sidewalk outside the place and sat down.

"So how's the sculpture coming…you know, the one you claim represents the mathematical concept of infinity?" I asked after washing down the first large bite of my sandwich.

"I'd say it's probably ready for you to take another look at but you know me, Church, nothing really seems finished to my eye. Perhaps if it pleases you, we can go up to my studio after we finish here. Now on to more important things, my friend, tell me about Chicago. Did Jerry's information prove helpful?"

"You mean the drug angle he threw out? Yeah, it was a good lead. Next time you see him give him my thanks."

"What can you tell me about it?"

I gave him a brief rundown, highlighting the links between the home invasion and the theft of the paintings but downplaying the street altercation and the shooting.

"So now you go to Europe in pursuit of those paintings?"

"If that's where they are…it's an assumption I'm making. I'll just have to check it out."

Boris nodded as he continued to eat. I could see he was ruminating about something but I didn't press him—just continued munching on my sandwich while enjoying the feel of the warm sunshine and gentle midday breeze.

"Maybe I come with you," he said suddenly.

"What're you talking about?" I asked.

"I'm thinking these are dangerous guys you're going up against. With Boris at your side it would be safer."

I put my hand on his arm and gave it a squeeze. "Look old friend, I appreciate the gesture. God knows, you've got the talent and experience to handle anything that comes down, and with fluency in the key European languages nobody would make you as somebody fresh off a jet from the U.S., but I work alone, always have, and with what you've taught me these past few years I'm pretty confident things will go in my favor should it come to that."

"So, you're not going to give poor Boris an opportunity for a vacation away from this lousy street, huh?"

"If you want a vacation tell your wife, Gloria. She'll jump at the chance…and knowing her she'll have it all mapped out before the day's through."

"Yeah, but she'll want to go someplace that's fun: you know, some place she's read about in the magazines."

"Nothing wrong with that."

"Like hell there isn't! It's been some time since I've had a chance to use a little muscle. Your operation promises some excitement, something my wife's doesn't."

"That may be, but the answer is still the same. Now let's get back to your place and have a look at that piece of sculpture," I said as I rose from my seat and gathered up the paper plate, napkins and empty plastic beverage bottle for dumping in the trash on the way out.

* * *

I got back to the flat a little after one o'clock—time enough to pack, give Guy Sanderson a call and change out of my city jeans and rough cotton blazer into something more in keeping with European sensibilities. Given the hour, I thought I'd better give Guy a call first—it'd be close to the end of the business day back East and Guy, who had a long commute home, probably wouldn't stick around the office like many of his colleagues.

I put the call through.

"He's been waiting for your call," said Betsy, Sanderson's secretary, once I'd had a chance to identify myself. "I'll connect you."

"Hey Church, it's about time you got back to me. You all right?"

"Couldn't be better. Emily fill you in?"

"Yeah, I have her report. Seems you scared the hell out of her with all that shooting."

"Couldn't be helped. She pulled her weight though…all during the time spent in Chicago. She say whether she learned anything?"

"Give me a break, all she talks about is you!"

"You give her any grief about the expenses we chalked up?"

"No. But I told her not to get any ideas she could operate that way when running solo. You heading for Europe soon?"

"I leave for the airport in less than two hours."

"So, what's your game plan? You thinking the art is stashed somewhere in Berlin?"

"Don't know about that but since I'm guessing both Betteldorf and his colleague, Herr Reichwein, are there it's the next link in the chain. I'll make contact with Reichwein and see where that leads. Chances are slim he'll know the identity of the party that commissioned the theft but I'm hoping he'll at least be able to finger the syndicate that engineered the whole thing."

"Well, take care of yourself and for God's sake keep in touch!"

"Will do," I said just before cutting our connection.

I packed a week's worth of clothes, mixing in both stuff I'd wear in more sophisticated circles with stuff meant for the street, but selecting only items with European labels in the hope I'd stand out a little less in both venues—not an easy undertaking given my build and height and what my European friends called my distinctively American body language.

I put in a call for a taxi after closing my two pieces of black leather luggage. It took only a few more minutes to finish dressing then, luggage in hand, I headed for the door. The cab was already parked in front of the entrance by the time the elevator let me off in the lobby. "SFO International Terminal," I said to the cabby as I settled back in the seat and closed my eyes, hoping to get a quick nap before confronting the throngs of travelers and the tedious officialdom of the airport.

* * *

"Welcome, Mr. Church," said the attractive, middle-aged attendant in First Class as she led me to my seat. "May I bring you something to drink—some champagne perhaps?"

"Nothing at the moment, thank you," I replied as I stowed my luggage in the rack above my seat. "But once we're airborne and you're free to move around I'd be pleased if you would bring me a martini—gin if you have it…and some nuts."

"With pleasure. And may I hang up your jacket?"

I removed my jacket and handed it to her then sat down and took inventory of the in-flight amenities of this airline's First Class accommodations.

Later, with a surprisingly good martini in hand, I began to work through in my mind the various steps I'd need to take to close in on the paintings. I suspected I'd be confronting at least three different individuals or groups of individuals: Reichwein, the criminal syndicate and the ultimate client. I couldn't be sure they would all be located in Berlin, or in Germany for that matter, but unless he's bolted I should at least find Reichwein there. I took out his business card Betteldorf had given me and studied the address. It was in the Charlottenburg District and appeared to be a flat just south of Kurfürstendamm on Fasanenstraße. I knew the neighborhood well, having rented a room—on Mommsenstraße, not more than a few blocks distant—during a stint in Berlin shortly after graduating from college.

Fasanenstraße was a fashionable street, with stately apartment buildings lovingly restored and sidewalks lined with tall leafy trees. In recent years it had become known for its cluster of fine art galleries and for the quiet ambiance one encountered as one turned off the crowded and noisy Kurfürstendamm onto its shaded path. Clearly, Reichwein had taste and the income necessary to sustain it. He wouldn't welcome my arrival, especially after hearing from Betteldorf how I threatened to blow the whistle on him. A similar threat should convince Reichwein to cooperate. Then again, he may have already sought protection from the syndicate, making my attempt to contact him somewhat more arduous than a pleasant walk down his arbor-covered street.

I leaned back, stretched my legs and closed my eyes, letting the mellowing effect of the martini silence further thoughts about what might lie in store for me in Berlin.

DAY 8

We landed at Berlin's Tegel Airport a little after eleven o'clock. I'd gone through customs earlier that morning at the Frankfurt Airport, completing the paperwork for the concealed weapon, so my exit from the terminal was swift. Chelsea, bless her soul, had arranged for the hotel to send a car. I learned of it as I approached the outer doors of the terminal and encountered a man holding a placard with my name on it. I nodded to him.

"Mr. Church, is it?" he asked in English.

I replied in German that, indeed, I was William Church.

"The staff of the hotel wishes to express its pleasure in having you as its guest. Arrangements have been made for me to drive you. Do you have any checked luggage?"

I assured him I didn't and handed him my two pieces of carry-on luggage. He led the way to a limo parked nearby. I climbed into the back seat while he deposited the luggage in the trunk. It felt good to settle into the soft leather seat. I was a little tired from the flights and from jet lag but put all that aside as we made our way out of the terminal complex and approached the access point for the autobahn. It had been a couple of years since my last visit and I was eager to take in all the sights of one of my favorite European cities.

"Are we expecting rain over the next few days?" I asked in German.

"No. The forecast is for pleasant weather," he replied, having now switched to German after it had become clear I was fluent in his native language.

"Take the scenic route I'm in no hurry," I said.

The driver nodded in agreement and pulled onto the autobahn, taking it only as far as the Spandauer Damm turn off. He cruised leisurely by the Schloss Charlottenburg, that beautifully restored Eighteenth Century Baroque palace, then turned onto the Otto Suhr Allee, taking us to Ernst Reuter Platz and the beginning of that grand avenue that runs through the Tiergarten: *Straße des 17, Juni.* A scattering of cumulus clouds against the soft blue of the sky offered a gentle background to the deeply green foliage of the Tiergarten. There was little traffic and the driver took his time working his way east along the avenue so I could enjoy the formal landscaping as we motored by. Eventually we passed by the Brandenburg Gate, crossed the Pariser Platz then turned left onto Wilhelmstraße, pulling up in front of the hotel only minutes later. The hotel, just off the Pariser Platz, the square immediately behind the Brandenburg Gate, is a starkly modern hostelry set in the legendary Mitte District—a district evocative of early Twentieth Century Berlin. At that time, the Mitte District was the heart of the city, with its museums, university and fashionable hotels. It was an era I was familiar with and appreciated, and staying at a hotel in the district always seemed to give me a sense of connectedness to that part of the city's history.

"Welcome back Mr. Church," said the attendant manning the reception desk once I checked in. "Your room is ready for you."

I followed the busboy to the bank of elevators, passing along the far side of the central lounge where a scattering of small groups and individuals were having their late morning coffee. My room was high up, overlooking the grand edifices directly across the street. And if I pushed back the curtains of my windows I could catch a glimpse of the Brandenburg Gate. I unpacked, took a long shower and dressed in street clothes—black jeans, white shirt and a lightweight black leather jacket of German manufacture that concealed the weapon holstered at my waist.

It was approaching one o'clock when I finally left the room and although I was hungry I resisted the urge to make a beeline for the in-house restaurant, preferring instead to slip out of the hotel and head on foot for the U-Bahn station at Potsdamer Platz not much more than a half mile away. Food could wait, I was anxious to get to the Charlottenburg District and make contact with Reichwein before my presence in the city was more widely known. Use of the subway system to get around was one further tactic at remaining inconspicuous and might put off any auto-based surveillance already in place. At least that was my thinking as I walked briskly down Ebertstraße, my attention directed at passing traffic—both vehicular and pedestrian—in the hope I'd spot anybody giving my presence any undue attention.

I reached the U-Bahn station without having detected any surveillance and purchased a ticket that would entitle me to ride at least as far as the Kurfürstendamm stop where I intended to get off. The ride was uneventful, with passengers calmly slipping on and off as the car advanced from one to another of the five intervening stops. No one appeared to glance in my direction, reassuring me that my efforts at trying to fit in were working at least to some extent. One couldn't be sure, however, since subway etiquette would minimize conspicuous staring in any case.

Once I exited the U-Bahn station I headed for Breitscheid Platz, a block to the east, where I could grab a quick lunch from one of the food vendors out in front of the Europa Center. Trying not to drop any of it, I carried the take-out food to a shady place across the square where I could watch the antics of a team of jugglers while I ate. They were pretty good, especially the girl.

After I'd finished eating I headed over to Fasanenstraße, three blocks to the west. Kurfürstendam was bustling as usual, with shoppers and other folks plying its spacious sidewalks, out enjoying a midday break from nearby offices and shops. I took my time, enjoying the sunny weather and the crowd, but eventually reached Fasanenstraße and turned on to it. I crossed over to the side of the street Reichwein's residence would be on, given its address, and walked on.

There weren't more than a handful of other pedestrians in sight as I walked past a small community park located to my right that was densely landscaped with trees and shrubs. Just then, two tall, well-built men walking behind me and apparently engaged in light-hearted banter overtook me but instead of passing on either side they crowded up against me, each taking hold of one of my arms and forcing me off the street and into the tiny park. After only a few steps they attempted to shove me violently to the ground but their timing was off, with the guy on the left letting go a fraction of a second earlier than the guy on the right. With the momentum provided by the first guy's shove I swung my body around in front of the guy on my right, grabbed hold of his right shoulder with my left hand and rammed my left knee into his groin. The blow forced him to release his grip on my right arm and I rolled aside as we both came crashing down. I sprung back up into a crouch just as the other guy leveled a vicious kick at my head—a kick I intercepted with a karate chop to his calf that momentarily knocked him off balance. I followed through on the motion of the chop, pivoting on my right leg and swinging my left leg in an arc that brought my foot up against the side of his head. As he went down, the other guy lunged at me, getting a chokehold on my neck before I could turn to face him. I arched my head backwards violently crashing into his face and breaking his nose, but he was a professional and didn't lose his grip despite the pain. As he tightened his hold, his eyes closed trying to ignore the pain, I suddenly bent forward, lifting him off the ground then twisting to the left and flipping him over my right side. We both went down but the impact of hitting the ground forced him to break his grip. I ended up on top of him and managed to throw a sharp elbow blow to his neck that cut off his breathing. As he fought to regain his breath I rose up and delivered a kick to his chest, breaking several ribs. He was done fighting.

The other guy, however, had shaken off my earlier blow and approached warily, looking for an advantage. I had about two inches in height on him and some twenty pounds of weight. He seemed to sense this and now knew I had serious martial arts skills. But he must have figured he could best me and assumed an offensive stance. I let him advance. His first move was to kick at my right leg, hoping to land a crippling blow, but I countered by lunging inside the arc of his kick and threw an old-fashioned right arm punch into his solar plexus. As he bent over in pain I grabbed his hair and brought my knee up into his face. It was all over.

I pulled out each of their wallets as they lay immobile on the grass in the tiny park and pocketed their identification. They must have known the park would be empty and planned the takedown accordingly for despite all the commotion no one seemed to have observed us. There was no reason to attempt an interrogation. I knew who they were, or at least had a pretty good idea who they worked for. I brushed myself off, wiped their blood from my hands and head with Kleenex from my back pocket and tossed the wad into a trash receptacle as I walked back to the street.

As I continued down Fasanenstraße I reflected on the implications of the attack. Clearly, word was out that I was in town and that there was every expectation I would be paying a visit to our Mr. Reichwein. That meant Betteldorf had been debriefed by the syndicate about my visit to his studio—either back in Chicago or here, assuming he'd already arrived. It also meant I'd been watched and that my ruse of using public transportation and dressing to fit in hadn't thrown them off. I kept thinking they had to have a fair amount of manpower to pull off a surveillance gig of that scope and to devise a takedown choreographed to take advantage of concealment by the tiny park's foliage. Whoever they were they weren't amateurs.

I reached the address given on Reichwein's business card and paused to examine the building. It was a four-story prewar structure done in sand-colored stucco with Romanesque ornamentation and window treatments. The registry plate beside the front entrance indicated Reichwein's apartment was on the third floor. I stepped back to get a glimpse at the facade on that level and noted his was the only unit to have a wrought iron balcony with large French windows opening on to it. The curtains were open and I wondered whether he'd been alerted somehow to my presence in his neighborhood and was at this very moment looking down in anticipation of my arrival. The front door was locked so I pressed the third floor button on the intercom panel, wondering whether he'd let me in.

"Who is it?" inquired a male voice with a pronounced south German accent.

"William Church to see Herr Reichwein, compliments of Herr Betteldorf," I replied in German.

"Please state your business."

"A sensitive matter regarding the disappearance of six Impressionist paintings in Chicago about two weeks ago. I've been asked to make enquiries. Perhaps you'd rather talk to the Berlin police?"

The electronically activated lock on the front door opened and I stepped into the front hall. A passageway led directly back towards the rear of the building but most of the hall was taken up with an elaborate staircase rising ornately towards the upper apartments. I climbed the stairs, marveling at the quality of the building's restoration. The door to the third floor apartment was already open when I reached that level and a man about Betteldorf's age stood there wearing what could only be regarded as a scowl. I smiled indulgently and offered my hand. "Herr Reichwein, I presume."

He motioned for me to enter his apartment and closed the door afterwards. I followed as he walked briskly down the hallway and into the drawing room. It was a large room with a high ceiling and walls covered with museum-quality art. A sitting area composed of deeply cushioned antique chairs and centered on a rich Oriental carpet was bathed in the afternoon sunlight coming through the French windows facing the street. Altogether a splendid room, marking the man as a person of cultivated taste and one with the means to live in such a style.

Satisfied he'd made the impression he'd sought he abruptly turned and fixed me with an imperious stare. "Now what is this business about artworks and what could my associate, Herr Betteldorf, possibly have said that would induce you to make your enquiries on my premises?"

"Oh I think you already know the answer to these questions," Herr Reichwein. "May I sit down?"

He shrugged as I allowed myself to take a seat facing away from the windows so as to avoid the glare while being able to continue enjoying the interior furnishings of the apartment. "I must say you have splendid taste," I said. "Is that one of the reasons you were selected to serve as an intermediary with Herr Betteldorf? After all, your associates could have approached him directly I would have imagined—seeing how anxious he was to live out his retirement years in Berlin. By the way, has he arrived yet?"

"You presume too much, Mr. Church. My connection to Herr Betteldorf is entirely professional and, I might add, confidential. At the moment, I have no business dealings with the man and therefore no reason to know of his whereabouts."

"According to Herr Betteldorf, you and he were close friends—a friendship going back some years…to the time both of you lived in Frankfurt."

"An impression quite profitable in a business built on personal contacts but regrettably not quite accurate, Mr. Church. Herr Betteldorf was a valuable conduit to a number of art collectors, both here and in the United States, that is all."

"I'm sure Herr Betteldorf would be distressed were he to learn of it, but it's not a matter that greatly concerns me. My only interest is your connection to the Walkers of Chicago, Herr Reichwein. Did Herr Betteldorf introduce you to them?"

"As a matter of fact he didn't. Apparently, they were not interested in being approached with regard to their Impressionist collection."

"But despite such reluctance—a reluctance well known to Herr Betteldorf—you were able to persuade him to divulge to you detailed information not only on the six paintings themselves but on the manner of their display within the residence and on what security measures the couple had taken to avoid theft."

"I deny that I ever received such information!"

"Yet you admit you are familiar with the paintings."

"Well, yes, my discussions with Herr Betteldorf did advance to the level of profiling the six Impressionist paintings in the Walker collection but certainly no further—certainly not to the level of detail you insinuate!"

"Herr Reichwein, you live well, you appear to enjoy the pleasures a generous income can provide, do you really want to jeopardize all this by refusing to cooperate with me?"

"What are you implying…that by some mysterious means you have the power to affect my life? That's preposterous?"

"It's not really mysterious at all. I have close contacts with the art theft team at Interpol. I believe they would find credible my description of your role in the international theft of a group of art works valued conservatively in the millions. And even if you could escape prosecution due to insufficient evidence word would quickly get out that you were a man tainted by rumors of supplying intelligence leading to the thefts of art. I suspect most collectors would not wish to take the chance of having any dealings with you."

"This is slanderous! Are you trying to blackmail me? Perhaps you wouldn't be so bold in your remarks if you knew there are others involved in my business dealings…others who have the means to make painfully clear to you the regrettable consequences of your insinuations!"

"You mean like the two thugs that attempted to prevent me from visiting you today? I hardly think you should feel secure having such personnel as protection. I suspect both are currently at some medical clinic getting their injuries seen to."

I could see the shock on his face. He clearly hadn't known about the assault, nor been alerted about the likelihood of my visit. The syndicate was keeping him in the dark. "So, Herr Reichwein, why don't you tell me how I can make contact with the syndicate who engineered the theft. That's all I want to know, I've no interest in you. My only interest is retrieving the art. You cooperate and our relationship comes to a close. You fail to cooperate and I make your life miserable, it's as simple as that."

"They can make my life miserable as well, Mr. Church, perhaps even kill me. Why should I risk such an eventuality?"

"Let me worry about getting you off the hook with the syndicate. They'll presume I got a line on them from having lifted the ID's from the two thugs and that's just what I'll tell them once we've had a chance to talk."

"But they'll know I talked to you."

"Yes they will, but they also know you're a guy who knows how to finesse a situation. I'll leak the news that you needed to think it over…that you'd get in touch with me soon. In the meantime I followed up on the ID's and made the connection. You're home free unless you panic under aggressive questioning."

Reichwein thought about it then sat down and began to talk. "They are very powerful. You don't want to get involved."

"Trust me."

"They are based here in Berlin…I don't know how many there are but they have connections and much money."

"Who is your contact?"

"A man called Werner. He represents himself as a private banker, with offices on Friedrichstraße—at this address," he said, writing down the address for me.

"How'd you get involved with him?"

"He approached me some years ago, in connection with a client seeking a Monet. He paid handsomely for my services. I've represented him and his associates ever since."

"What's his full name?"

"I don't know. He simply identifies himself as Herr Werner."

"But surely the building directory where he has an office would list his full name or at least his surname?"

"Yes, one would think so but surprisingly it doesn't, and when I call on the phone and ask to speak with Herr Werner the receptionist doesn't display any puzzlement."

"Can you describe him?"

"A man of average height, well-groomed with thinning gray hair and always conservatively and expensively dressed. I would guess he's about sixty years old, speaks with a decisive and authoritative tone...in good Berliner German I might add."

"The man you describe doesn't seem all that frightening. What is it about him that makes you so fearful?"

"There is a brutish manner about him...I can't put my finger on precisely what it is that alarms me but to be in his presence is to feel an uneasiness...a sense that disagreeable things can happen if one incurs his displeasure."

"I take it you've been in that situation from time to time?"

"Yes, yes I have, Mr. Church, and I have no desire to invite any repetition."

"But did he actually threaten you or harm you in any way those times you incurred his displeasure?"

"It was in his eyes. He stared at me the way a predator might stare at an easily dispatched object of prey, calculating whether it should execute a kill or allow the animal to walk by. In the few times I was meant to feel like that animal I somehow managed to gain a reprieve so the answer to your question is no, but there was no escaping the sense of dread that haunted my thinking for weeks afterwards."

"I'm getting the impression you'd be inclined to regard this Werner person as not simply a front for the syndicate but more than likely its actual leader."

"I have no way of knowing but, yes, if I had to guess I'd say the chances were good that Herr Werner is a principal player within the syndicate."

"One last question, did all your dealings with Herr Werner result in the acquisition of the desired art works by means of criminal acts such as in the case of the Chicago heist?"

"No, not always. I had the impression legitimate means would be used to secure the desired object or objects should that be possible but if not other less savory methods would be employed—the lesson being that the syndicate always managed to get its way, one way or another."

"What you're implying is that this syndicate is a quasi-legitimate organization with a reputation for always succeeding on behalf of its clients, no questions asked."

"Yes, I believe that would be a fair way to describe it."

"This syndicate must have a name. How else could it market its services?"

"No, I'm afraid it doesn't…at least not one that I'm aware of. It seems potential clients are informed by a trusted confidant, maybe a private banker, an attorney or a freelance art broker such as myself. One way or another they learn of the availability of a group of expeditors who guarantee the acquisition of a particular work of art. In my experience, private collectors are not put off by the fact these people choose not to have any public identity despite having to pay them a very generous commission for their services."

"So the syndicate has no public identity, its membership held secret, and its only known contact is a man without a surname."

"Yes, I'm afraid that's the case."

"Interesting. Well, despite your misgivings you've been helpful, Herr Reichwein, and as I said earlier I'll make an effort to keep confidential your role in the enquiry." I stood up and allowed him to escort me to the front door. "Just keep to the story I outlined regarding your success in stonewalling me during my visit and you should come through this without suffering any harm," I said as I shook his hand. "I shouldn't think we'll be meeting again," I added as I started down the stairs. He nodded, but with a troubled look on his face, and slowly shut the door.

* * *

There was no welcoming committee waiting on the street as I stepped on to Fasanenstraße. Apparently, the two men with whom I'd had a run-in earlier were gone and a second team had not been deployed. I headed for Kurfürstendamm where I knew I could catch a taxi. Although it was late in the afternoon I thought I'd swing by the office of the mysterious Herr Werner. Once I reached the taxi stand at the corner I climbed into the first one in the queue and gave the driver the Friedrichstraße address and settled back for the ride.

I had no intention of actually making contact with Werner this soon after arriving. He'd quickly deduce I'd persuaded Reichwein to talk—something I'd promised not to reveal. No, I simply wanted to get a feel for the location and see what possibilities presented themselves for a discreet takedown should I catch him on the street.

The driver worked his way up Budapester Straße to Tiergarten Straße—the avenue bordering the southern perimeter of the Tiergarten—then dropped down to Potsdamer Straße and on to Potsdamer Platz, passing the spectacular Sony Center in the process. Once across, we were on Leipziger Straße and just minutes away from the intersection with Freidrichstraße. I asked the driver to pull over once we arrived at the corner, explaining I'd like to walk the rest of the way.

The office was on the second floor of a restored pre-war commercial building. The directory listing simply gave the office suite number, no company name or that of any principal agent. Clearly, the uninitiated would have no easy way of learning what went on behind such anonymous labeling. I stood some distance away, checking to see if he'd mounted some sort of security screen. No one seemed to be providing surveillance of the entrance to the building, suggesting he'd not been overly alarmed by my altercation with his two subordinates. The man had style I'd give him that. A stroll around the surrounding blocks revealed a park several blocks away with ample foliage. Other possible intercept points also presented themselves. But whether he would expose himself in such a fashion seemed highly problematical. Having reconnoitered the area I chose to walk back to the hotel. It was getting on to cocktail time and I wanted to freshen up before making my way down to the hotel's central lounge.

* * *

"A martini, straight up with a lemon twist," I said in German to the young woman working my section of the central lounge. It was after five o'clock in the evening and the cocktail lounge was full. I carefully screened the seated parties, looking for someone who exhibited an interest in my presence. None were apparent but given my inability earlier in the day to detect surveillance I wasn't surprised. My drink arrived, along with a concoction of mixed nuts and other tidbits. As I sipped the drink I thought about the day's events. I was particularly surprised by the absence of any sign of the arrival of Herr Betteldorf. Reichwein was convincing in his denial of any contact with the man here in Berlin. It was hard for me to be persuaded that he simply chose to remain in Chicago despite the imminent possibility of police enquiries. I imagined it would all be made clear once I contacted Herr Werner, something I planned to put off for a couple of days. As I finished my drink and checked my watch I realized the hour had come and gone. I signaled the attendant to bring the bill. I'd made reservations at the hotel's fifth floor restaurant for a table overlooking the Brandenburg Gate for seven o'clock—an early time for Europeans but strategic should one wish to secure such a table. I gave my room number and signed the chit then rose and headed for the restaurant.

The sun had not yet set but was expected within the hour when artificial lighting would bathe the Brandenburg Gate in a soft, irresistible marbling of shadows and light. It was a sight I always regarded as a signature portrait of the city and one that I looked forward to contemplating as I enjoyed my dinner. I was seated next to a supporting column, not far from the large floor-to-ceiling windows overlooking Pariser Platz and the monumental gate. I ordered a bottle of Chateauneuf-du-Pape—a Rhône wine of blended delicacy and body I'd come to appreciate in recent years. As I waited for it to arrive a young woman of striking beauty was seated at a table directly across from mine but also one with a generous view of the outdoor scene. Our eyes met and I nodded in acknowledgement.

She wore a black sheath number of elegant simplicity that complemented her pale skin. A stylish rope chain gold necklace and gold earrings finished off the ensemble. I waited for her companion to arrive, thinking he must have been delayed by one task or another, but after enough time had elapsed for the wine steward to bring over the bottle, open it with all the ritual such a task required, and allow me a taste, I came to the conclusion she would be dining alone. The waiter's subsequent removal of the second place setting at her table confirmed my suspicion.

She'd ordered a glass of champagne. Only after it had arrived did she study the menu, delicately sipping the almost transparent liquid as she sought to make up her mind. I watched her as unobtrusively as I could, given the proximity of our tables. My salad had just arrived when she signaled to the waiter she was ready to place her order. Once he'd been given instructions and had set off briskly towards the kitchen, order in hand, she looked over at me and smiled. I smiled in return and raised my wine glass in salute. We were the only two in this section of the restaurant and camaraderie of sorts had already built up between us.

"I take it we're both eating alone," I said. "Conversation being a fine ingredient in any dining experience I wonder if I might suggest we join one another?"

"I believe your table commands the superior view," she said with a smile.

I rose and came around to hold the chair across from me as she got up from her seat and crossed the short distance separating us. A busboy noticed the shift and quickly came over to transfer her champagne glass to my table.

"I'm William Church," I said as we stood looking at each other.

"Very pleased to meet you, Mr. Church," she said in faultless English with just a slight hint of a German accent, despite my having addressed her in German. She shook the hand I'd extended then gracefully seated herself in the chair across from mine.

"I take it my fluency in German didn't mask my American identity," I said as I returned to my seat.

"No, it was the way you carry yourself not your linguistic skills—which by the way are excellent—that gave you away. I hope I didn't embarrass you."

"Not at all."

"Allow me to introduce myself. I am Beatrice Dahlem."

"Well, Miss Dahlem, it's a pleasure to meet you and a delight that you've agreed to share a table with me. Are you a guest at the hotel?"

"Please call me Beatrice and no, I'm not a guest. I have a flat not far from here and on occasion I treat myself to a dinner and this exquisite view."

"Yes, I can well understand such an inclination, and it's clearly my good fortune that your impulse so perfectly coincided with my arrangements. Tell me, are you a native of Berlin?"

"Yes I am. But I've spent a number of years outside the country…both as a student and on business."

"From the quality of your English I take it some appreciable amount of time was spent in the United States."

"You're correct in thinking that, but enough about me, you are a guest at the hotel, yes?"

"I am—just arrived this morning."

At this point her salad arrived and we both concentrated on our food. I was charmed by the delicate and precise way she handled her knife and fork—the European way: her knife in her right hand and her fork in the left. She caught me noticing.

"I see you also eat holding the knife and fork as Europeans do," she said.

"My mother was German," I said. "There was never any question how I would conduct myself at table. But as I grew older and studied the awkward way Americans wrestled with their food I came to see the sense in her training."

"Was your father also German?"

"No, American…as American as they come, with roots going all the way back to colonial times."

"So you did not learn your German at home."

"No, that was a product of classroom instruction and lots of travel, though I don't suppose having heard the language while growing up hurt at all: my mother's family all spoke to one another and to German friends in that language."

"And you are here on business?"

"Business and pleasure…like most travelers I suppose. And you? I take it your business career didn't stop just because you're now living in your native land."

"Of course not," she replied with a laugh. "I continue to work, though perhaps without as much traveling as before."

"And the nature of your business? Or is that too crass a question to ask a lady with whom one is dining?"

"There's not much to tell. I take on special assignments for various employers…what I believe you Americans refer to as a freelance consultant."

"May I ask what special skills you bring to the table, so to speak?"

"I like to think they are numerous…some having to do with human resources, others having to do with information management. And you? What can you tell me about your work?"

"Like you, I'm a freelance consultant—mostly working for insurance companies…in the area of claims administration. Nothing particularly interesting I suppose but it does entail a fair amount of travel—something I find agreeable, particularly since I've no family or other domestic responsibilities keeping me tethered to a particular place. How about yourself? Are you tethered to Berlin by a relationship?"

"My, we are getting personal! But to answer your question honestly is not an easy thing for a woman. We are always in relationships, though often we can choose to manage them in ways that free ourselves for travel or, on the other hand, use them as an excuse to remain tethered as you so elegantly put it."

Before I could pursue my line of enquiry the busboy approached and removed our salad plates. Almost immediately afterwards, our waiter arrived carrying our entrée. He excused himself for interrupting our conversation and proceeded to place the dinner plates on the table. "Would the lady wish another glass of champagne?" he asked as he replenished my wine glass from the bottle of Chateauneuf-du-Pape.

"Or would you like to share my bottle of wine?" I asked. "I believe you'll enjoy it, particularly with the entrée you ordered."

"Yes, that would be very nice. Thank you Mr. Church."

As the waiter left to retrieve a wine glass I placed my hand on hers and said: "Please call me William. The evening seems to be developing in an unexpected direction—one that I believe calls for us to address one another a bit more familiarly. Do you agree?"

"As you wish, William. But in truth I suspect we're both rather under the spell of the lights of the Brandenburg Gate. They are lit now, as you can see, and the beauty of such an evening's landscape is irresistibly romantic, is it not?"

"That it is, and it's the principal reason why I always choose to enjoy my first evening meal right here whenever I'm in the city, but surely our serendipitous encounter is in itself a romantic event, whatever else it might be?"

"Perhaps so, William, but if not romantic it's at least proving to be pleasurable," she replied as she turned her attention to her dinner.

The waiter returned with a glass and proceeded to pour wine from the bottle. She took a sip and smiled. "Yes, it will do very well. Thank you, William."

We dined quietly for some time, savoring the food and wine and taking long moments to gaze out the window at the evening landscape. It was only after our dinner plates had been removed and we'd settled upon coffee and desert that conversation again ensued in earnest.

"Do you plan on being in Berlin for some days?" she asked.

"Very likely, although it all depends on how successful I am at scheduling my various appointments. Still, it's a city that cries out to be explored so any delay just means I'll be profitably engaged otherwise, such as in attending the current exhibition of German Expressionist painters on Museum Island."

"Yes, that is something I would also like to do," said Beatrice.

"Perhaps we can attend together?" I suggested. "What about tomorrow?"

"But won't you be busy?"

"I'll do what I can in the morning then leave the rest for the following day. Can you arrange to be free?"

"Well—," she said, hesitatingly, thinking about it, then abruptly looked up at me with an enquiring stare. "Do you really wish it?"

"I can't imagine why not," I said. "Given the success of this evening's encounter I think both of us would enjoy a few more hours in one another's company."

"Then…perhaps tomorrow afternoon?"

"Perfect! Let's meet for lunch somewhere on the Unter den Linden perhaps that lovely terrace café next to the Staatsoper—the one across from Humboldt University."

"Yes, all right."

With our plans for the next day settled we got up from the table and headed towards the exit. An attendant carrying Beatrice's coat met us at the door and helped her put it on.

"I'll say goodbye to you for now," she said once we reached the hotel lobby. "It's been a perfectly delightful evening," she added as she extended her hand for me to shake.

"I agree, but please, allow me to escort you home. I know you say you only have a short distance to walk, but it's evening and I'm kind of an old fashioned guy and would feel remiss if I didn't."

"As you wish," she said, taking my arm."

The evening air was pleasantly cool as we walked arm in arm down Wilhelmstraße and up Unter den Linden. We turned at the next corner.

"That's my building over there," she said, pointing to a large apartment building with vaguely Romanesque architectural treatments at the far corner of the next block.

"I have to say, you are close," I said. "Been living here long?"

"It was my parents apartment…the place where I grew up so, yes, I've called it home for a very long time."

We continued to walk towards the building, not saying anything. But as we approached the front entrance she turned to me and asked: "Would you like to see it?"

"By all means," I replied.

Her apartment was above the main entrance, requiring a short but vigorous climb up wooden stairs. She unlocked the front door and I followed her in. As she advanced through the apartment she switched on overhead lights. I followed her down the hallway and into the main parlor but in passing I was struck by the lack of modernity in the interior furnishings. It seemed as if I'd entered a Victorian home of turn of the century age. Towering bookshelves in ancient oak filled with books of comparable age covered one wall of the parlor. An antique grand piano, its surface strewn with piles of piano compositions, stood on a large oriental carpet— one of several covering the ancient wooden floor. A sitting area of upholstered couches and chairs surrounded a large antique coffee table, its surface cluttered with objets d'arte, took up about a quarter of the room. A remarkably graceful secretaire of highly burnished wood was positioned where it could best capture the light from the large windows facing the street.

Access to the dining room from the parlor was through a broad opening in the wall separating the two rooms. Through it I could see the dining table—one that could easily seat at least ten people. It too seemed to be another surface that functioned as a catchall—in this case for various piles of documents and books. A large buffet held a collection of brilliantly polished sterling silver commemorative bowls. And resting above it was a large wooden hutch with glass doors, filled with what appeared to be fine quality antique china. Framed oil portraits of persons whom I could only guess were family ancestors were hung on the walls of the dining room but in no apparent pattern. Beatrice stood off to the side, watching me as I studied the scene.

"You are surprised," she said.

"Yes, I suppose I am," I replied. "It didn't occur to me I'd find you living so graphically in the past."

"It's not what you think. I've kept these few rooms just as they were when my parents were alive. They offer me a kind of tangible link to my past...to a life I once enjoyed but which no longer exists. Come, I'll show you where I really live."

She took my hand and led me back down the hallway we'd come through earlier. We passed by the entrance door and continued on into the section of the flat that held the bedrooms and bath. She opened the first door on the right, worked the light switch and stood aside so I could enter. What must have once been the master bedroom—a room almost as large as the parlor, with a comparably high ceiling and stately windows—had now become an extremely modern living room done in glass and chrome and soft black leather, with artwork by recognizable contemporary artists.

"Only my most thoughtful guests are shown what I like to refer as my 'memory rooms'," she said as she once again took my hand. "Most are steered to the left into this room."

"It's stunning!" I said, "and more in keeping with the image I have of you."

"We're not finished," she said, leading me out of the room and back into the hall.

The next door she opened was a short distance further down the hall and faced us. She flicked on the lights and led me in. "This is my bedroom," she said.

A queen-sized bed of Scandinavian design covered with contemporary linens and a luxurious comforter dominated the room. An assorted array of throw pillows was piled up against the teak headboard. Over the bed was a large, brightly colored Batik textile framed in teak. Other pieces of furniture were also of teak: the night tables, a wall unit holding a hi-fi system and flat screen television, and over against the wall immediately to my right a slender 'library' table that held a vase of freshly cut flowers and several piles of recently published books. What appeared to be an expensive and authentic lounge chair and ottoman of Scandinavian design rested on a thick Armenian carpet off in the corner. It's abstract design in red and brown lent added richness to the room.

"It's beautiful and very much to my taste," I said, giving her hand a squeeze.

She led me back into the main hall and pointed to a door off to the right. "That's the third bedroom. It's rather small," she said, "so I converted it into a dressing room with walk-in closets and all the rest. And that door next to it leads to the bathroom. It's been fully modernized as has the kitchen and pantry."

"What, no guestroom?" I said, jokingly.

"Actually there is one. It's small and used to be the live-in maid's room. It's off the kitchen so it's a bit noisy…just the thing to induce guests to limit their stay," she said with a laugh.

"Well, Beatrice, I'm very impressed," I said, "and appreciate the special honor of being given a full tour."

We were still walking down the hall towards the front door when she stopped and turned to me. "Would you like some brandy before you go?" she asked.

"I'd love some…that is, if it's not too much of an inconvenience."

"Not at all. Come." She took my arm and led me into her private living room.

While she went to the chrome and glass sideboard immediately to the right of the door to retrieve a bottle of brandy and two glasses I walked over to the large windows facing the street and drew back the drapes. The street was quiet. Unless someone was concealed directly beneath me, in the recessed entrance area of the building, it appeared the syndicate had let up on its surveillance; probably figured I'd remain in the hotel after dinner. I drew the curtains closed and went over and sat down on the couch.

Beatrice came over carrying a bottle of vintage Cognac and two fine quality crystal cognac glasses. She placed them on the table and sat down beside me.

"You want to pour?" she asked.

I nodded and leaned forward, picking up the distinctive bottle. After removing the cork stopper I poured a generous amount in each glass and handed one to her. "Here's to the end of a very special evening," I said, touching my glass to hers—then taking a drink.

"Perhaps not the end," she said quietly, removing the half-empty glass from my hand and placing it back on the table along with hers. She then placed her hands around my neck and drew me closer. Her lips met mine and she held them there, letting the passion build.

I folded her into a full embrace and returned the kiss, surprising myself with the sense of urgency I felt as she caressed the back of my neck. I located the zipper tab at the back of her dress and started to gently unzip the garment. She pulled away, smiled, and gave me a quick kiss on the lips.

"I'll be just a moment," she said as she rose from the couch. "Make yourself comfortable in the bedroom." She then quietly slipped out of the room.

I finished my Cognac then rose and followed her into the hall. The door to the bedroom was open and I walked in. She'd removed the throw pillows and had folded the comforter up at the foot of the bed. I studied these preparations, idly wondering how she could approach sex in so matter-of-fact a manner, then walked over to the ottoman and sat down. After a pause, I removed my shoes and socks, then the rest of my clothing, and climbed under the sheets. I lay there thinking I'm in the presence of a 'fully together' woman—one who knows what she wants and how to get it. I smiled to myself, thinking she probably has a similar impression of me. Just then the lights went out in the room and I could sense her approach as her perfume gently wafted its way towards me. I felt the top sheet move and seconds later the cool, silky contours of a perfectly proportioned female made its presence felt from one end of my body to the other.

* * *

It was close to midnight when I stepped back out on the street and headed for the hotel. Beatrice was a little surprised I'd not accepted her offer to spend the night but I needed a good night's sleep after last evening's transatlantic flight and I didn't suspect that would be in the cards were I to stay. She handled it well, reminding me of our luncheon appointment and museum visit scheduled for the next day.

The streets were quiet this time of night—even Unter den Linden. I walked slowly, giving myself time to enjoy the stillness and the cool, crisp air. The Brandenburg Gate was still illuminated—and starkly elegant as the play of shadows and light animated the otherwise empty expanse of the Pariser Platz. I stopped to admire the scene then turned and headed for the hotel's main entrance.

DAY 9

THE MORNING'S PAPER ACCOMPANIED the breakfast cart I'd arranged for—once I'd finally pulled myself out of bed. Half the morning was gone—slept through I kept thinking as I made my way to the shower. But once out of the shower and freshly shaved I felt surprisingly free of any jet lag. A good use of those so-called 'wasted morning hours' I thought to myself as I dressed. I put on a fresh dress shirt—a dark French blue—together with a matching paisley tie, a pair of gray slacks and blue blazer, as well as a pair of black leather street shoes with cushioning rubber soles that I knew from experience handled the hard surfaces of city streets and museum marble floors with ease while keeping my feet feeling fresh despite hours of walking.

The coffee was piping hot and delicious. Only after I'd taken several leisurely sips did I turn my attention to the newspaper. I scanned the headlines, searching for stories having to do with the city of Berlin. One caught my eye immediately. It was a police report about the recovery of a body floating in the river Spree, not far from Mühlendamm Bridge. Preliminary identification, based upon identity papers found with the body of the deceased, indicated the victim was a Mr. Betteldorf—a resident of the United States but a citizen of Germany. Cause of death had not been conclusively determined but foul play was suspected.

I put the paper down and took another sip of coffee. So that's why Reichwein hadn't heard from him, I thought. The syndicate must have picked Betteldorf up shortly after he arrived, questioned him then killed him. That's how they knew of my imminent arrival and of my plans to pay Reichwein a visit. Christ, I thought to myself, once old Reichwein reads about this he'll panic and blurt out everything, hoping to ingratiate himself before he's even questioned. I quickly figured I didn't have a lot of time to make my move before they'd be coming after me or, worse yet, before they did a disappearing act. I got up from the breakfast table and walked over to where my hand luggage was stowed. The identity papers I'd lifted off the two thugs were inside the side pocket. I pulled them out and laid them on the desk.

Both were German citizens. The one named Heinz was a native of Berlin, the other, named Walter, was born in Stuttgart. Their locally issued driver's licenses showed them residing at different addresses in the Friedrichshain District. Employment papers identified their employer as a freight expeditor also located Friedrichshain—in a warehouse on the Spree not far from the Michaelkirche Brücke.

I quickly changed clothes, removing the outfit meant for today's date with Beatrice and putting on a pair of jeans, canvas shirt and leather jacket. I didn't know what I'd find at the warehouse but the fact that Betteldorf's body showed up downstream from the warehouse couldn't simply be a coincidence. I hurriedly finished the rest of my breakfast, removed the holstered semi-automatic from the room safe, swept up the identity papers lying on the desk and headed for the door.

I didn't want there to be a record of my comings and goings this morning so I avoided taking a taxi. Instead, I walked over to the S-bahn station at Unter den Linden and Friedrichstraße, caught the next train and within minutes arrived at my destination: the Ostbahnhof Station—next to the Spree and a short distance upstream from the warehouse.

I approached the building carefully, not sure who I would encounter or what I'd find. The building itself was one of a whole collection of non-descript structures dating back to the time the neighborhood was part of the Eastern Zone. Like most commercial warehouses it had a large entry for trucks and a standard-sized door for people. Both doors were shut but a man was sitting on a wooden box outside the smaller door smoking. It was Walter. I figured he's either out for a smoke or he's been assigned security duty. Either way, the only chance I had of getting close enough without arising suspicion was to bluff. "Hey Walter! I shouted in German, "How've you been? You got a cigarette for me?"

He stood up quickly, trying to figure out who it was that was approaching. I counted on his not recognizing me right away and hoped he'd assume I was some friendly acquaintance who just happened to be passing by.

"Where's your buddy, Heinz," I said as I extended my hand for him to shake. It was only as he shook my hand that he realized who I was but by that time it was too late. I dug the barrel of the gun into the soft spot below his ribs, turned him around and shoved him up against the building. "Nice and quiet, Walter," I said as I did a quick body search, coming up with cheap revolver that I tossed aside. "Now, we'll be going inside, you in front. That where Heinz is?" I asked.

He nodded.

"Who else?"

"One of the warehousemen…Willie."

"You sure that's all?"

He nodded again.

"Okay, but any surprises and it'll be your back that gets a hole blown in it. Now open the door."

The inside of the warehouse looked anything but industrial. The floor was spotlessly clean and the lighting brilliant. Packing materials of the sort one would expect to encounter in the studio of a museum curator were neatly stacked on shelving along the left side of the interior wall. Large tables stood in the middle of the room and both vertical and horizontal shelving took up the right interior wall. An office area of sorts was positioned closest to the smaller outside door and both Heinz and Willie were huddled over a desk examining some sort of document. They both looked up at the sound of the door shutting behind us.

"Take it easy, both of you," I said, pushing Walter over to where they were standing and letting them see my weapon. "Just came by to return your identity papers," I added, tossing the two packets of identity papers on the desk. "No hard feelings, eh?"

"You bastard!" growled Heinz, fingering his bandaged broken nose. "We should have killed you!"

"You mean like you did poor old Betteldorf? By the way, where'd you do the deed? Can't imagine your bosses would want you dirtying up this place with…ah, I get it," I said, looking down at the highly polished chemical seal overlay on the concrete surface of the floor—no problem tidying up afterwards. Pretty neat!"

"Who is he?" asked Willie.

"The bastard we had a run-in with yesterday," replied Heinz.

"Now I want the three of you to each take a chair and sit down," I said as I edged over to the desk and lifted the receiver on the phone. "You've got a choice: either show me the shipping receipts for the six paintings obtained in Chicago that went out within the past week or sit here while I put a call through to the Berlin police. Chances are they'll be interested in following up on my suggestion the killing of the guy they pulled out of the Spree yesterday somehow involved you three guys and this address."

"Who the hell are you?" shouted Walter. "You an American cop?"

"Shut up!" said Heinz to Walter. "He's going to call the cops in any case so don't do or say anything…that right asshole?"

"I'm afraid he is," I said, punching in the Berlin equivalent of the "911" number and putting the receiver to my ear.

Figuring I'd be distracted by the call, Willie leaped out of his chair and made a lunge for me. I shot him in the thigh then quickly moved to the other side of the desk so it was between me and the other two men. Willie dropped to the floor, moaning and holding his leg. "Let's not have a repeat of that," I said gripping the semi-automatic steadily and aiming it at the two of them.

I requested a homicide unit be dispatched to this address along with an ambulance and a patrol detail. When asked to identify myself I simply repeated the request, adding it had to do with the body recovered from the Spree yesterday, then hung up. They'd be able to trace the call to the same address, reassuring them it wasn't a crank call.

"Okay boys, I'm thinking you'd like to get word to Mr. Werner just about now," I said soothingly as I walked around the desk and stood behind their chairs. "I'll be sure to let him know," I added as I pulled a length of duct tape off the roll I'd picked up off the desk and used it to tie Heinz's hands together, lashing them securely to the back of his chair. I did the same for Walter then dragged Willie, moaning and cursing, around to the far side of the heavy steel desk where I pulled his hands around one of the desk legs and secured them with more tape.

With the remaining time left before the cops were due to arrive I rifled through the files in the desk and in the cabinets nearby, looking for a manifest that would give me some idea of where the paintings had ended up. The only thing I came up with that I thought might be what I was looking for was an order for a shipment having left by truck five days ago, heading for Geneva, Switzerland. No inventory notes were present other than gross weight. And the destination was identified only by a street address in a neighborhood somewhere in the metropolitan area of the city. Before I could question Heinz about the manifest the sounds of vehicles coming to a sudden stop outside the building signaled the arrival of the police. I quickly stuffed the manifest into my pocket and pulled out my Interpol and federal concealed weapon permits. I stood there holding the permits in one hand and my gun—now with a chamber racked-open and absent its clip—in the other.

* * *

I watched as the Stadtpolizei escorted the handcuffed crew out to a waiting squad car and as paramedics wheeled Willie out to the ambulance. They'd reported Willie only suffered a flesh wound and that he'd probably be up and about in just a matter of hours. I, on the other hand, had been instructed to remain at the warehouse—that the homicide team needed to question me further. I figured this would take some time and since it was already half past eleven there was no way I'd be able to make my luncheon date with Beatrice. I slumped into a chair near the desk and punched in her number on my cell phone.

" Hello?"

"Beatrice? This is Church."

"Yes, hello, William."

"Listen, something's come up…a business matter requiring my immediate attention. It doesn't look like I'll be able to make our date."

"I understand…these things happen…but, please, let me be of some help. Perhaps I can drive you around in my car?"

"That's a kind offer but I'm afraid this matter will keep me holed up in an office—not running from one place to another."

"So when will I see you?"

"Let's plan to meet for drinks at the hotel…say about six-thirty?"

"As you wish," she said before breaking the connection.

I closed my cell phone and put it in my jacket pocket, puzzled by Beatrice's seeming abruptness in ending our phone conversation…almost as if she needed to attend to something upon hearing I'd not be able to make our afternoon get-together. Well, I thought, she did have her own business to look after and probably decided to make use of the newly available time. Still, that didn't quite jive with her offer to act as my chauffer for the rest of the afternoon. I was still trying to figure it out when the two homicide cops from the Berlin Stadtpolizei pulled up chairs across from me.

"So, let's go over everything," said the older guy. "You say you got a lead on this place after being mugged by those two we just took away, that right?"

"That's right. It happened on Fasanenstraße, just off Kurfürstendamm. They jumped me but I managed to subdue them and remove their identity papers."

"That how they got all banged up?" asked the younger cop.

I nodded.

"So you're saying these guys were trying to get you to stop pursuing an investigation into the theft of some artwork that occurred a few weeks ago. What makes you think that?"

"The murder of Herr Betteldorf for starters," I said. "He was my link to the instigators of the theft—an outfit based in Berlin according to him. It's the reason I traveled here. With Betteldorf dead and me also dead, or sufficiently intimidated that I'd give up the search, the Berlin connection would be broken and whatever criminal investigation took place would most likely be confined to the States."

"So you used the identity documents to locate their place of employment and decided to check it out, that right?" asked the older cop.

"Actually, I only decided to check it out after reading about the discovery of Betteldorf's body in this morning's paper. That made me think things were developing faster than I anticipated and that I'd better make a move sooner rather than later. Then once I learned about the location of the warehouse—just upstream from where the body was found—taking a crack at the warehouse seemed a no-brainer."

"So, it's your opinion Betteldorf was murdered right here, then dumped into the Spree where it floated downstream to where it was finally discovered, and that the three guys we've placed in custody stand a good chance of actually having participated in the killing," summarized the older cop.

"That's my take on the matter," I said.

"Well, we'll check it out. The forensics team should be here momentarily," said the younger cop.

"But I take it you didn't find the paintings you were looking for, or any other pieces of artwork for that matter. How do you account for that?" asked the older cop. "You think maybe this isn't the location you were searching for...maybe the whole thing is a mix up...that this place has nothing to do with the theft of art or with the murder of Herr Betteldorf?"

"Don't think that's possible, officer. Just look around. This is not your average industrial warehouse—not with the way it's furnished or the degree to which it's kept immaculately clean. And the shelving—not to mention the packing materials—is what you'd probably see in the basement of any museum. As for the absence of any artwork, you have to understand these men deal in items worth millions. They don't need to fill a warehouse with inventory. All they probably handle at any given time are a handful of objects—artworks that most likely remain in the warehouse for only a few days before being shipped out to whoever commissioned their acquisition."

"So who are the guys who head up this alleged art theft ring?" asked the older cop.

"I don't know for sure, but I've a couple of leads. It'd help if you'd release me so I could follow up before word of your raid on this warehouse and the arrest of their men gets back to them. If I don't move fast I'm afraid they're likely to disappear."

"Well that's a little complicated," said the older cop. "You're involved in a shooting, and it's not yet been proven the man you shot was guilty of anything other than trying to protect himself from you—a stranger with a gun...a foreigner to boot!"

"Let me talk with a BKA Interpol representative...can you get one on the phone?"

The older cop nodded to the younger one who pulled out his mobile and punched in some numbers. As he waited for the phone to be answered he walked some distance away. A conversation ensued, with the younger cop strenuously insisting on something—probably that the guy be called to the phone immediately. Whatever he'd said seemed to work since the younger cop returned to where we stood and handed the phone to me.

"This is William Church, ex-Interpol liaison from the art theft team at FBI, with whom am I speaking?"

"Yes, we know who you are. The Berlin Stadtpolizei put a call through to us earlier and we've done some checking. You are speaking with Inspector Bleibtreu of the Bundeskriminalamt."

"Inspector Bleibtreu, I'm engaged in an active search for six French Impressionist paintings stolen about two weeks ago from a home in the Chicago area of the United States. I have reason to believe the theft was engineered by a criminal syndicate based in Berlin the leadership of which is at least momentarily unaware of the raid on their warehouse. I'd like your assistance in persuading the Berlin Stadtpolizei to release me so I can pursue my investigation without delay."

"I understand there are complications…a shooting."

"Yes, that's correct but I'm a trained law enforcement officer with full concealed weapon privileges in all EU countries. This shooting was clearly within the scope of my license as I believe the officers present will attest."

"Yes, I understand, but surely you must see that an enquiry is essential in such cases, and until a magistrate has ruled on the matter your whereabouts is a matter of some official concern."

"Of course, but I suspect my whereabouts can easily be monitored without limiting my ability to move about in the city. After all, I'm staying at a prominent hotel and should my presence be required on short notice I'm easily reached on my cell phone."

"But what precisely is it that gives this matter such a sense of urgency?"

"Inspector Bleibtreu, as an Interpol liaison for the BKA you are surely aware of the difficulty of tracking the movement of stolen artwork across international boundaries. I've reason to believe the stolen paintings might already have left Germany and the trail will only get colder with every hour. My best chance of remaining in pursuit is to make contact with one of the principals involved in the syndicate before word of the raid on the warehouse reaches them."

"And I suppose you've no interest in allowing the Stadtpolizei to follow up on your lead?"

"No disrespect intended, Inspector, but as a criminal investigator you can appreciate the advantage one such as myself acquires by pursuing an enquiry without the impediment of an organizational infrastructure, especially when time is of the essence."

He laughed. "Okay, I'll see what I can do. Let me speak with the officer in charge."

I handed the phone to the older cop who listened attentively then broke off the call without saying a word. "He'll be talking with my superior and the presiding Magistrate," said the older cop. You're to accompany us."

"Where to?" I asked.

"Back to headquarters where we've been asked to await further developments."

"We all piled into a non-descript four-door sedan without police markings—the younger cop driving. The ride was accomplished without further conversation. Clearly, the Stadtpolizei homicide detectives weren't thrilled by the prospect of my getting released. Once we arrived I was allowed access to the staff lounge where I secured a cup of coffee and found reasonably comfortable seating. Meanwhile, the older cop went to check on the results of a background search on the three men brought into custody from the warehouse. After about a half an hour he returned—also holding a cup of coffee.

"Seems the guys you confronted at the warehouse all had records…including assault and battery. And the forensic team confirms the presence of blood traces on the warehouse floor. Looks like your story's going to hold up, Church."

"So when can I leave?" I asked.

"Magistrate's on the phone with Bleibtreu right now."

Just then, the younger cop stuck his head in through the open door to the lounge and called out: "They want you."

"Must mean the Magistrate's ready to make a ruling," said the older cop as he took one last swig before dumping his coffee cup into the waste can and heading for the door. I followed suit.

The Magistrate was a middle-aged woman of slender build with short-cropped gray hair and eyes to match. She wore an unexpectedly stylish and rather feminine pants suit of lightweight black wool with a white scooped-out cotton jersey underneath. I approached her desk with as submissive a demeanor as I could muster. She stood as I approached.

"Mr. Church, I've spoken with Inspector Bleibtreu who has appealed to our local jurisdiction to provide you with every courtesy in the matter at hand. The detectives in charge of this investigation, whom you've already met, report there is evidence to corroborate several of your allegations. Although I customarily take a hard line when the use of a firearm is involved, especially so when a citizen is wounded, in this case I'm obliged to overlook such matters and to authorize your immediate release. I do this without enthusiasm, you understand, and should further police incidents arise in which you are involved be assured I will regard this expression of leniency to have been a mistake and will order you placed in custody until all matters are exhaustively investigated. Is that clear?"

"Yes, Your Honor."

"You are dismissed," she replied, returning to her seat and returning her attention to the documents on her desk.

I nodded in acknowledgement, turned and headed for the door—the two cops right behind me.

"If I learn anything more that relates to the homicide case you boys are working on I'll give you a call," I said as I shook their hands. "But before I leave I'll need you to return my gun. Has forensics finished with it yet?"

"I'll check," said the younger cop as he hurried down the hall.

The older cop and I stood awkwardly in the spacious hall just inside the main entrance waiting for him to return. "They come up with a preliminary cause of death yet?" I asked just to break the silence.

"Apparently there were knife wounds, several of which could have been the proximate cause of death. It doesn't appear Herr Betteldorf died of drowning."

"So accidental death has been conclusively ruled out?" I asked.

"It would seem so," he replied.

"Well, I suppose that means you and your partner will be on this case until it's resolved."

"Yes, and it also means we have every reason to continue regarding you as a material witness so don't imagine the Magistrate's ruling means you're out of the woods. We'll want to keep a close eye on you."

"As I said, I'm not hard to find or to contact. Just let me know what you need and I'll be happy to oblige…if I can."

At that moment, the younger cop returned with my handgun. "Forensics' all done with it," he said breathlessly as he handed me the semi-automatic. I thanked him, nodded to the older cop and headed for the main entrance doorway.

* * *

It was almost two o'clock in the afternoon before I finally reached the hotel. I headed directly for my room and gave a call down to room service as soon as I walked in. A club sandwich and a bottle of one of Berlin's favorite beers would soon be up, so I was informed, and with relief from a growling stomach close at hand I headed for the shower. Afterwards, I dressed in the outfit I'd originally selected earlier—when the prospect of a luncheon and a museum tour seemed in the offing. But this time my plans involved getting in the face of our mysterious Herr Werner.

The food arrived just as I finished dressing. I thanked the attendant as I escorted him to the door of the room, discreetly tipping him in the process, then eagerly sat down for a quick bite of lunch. I flicked on the television, thinking a local news channel would be the best indicator of whether the story of the raid had already gone public. If local TV networks in San Francisco were any example, fast-breaking local stories with a twinge of sensationalism were often allowed to preempt scheduled coverage. I was counting on that. Sure enough, the discovery of Betteldorf's body in the Spree was being treated as a breaking news story now that it was being tied to a police raid on a warehouse just upstream. I had to figure Werner and his partners had by now been apprised of these developments. The big question was whether I'd be able to intercept him before he skipped town. I hurriedly gulped down the rest of the sandwich, finished off the beer and headed for the door.

No longer having any need for surreptitious movement I jumped into a cab out front of the hotel and instructed the driver to drop me off directly in front of the Friedrichstraße building where Werner had his office.

Fortunately, the front door of the building was unlocked, allowing me to quickly make my way upstairs and through the well-lit hallway to the doorway of the suite belonging to Werner and his associates. I passed it by and paused outside a door to another suite some distance down the hall. I hadn't yet made up my mind how to proceed: should I attempt to gain access to the suite through some sort of ruse, simply break through the door, or remain out in the hall hoping he'd materialize. As I pondered these options the door to the suite opened and an elderly man rushed out, his suit jacket askew. He matched Reichwein's description of

Herr Werner so I decided to follow him, hoping my assumption about his identity wasn't faulty. He seemed rather distraught and took no notice of my presence as he hurried down the staircase and out the front door of the building.

A waiting limo stood by the curb, the door to the rear compartment was open and a well-muscled attendant stood next to it. The chauffer remained behind the wheel with the motor idling. The man I hoped was Werner headed straight for it and as he climbed in he spoke loudly to the driver to take him to an address in the Grunewald District. Acting on impulse, I lunged for the bodyguard just as he was about to close the door, striking him on the back of the neck with edge of my right hand. He crumpled to the sidewalk, unconscious. With my gun pointed at the old man's head I eased myself slowly into the back seat and closed the door.

"Please proceed," I said in German to the driver. "You've been given your instructions…and no funny business—I know the city."

The driver glanced into the rearview mirror to gauge the old man's wishes. The old man nodded affirmatively, his eyes—those predator eyes that had so disconcerted Reichwein—fixed on me. The driver immediately pulled out into traffic, leaving the bodyguard lying on the sidewalk.

"So you are the William Church who's been giving my people such a headache," he said dispassionately, his hands comfortably folded on his lap.

"Yes, and I take it you are the mysterious Herr Werner who fronts for whatever outfit it is I've been running up against."

"Well, now that you've taken it upon yourself to join me perhaps you'll have a chance to meet the members of our small group...although I don't imagine you'll live long enough to share such knowledge with the authorities."

"I take it, then, we're heading for just such a meeting...at a location which I suppose is staffed with well-armed men, among others."

"Yes, that would be a very correct supposition. Perhaps you would like to reconsider...instruct the driver to pull over so you can get out, thereby avoiding any further unpleasantness?"

"Actually, the choice is up to you. I've no strong interest in exposing your associates. My only interest is in recovering the six French Impressionist paintings stolen just outside Chicago and smuggled into Europe. Just tell me where the paintings can be found and I'll cheerfully be on my way."

"Ah, but that would be unprofessional of me, Mr. Church. My clients insist on strict anonymity as you can well understand."

"But anonymity works both ways does it not, Herr Werner? I don't imagine your clients would rejoice to learn the identities of you and your associates have fallen into the hands of the Bundeskriminalant."

"I don't foresee that happening, Mr. Church," he said with a chuckle."

"Yes, I can understand your complacence...you figure I'll be subdued in short order once we arrive at the address you've given to your driver. But what if the BKA is apprised of the existence of this meeting prior to our arrival. A simple phone call to a certain

Inspector Bleibtreu conducted right here—as we drive—should accomplish just that."

"You wouldn't!" he said with evident alarm. "Then you would have no way to trace your precious paintings!"

"From what you've intimated, I'll have little or no chance in any case," I said as I calmly reached into my breast pocket and pulled out my cell phone. I thumbed through the commands to reach speed dialing and touched the "Bleibtreu" entry.

"Stop it!" he yelled, now fully agitated.

"You've got just a few seconds before we're connected. What's it going to be?"

"Yes, yes, I'll tell you. Just turn that thing off!"

I pretended to end the call but discreetly pressed the mute button. "Well, I'm listening," I said.

"The paintings are no longer in Germany," he said.

"I sort of figured that out for myself," I said, "so where are they?"

"In Switzerland…just outside of Geneva."

"I need an address," I said.

"That I can't supply without looking at my records. All I remember is that the location was north of the city—not far from the lake."

I reactivated the audio feed and pressed the loudspeaker button just as Inspector Bleibtreu came on the line. We could both hear him through the phone's speaker.

"Inspector Bleibtreu," I said, "this is William Church. I'm riding in a limo in the company of a certain Herr Werner who I believe to be the ringleader of the criminal syndicate behind the art thefts I've been investigating, as well as the one who most likely ordered the killing of Herr Betteldorf."

"You betrayed me!" shouted Werner as he lunged for the cell phone. Before he could reach it I smashed his wrist with the semi-automatic then pushed him away.

"Are you in control, Mr. Church?" asked Bleibtreu.

"At the moment, yes, but we are heading for a meeting of the entire syndicate at this address in the Grunewald—I gave him the address—and I imagine if the Stadtpolizei aren't there in force by the time we arrive I'll have lost the advantage and perhaps my life."

"I understand. I'll see that they are there in time, Mr. Church, and thank you."

I broke the connection and slipped the cell phone back in my breast pocket.

"That was a serious mistake," said Werner as he rubbed his bruised wrist, "you'll receive no further information from me and I doubt very much the authorities will be able to establish any connection between myself, or the others at the Grunewald estate, and the matters you alleged would implicate us."

"You're suggesting the men already in custody will not be in a position to identify you?"

"Yes, that's exactly what I mean!"

"But there is always Herr Reichwein—is that not the case?"

"He will not talk, I assure you. He knows I have other agents in my employ who would willingly silence him."

"Perhaps not, but surely you don't suppose the authorities are so unimaginative as to not figure out a way to establish evidence in support of the operational blueprint I'll supply, even without the testimony of Herr Reichwein?"

"If you live long enough to provide such a blueprint, Mr. Church."

"Yes, you keep coming back to that. I suppose that form of intimidation has worked well for you, Herr Werner, but I assure you in my case it simply doesn't work. So let's focus our attention on the matter of the Impressionist paintings: would this shipping manifest happen to be the document you'd need to refer to in order to provide a specific address in Geneva?" I asked as I pulled the document from my coat pocket and allowed him to glance at it.

Werner's sense of alarm was palpable as he scrutinized the manifest. "Where did you get this?"

"From the files at the warehouse. I was a little troubled by the absence in the manifest of any description of the item or items being shipped, but between your admission that the paintings went to Geneva and your apparent discomfort arising from my possession of the document I'd have to conclude that the address given on the manifest does in fact indicate the present location of the paintings."

"I guarantee they won't be there by the time you arrive!"

"Yes, I would imagine you'd place a call to that effect…that is, if you were in a position to do so."

"And why wouldn't I be?"

"We'll see, won't we," I replied.

The Grunewald address turned out to be an estate in the truest sense of the word, with extensive grounds bordered by a dense wall of mature trees surrounding a mansion-sized villa set deep within its boundaries and approached by a long, gravel-paved drive. I could see at least a half-dozen police cars. Some were parked haphazardly at varying points on the property, others were parked on the street out front. A uniformed policeman gestured for Werner's driver to stop just as we turned into the driveway. I identified myself and indicated we were expected. He radioed to whoever was in charge, received an okay and motioned for us to proceed. The driver drove slowly and carefully, not entirely confident the police wouldn't react nervously upon seeing us approach.

A tall, well-dressed man with steel-gray hair walked briskly over to the car as the driver brought it to a stop alongside a line of expensive German cars just off to the right of the front entrance steps. He was accompanied by the two homicide detectives I'd dealt with earlier.

"You must be William Church," said the man as he extended his hand in greeting, "I'm Inspector Bleibtreu."

"Didn't expect to see you here," I said, shaking his hand, "but I'm glad you are since I've got a problem I think only you can resolve."

"What's that?" said Bleibtreu.

"Our friend in the back seat is Herr Werner. I believe you'll find he's the linchpin in the syndicate. He's revealed the location of the stolen paintings I'm after but intends to alert the people currently in possession thereby preventing me from recovering them. I'll need about thirty-six hours with him incommunicado—

no lawyer, no phone calls, no talking with the others you've placed in custody. Can that be arranged?"

"It's quite irregular—given our laws—but in special circumstances it can be authorized. I'll see if I can secure the cooperation of the courts in this case."

"Great! So what did you find here?"

"As you predicted, we encountered several men with unauthorized concealed weapons, some household staff who've been released and four gentlemen who claim to be assembled for entirely lawful purposes."

"Since it seems likely these gentlemen don't know of my presence, or of my intentions regarding the stolen paintings, I don't see any harm in allowing them to be released once your initial enquiries have been completed."

"That go for the Betteldorf matter as well?" asked the older homicide detective.

"I think so," I replied. "I can't help thinking Herr Werner acted alone from an operational standpoint, consulting with the others only at the beginning and end of any given commissioned acquisition."

"Well, if we hold him incommunicado as you request it'll mean we're unable to question him until after that point in time," said the older homicide detective.

"True, but there's probably lots of useful evidence to be gleaned from the files at the warehouse as well as what you'll find at Werner's office and home. And I'll be happy to give a written deposition regarding what he's admitted in my presence during the ride over here—some or all of which can be corroborated by his driver if you can get him to talk."

"We'll follow up on that," said Inspector Bleibtreu. "Perhaps you'll agree to ride back to my office with me. I'd like that deposition now if possible."

"Certainly, but it'll have to be fast. It's already almost four o'clock and I've a six-thirty appointment for cocktails with a certain lovely young lady. Having already stood her up at noon today for a luncheon date I'd probably find myself in hot water if I did it again, especially on the same day."

"I'll use my emergency lights on the way over," said Bleibtreu with a chuckle. "Let's go."

We both climbed into his car—one of the expensive vehicles parked out front—and drove off.

* * *

She was sitting at a table up near the bar, a glass of champagne in her hand. I paused for a moment before walking over—eager to take in the crisp, cool elegance of her outfit, the lustrous beauty of her amply exposed skin and the exquisite way she'd done up her long blond hair. She spotted me just as I began moving in her direction, giving me a little wave and a welcoming smile.

"Well, William, you didn't stand me up," she said impishly. "I was a bit worried after this morning's mix up."

"Sorry about that," I said as I slipped into the seat next to her and gave her a quick kiss on the cheek.

"Did everything turn out all right at least?" she asked.

"It's been a long and very busy day…but yes, I'd say things turned out pretty well. How about you? How'd your day go?"

"A little crazy, what with hectic phone calls and a client who's become a bit overbearing—but nothing I can't manage."

Just then the attendant responsible for our table came over with a frosted martini glass, a small dish with a twist of lemon and a small shaker. Before I could say anything, Beatrice touched my arm, saying: "I ordered your drink before you arrived and signaled the bartender to prepare it up as soon as you sat down. So now it's here and ready for you to enjoy with no wait involved. Are you pleased?"

"Very!" I said, taking her hand and kissing it.

The attendant shook the iced gin vigorously then poured it into the glass. He stepped back, waiting for my assessment. I dropped the twist into the ice-cold martini and took a sip. Perfect! "Give the bartender my thanks," I said. "Tell her she has managed to mix up a drink that would make a top bartender in San Francisco proud." The waiter smiled and headed for the bar.

"So what are your plans tomorrow," asked Beatrice once I'd had a chance to take a few more sips and to munch down a handful of nuts.

"Looks like I'll have to take off first thing tomorrow morning. I'm needed in Geneva."

"Will you be back the same day?"

"No, it'll take a couple of days I figure. Anyway, I've decided to make the trip by car—give me a chance to revisit some of the countryside."

"Let me come with you! We can take my car...I'll even let you drive."

"It's a business trip, Beatrice, you'd be bored stiff."

"Nonsense. The drive will give us a chance to spend some time together, and once we're in Geneva I'll busy myself with friends and perhaps do a little shopping."

"You're serious?"

"Of course I'm serious, William. Anyway, you owe me after having stood me up," she added with a mischievous grin.

"You're right, it would be nice having you along. So, can you be up and ready to roll by seven o'clock?"

"Boy, you don't cut a girl any slack do you? Yes, William, I'll be parked out front of the hotel at seven sharp."

"It's only that I need to make it to Geneva that same day, otherwise I'd have suggested we leave closer to ten."

"It's okay. I'm up for it...whatever the time."

"Then you'll understand a leisurely dinner is out of the question this evening. I've got phone calls to make, as I'm sure you do. And we both need to pack, not to mention a need for some sleep, so let's order sandwiches here at the bar—what do you say?"

"As you wish, William," she replied, taking hold of my hand.

I signaled for the attendant to come over. When he arrived, I ordered a club sandwich for each of us as well as another round of drinks, and let him know we'd be finishing up with coffee and a look at the dessert cart.

"So what's our route tomorrow?" I asked once the attendant had left with our order.

"I'm thinking we'll take the B2 out of the city, make our way over to the A9 and stay on it as far as Nürnberg where we'll pick up the A6. Sometime after stopping for lunch we'll connect with the A5 and take it all the way to Basel where we'll pick up the A2 then shortly afterwards the A1, which should take us into Geneva."

"I take it you've done this drive before," I said with a laugh.

"Yes, and I can tell you it'll take close to ten hours of driving time," said Beatrice with a triumphant look.

"Okay, now to the important part: where do you plan for us to stop for lunch?"

"Ah, that's a secret. You'll find out in good time."

Soon, our sandwiches arrived, along with the drinks, and we gave the food our full attention. But it was close to eight before we finished. I signed the bar tab, walked Beatrice to the front entrance of hotel where I kissed her goodnight and watched as she headed for home.

Before heading up to the room I stopped off at the registration desk and notified the attendant I'd be checking out early the following morning and to have my bill ready. He assured me a copy of the bill would be slipped under my door well before I woke up and would include any arrangements I made later this evening for an early breakfast to be brought up to the room. I thanked him and headed for the bank of elevators.

When I reached the room I poured myself a brandy from the courtesy bar and settled into a comfortable chair. I had two phone calls to make. The first had to be to Guy Sanderson, my contact in the claims office of the insurance company footing the bill for this operation. I figured it would be mid-afternoon in New York about now and Guy should be at his desk. I was right.

"So what's the story, Church?" said Guy once he picked up the phone.

"I've got a lead on the present whereabouts of the paintings— at a lakeside house on the outskirts of Geneva. I'm heading there tomorrow morning."

"Do you need anything?"

"That's one of the reasons I'm calling. I'm going to have Chelsea arrange for an executive jet to be on standby in Geneva to take out the paintings once I've recovered them. I'll need you to authorize it...don't think the leasing company will sign on without some corporate guarantee."

"No problem. The last thing we need is for those paintings to get snarled up in some jurisdictional fight involving the police, customs, and God knows how many lawyers!"

"I'll let Chelsea know...and thanks."

"You want to fill me in on how you've managed to trace the paintings?"

"It's a complicated story...but I tell you what, you meet the jet at Midway Airport in Chicago and I'll lay it all out for you over a couple of drinks."

"You can't fool me, Church, you'll need me there to get you and the paintings through customs."

"There is that...but just think of the debriefing as a kind of reward for having to drag yourself out of Manhatten."

"You forget I happen to live in the suburbs. I drag myself in and out of Manhatten every Goddamn working day!"

"Okay, let me put it another way: believe me, you won't want to know about the complications arising from the search until it's all behind us, and that goes for whatever complications still might develop."

"Your saying it'll give me a headache?"

"I'm saying you need deniability, and yes, it'll give you a headache."

"I'm getting one already...just talking with you."

"So hang up. Anyway, I need to call Chelsea."

"Give her my love...and listen, you take care of yourself, Church," said Guy as he hung up.

I put the call through to the concierge desk of my condominium building. It was half-past eleven in the morning California time and unless she had a dance rehearsal scheduled Chelsea should be manning the desk. I lucked out—she answered the call.

"Chelsea, it's Church."

"Hey, Church, where are you?"

"I'm still in Berlin but just about to leave."

"You need reservations?"

"No, I'll be driving...a friend's making herself available to chauffer me."

"I'll bet! Tell me, is she as pretty as Emily? You do remember Emily."

"Don't be catty. But, yes, she's very pretty and, yes, we've kind of got a thing going."

"Does she know what you do?"

"No, and I've no intention of letting her in on it."

"That's going to be kind of hard, Church, if she's hanging on your arm while you do what you do."

"I'll manage. Anyway, let's get back to business. I need you to arrange for an executive jet to be on standby at the Cointrin International Airport in Geneva, Switzerland, twenty-four hours from now."

"Wow! That's going to cost a pretty penny."

"I know. Tell the chartering company to call Sanderson. He'll front the contract on behalf of the insurance company."

"They'll want to know how many passengers, the weight of any freight, destination…things like that."

"I'll be the only passenger, cargo will be light enough they won't need to factor it in on fuel load. Destination will be Midway Airport in Chicago."

"Got it," she said as she scribbled away.

"Another thing," I said, "I need you to book us into that hotel I like that's near the Quai des Bergues in Geneva."

"I know the one you mean. I take it you'll only be needing the room for one night."

"That's right. Also, have the concierge arrange for a rental car. I'd like to take possession of it as soon as I check in."

"Will do. So, can I expect to see you back here in a day or so?"

"With any luck, Chelsea, but don't lay in any fresh oranges just yet. Lots can happen between now and then. Talk to you later."

After breaking the connection with Chelsea I picked up the brandy snifter and drained the remaining fluid. I was too tired to worry about packing so decided to put it off until I woke up next morning. Only thing left to do before turning in was to call down to room service and order a wake up call for five o'clock and a breakfast tray for six. Moments later, I shed my clothes, hit the bathroom, then slid under the covers confident I'd fall asleep as soon as my head settled comfortably in the cushiony folds of the pillow.

DAY 10

BEATRICE WAS TRUE TO her word, sitting regally on the passenger side of the front seat of a sleek sports car, the top down. Despite the haze of the early morning hour I noticed she was wearing fashionable sunglasses. She turned towards me as I walked over to the car carrying my two pieces of luggage. Her long blonde hair—done up in a ponytail—shook provocatively as she followed my progress.

"Be a sport and unlatch the trunk," I said as I leaned over and gave her a kiss.

"It's unlocked," she replied, "just give it a pull."

I opened the lid, repositioned her luggage to make room for mine in what must be the smallest luggage compartment imaginable then shut it carefully, hoping it would clear the tops of the bags and lock securely. It did.

"Good morning," I said cheerfully as I slid behind the wheel. "This is some car you drive!"

"You like it?"

"It's a bit like entering the cockpit of a jet fighter but, yes, I certainly do."

It was a late model product of German manufacture, done in metallic gray with black leather seats. A conventional gear shift with multiple speeds forward promised a high level of responsiveness both in traffic and on the hilly segments of highway we'd most likely encounter as we approached Switzerland. I switched on the engine, engaged the clutch and nudged it gently into first gear. There was scarcely any traffic this early in the morning allowing me to pull onto Wilhelmstraße with ease. After a short interval I turned right onto Unter den Linden and headed west towards the Brandenburg Gate and the Tiergarten.

"You know how to navigate out of the city?" she asked.

"Correct me if I make a mistake but I think I can manage," I replied with a smile.

A quarter of an hour later we were on the A100 and heading south. The traffic picked up considerably as we merged onto the A115 and headed southwest.

"So what do you think?" she asked as she watched me maneuver the car through the thickening traffic.

"It handles like a dream!" I exclaimed, watching the tachometer respond to the shifts in acceleration.

Minutes later, we turned onto the A10 and headed west towards the junction with A9, passing the town of Michendorf on our right as we sped along. Less than an hour had elapsed before we found ourselves on the A9 heading southwest towards Leipzig and Nürnberg.

The sun was well above the horizon by this time and with nothing more than scattered cumulus clouds to contend with Beatrice's plan to make the entire trip with the top down seemed eminently doable. I picked up the rhythm of the fast-moving autobahn traffic and settled in for the 380 kilometer run to Nürnberg. Despite the slipstream hiss of fast-moving air passing over the windshield or the roar of vehicles overtaken in the slower lane Beatrice seemed determined to carry on a conversation.

"So, William, can't you tell me anything about the business that requires you to be in Geneva on such a short notice?"

"Sure I can. It's nothing earthshaking. I've been asked to soothe the feelings of a prominent customer of an insurance company I occasionally work with who seems somewhat discomfited by a claims settlement. Seems he feels the settlement was less than generous."

"But why you? Why couldn't the company's agent in Geneva handle the matter?"

"It's the office in Geneva he's got a bone to pick with. By sending me the customer gets the impression he's being treated as special, and of course he is."

"You mean it's just a public relations gig?"

"A little more than that. The kind of loss he's incurred happens to be in an area I've managed to develop some expertise in. The client knows that and asked for me specifically."

"But you can't tell me the nature of the loss I take it."

"That, I'm afraid, has to remain confidential. I can tell you, however, that from the standpoint of the insurance company it involves a considerable amount of money."

She seemed to want to think about that and sat back, letting the conversation come to an end. I switched on the radio and began searching for a classical music station. She reached over and punched the third selection button. A Chopin etude emanated from the car's eight speakers.

* * *

"Turn off at the next exit," said Beatrice. It was a little before noon and we'd shifted to the A6 at Nürnberg about a half-hour earlier.

"So, are you finally going to tell me where you've planned for us to have lunch?" I asked as I shifted to the right-hand lane and slowed down.

"You'll see," she replied with a smile.

We turned off, dropping down into a lovely valley named after the river flowing at its base—the Neckar.

"It's beautiful," I said as we drove, passing one small village after another.

"Stop at the next village," she said.

It was small, but perched as it was high on the side of the valley it offered a splendid view of the river flowing lazily past the clustered settlements lined up on the opposite bank.

We'd almost reached the end of the village when Beatrice instructed me to pull up next to several other cars parked in front of a rather ordinary-looking building.

"It's rather disappointing from the outside," she explained, "but wait until you see the garden terrace."

The sign out front identified the establishment as a hotel-restaurant, though given the modest size of the building it couldn't have offered more than a half-dozen rooms. I didn't have much time to study the layout before Beatrice took my hand and led me towards the front entrance. We passed through a tiny unmanned registration office—presumably for the hotel operation—and out through a narrow passage to the dining area.

"What do you think?" she asked.

I had to admit it was stunning. Perhaps a dozen generously spaced tables occupying a wooden terrace edged in low-lying evergreen shrubs that seemed to offer a decorative frame to the spectacular landscape down below. A matronly-looking lady greeted us and showed us to a table shaded by an adjacent awning. A simple menu was given to each of us and we were left alone to ponder our choices from the limited set of options.

"Don't be distressed by the simplicity of the cuisine," she whispered in English, "every dish is exquisitely prepared. I know…I've eaten here before."

"So what do you suggest?" I asked.

"One of the regional Schwäbische dishes I should think, along with a bottle of the local wine."

I complied, selecting a local fish entrée recommended by Beatrice. As we waited for the food to arrive we sipped our wine and enjoyed the scenery. All but two of the tables were occupied by what appeared to be local residents, making our presence a subject of some interest. But we ignored the furtive stares and relaxed under the soporific effect of a pleasantly warm and gentle breeze and the background murmur coming from the other diners. Our food had just arrived when my cell phone gave off its distinctive ring.

"Hello, this is William Church."

"Mr. Church, this is Inspector Bleibtreu. I'm afraid I've got unpleasant news to report."

"Yes, and what is that?"

"The courts would not authorize holding Herr Werner incommunicado as you had requested. His lawyers arranged for his release about two hours ago. I only learned of these developments upon returning to the office and thought you'd wish to be informed immediately."

"Of course. Thank you for letting me know…tell me, is he under surveillance?"

"Yes, and he is instructed not to leave the city, but there are no limits to his freedom of movement or of communication beyond that."

"I understand. Well, this presents some serious difficulties."

"Yes, I imagined that it would. Perhaps there's still time."

"That would be true if I were presently in Geneva. Unfortunately, I chose to drive and am currently a little less than half way there. But thank you anyway for your good thoughts and for so promptly informing me. I'll let you know how it all turns out."

"I'd appreciate that," said Inspector Bleibtreu.

I broke the connection and returned the cell phone to my pocket. Beatrice was staring at me, obviously engrossed in trying to discern the full meaning of my conversation. I smiled and gave a small shrug…as if to say it was a matter of no great import but I could tell she wasn't buying it.

"What's going on, Church?" she asked. "From what I could gather from your side of the conversation something involving the police seems to be connected with your business in Geneva."

"It's a little complicated, Beatrice."

"I'm a smart girl, William, you can tell me."

"Of course you are, but I really don't wish to get you involved. Anyway, it's something I can handle…we'll just have to get ourselves to Geneva as quickly as possible."

"Well, whatever it is it'll have to wait until we've finished this very special meal."

"We'll take our time, Beatrice, don't worry," I assured her as I refilled her wine glass.

And we did. An hour and a half went by before we finally rose from the table and headed back to the car.

"You want to drive?" I asked.

"Please," she replied, taking the car keys from my hand and walking over to the driver's side. Before I was fully settled in the passenger seat she started up the engine and began to briskly back out onto the road, pointing us in the direction we had come. She maneuvered the car expertly through the circuitous streets of the small villages and had us back on the A6 in no time at all. My concern her driving habits would be timid and slow was quickly erased as she accelerated swiftly and aggressively, putting us into a cruising speed that promised to get us to Switzerland in record time.

A little over an hour later we merged onto the A5 and headed south, picking up traffic heading for Karlsruhe and Strasbourg. She caught the tempo of the traffic and maneuvered expertly so as to maintain her cruising speed. But I could see it was taking all her concentration. That was all right with me. I needed the quiet time to rethink my strategy for recovering the paintings now that Werner was free to alert the people in Geneva who presumably still had them in their possession.

* * *

It was a little past four o'clock when we entered Switzerland. Beatrice pulled over just after we passed border control and brought the car to a halt. "I'm bushed," she said, "do you mind taking over, William?"

"No problem," I said, opening my door. I walked around to the driver's side and helped Beatrice climb out. She stood and stretched, then walked to the other side of the car. While she made herself comfortable on the passenger side I readjusted the seat, put the car in gear and pulled swiftly back into the stream of traffic.

The A5 had become the A2—a toll road bypassing Basel—and we were on it for only a short time before connecting with the A1—the highway that would take us into Geneva.

"So where do you have us staying in Geneva?" asked Beatrice as she fiddled with the built-in GPS display in anticipation of navigating us to that destination.

"A fine old hotel near the Quai des Bergues," I replied. "You'll like it. It has a fine view of the lake, an exquisite dining room and luxuriously-appointed rooms."

"I take it you've stayed there before."

"Often. It's one of the reasons I'll not be needing your assistance in getting us there."

"Very well," she said, shutting off the GPS.

The air was getting cooler and I could see she was shivering a bit. I reached behind her seat and grabbed the black leather jacket she'd placed there earlier in the day when the heat of the sun was a lot warmer. "Here, put this on," I said, handing it to her.

She was wearing tight-fitting spandex-cotton jeans, a pale blue cotton shirt and sandals. The jacket, a nicely tailored design of European manufacture, went well with the outfit and gave her a more urban look—just right for our arrival in Geneva. I had on a pair of lightweight gray woolen slacks, a white sports shirt and my blue blazer. I hadn't removed the jacket at any time during the day in order to keep my gun concealed, thinking it would not only lead to endless questions but might actually frighten her.

We pulled up to the hotel at about six o'clock. Two porters immediately came to our assistance, extracting the four pieces of luggage from out of the trunk and carrying them inside. I handed the keys to the valet and Beatrice and I—stiff from all the sitting—slowly made our way through the hotel entrance doors and over to the reception desk.

"Welcome back Mr. Church," said the young woman behind the desk. "I see the last time you stayed with us was six months ago. Will you be wanting the same room?"

"That would be nice, Stephanie. By the way, this is Beatrice Dahlem…a friend from Berlin."

"Please to meet you, Miss Dahlem. I hope you'll enjoy your stay at our hotel."

"I'm sure I will, Stephanie, especially if the room has a comfortable bathtub and lots of hot water."

"I think you'll find everything to your satisfaction, Miss Dahlem."

"I believe my assistant, Chelsea, arranged for a rental car."

"Yes, she did. I've got the papers right here. All you need to do is sign the rental agreement document. The car is with the valet, under your name…just call down a few minutes before you need it and they'll bring it around front."

"Thanks, Stephanie."

The room offered a spectacular view of the lake and even before I'd taken care of the porters who'd brought our luggage up Beatrice was at the window mesmerized by the view.

"Oh, William, it's glorious!"

"Thought you'd like it," I said as I began to remove my clothing in anticipation of a shower. "You going to join me?" I asked.

"You go ahead. I'll wait until you're done," she said, unwilling to give up her rapt contemplation of the Jet d'Eau, that famous water fountain out in the lake.

* * *

It was well past seven o'clock by the time we took our seats at the table I'd reserved in the hotel's restaurant. The menu featured French cuisine and the wine list was decidedly French. A bottle of Bordeaux wine seemed appropriate so I selected a reasonably priced Margaux. Beatrice ordered *filet of sole* while I indulged my preference for beef by ordering a *filet mignon*. We were both tired but gamely sought to engage each other in conversation. Beatrice took the lead.

"When did you plan on seeing that client?" she asked.

"Ordinarily, I would wait until a civilized hour tomorrow morning but given the urgency reflected in that call from the office while we were having lunch I thought I'd drive out there right after dinner."

"Do you know the way? I could navigate for you."

"A kind offer, particularly seeing how tired you are, but there's no need. The rental car I ordered has GPS navigation."

"And I had such a nice evening planned for us," she pouted.

"I'm sure your intentions were the stuff of dreams," I said, touching her hand, "but it's more likely that after dinner and a couple of glasses of wine all you'll really want to do is go to sleep."

"What about you?"

"The same, but unfortunately I'm here on business and fatigue has simply got to be shunted to the sidelines. Anyway, it probably won't take all that long…before you know it I'll be snuggling up close in our cozy bed."

"Promises, promises," she said with staged exasperation.

Our food arrived and the wine was poured. The Margaux— from a winery I wasn't familiar with proved to be delicious and I made a mental note to remember it for next time.

We ate in silence, letting the stress of the all-day drive drain away. I actually wasn't as tired as Beatrice, having had an opportunity to catnap the second half of the trip while she was driving, but I wanted to get her mind off my business—particularly tonight. I had to struggle to refrain from rushing through dinner but did manage to gracefully decline dessert and to urge Beatrice to limit herself to just one cup of coffee, ostensibly to avoid being kept awake. But before she finished that cup her cell phone rang. She quickly removed it from her small clutch bag and flipped it open.

"Beatrice Dahlem here," she said once she'd managed to get it into position. She listened intently to the caller, nodding her head in agreement with whatever was being said. "Yes, of course," she replied, "I understand the gravity of the situation…you can count on me." With these words, she terminated the connection and woodenly returned the phone to her clutch bag. She then turned her attention back to me.

"William, I'm afraid our little holiday has got to end.

"What do you mean?" I asked.

"That was a principal client instructing me to drive to Paris. It seems there's a personnel issue requiring my attention at the firm's branch office."

"But surely you'll spend the night here and leave in the morning?"

"No, I'll leave right away…that is, after a second cup of coffee. It's only a five-hour drive and at this hour the principal highway will have light traffic. Tomorrow morning it will be heavily congested with commuters and all sorts of trucks."

I didn't try to change her mind, just nodded sympathetically and joined her in drinking a second cup of coffee.

We managed to return to our room by nine o'clock whereupon Beatrice quickly changed back into the casual outfit she'd worn during the day, repacked her bags—all the while chattering on about how we must not let work ruin our relationship—then arranged for her car to be brought around. While she was busy doing all that, I was changing into black jeans, black cotton shirt and black leather jacket, deftly concealing my holstered semi-automatic at my belt while her back was turned.

"Let me help you with the bags," I said when it became clear she was about to leave the room.

"I can handle them," she replied with a smile. "What I'll have less success in handling is this interruption in our holiday. You will come back to Berlin once this Geneva business in over with won't you?" she asked coyly.

"That certainly would seem to be my plan," I replied as I took her in my arms and kissed her. "Drive carefully and don't hesitate to put up at a hotel if fatigue gets the better of you," I cautioned.

She kissed me back, took one last look around the hotel room then picked up her bags and headed out.

I closed the door behind her and began repacking my bags, all the while thinking that, however fortuitous, the suddenness of her disappearance was somewhat troubling. I was particularly struck by her utter lack of indignation at whoever was making such an unreasonable request. Surely, she was in a position to resist—to come back with the counter argument that the problem could await resolution until perhaps a few days later. I didn't know what it all meant but I couldn't help feeling uneasy.

When I finished packing I called down to the front desk. "Yes, this is Mr. Church. Something's come up and my companion and I will not be staying the evening. Could you please have my bill ready for when I come down? Thank you. Also, please inform the valet that I'll need my rental car to be brought around."

* * *

I was traveling north, more or less following the lakeshore—my eyes glued to the GPS display, counting on it to signal when I'd need to turn. Streetlights were infrequent and clouds blocked any available moonlight, making any effort on my part to monitor the names of passing streets fruitless. Anyway, I wasn't familiar with the outlying bedroom communities of Geneva so it wouldn't have done me any good. Fortunately, traffic was light. Finally, the display lit up a turn and I hastened to comply. I was now on a narrow paved road that meandered through a neighborhood of large estates. I slowed down to a crawl. I noticed the further up the road I drove the longer the interval between houses. Were it not for the formal grounds and the size of the homes one would almost be forgiven for regarding this as an essentially rural part of the countryside.

Another turn indicator lit up on the display, guiding me into an even narrower lane. I followed it slowly, dimming my headlights so as not to betray my presence. I was now in an area where I could only see one lit-up home, presumably my destination. I quietly maneuvered the car into a u-turn and parked. I climbed out and stood silently, trying to gauge the distance to the solitary house and what security precautions might have been employed. I could see a wrought iron gate set in stone masonry about fifty yards ahead. It was closed, blocking the driveway. A stone wall about four feet high seemed to surround the property—easily surmountable but probably secured through the use of sensors. No lights shown on the upper floors, only a few rooms on the ground floor revealed interior lighting, together with a single exterior floodlight above the main entrance.

The night was still, making even the slightest noise conspicuous to anyone listening. I tried to walk stealthily as I headed for the front gate. I removed the black leather gloves I always carry in the pocket of the jacket and put them on. They'd protect my hands during what might prove to be rough going across the tree-studded grounds while eliminating any possible evidence of my presence once I gained entry.

I had to believe going through the front door was preferable to breaking in so with that thought in mind I headed for the stone wall and hopped over. I began a fast run towards the house, reaching the base of a large tree trunk about halfway just as a cluster of floodlights lit up the terrain I'd just come through. I hunkered down waiting to see what would happen. The front door crashed open and a big, athletic guy in what looked like a chauffeur's uniform came rushing out, gun in hand.

I stepped away from the tree—just long enough for him to catch a glimpse of my profile then quickly stepped back. He picked up on the movement and the profile and fired a shot.

"Come out and show yourself!" he shouted in thick Swiss German. "You're trespassing on private property."

I didn't answer.

"Come out, I say, or you risk being shot like a dog!" he shouted, stepping off the front porch and advancing cautiously towards my location.

I waited until he was beyond the perimeter of light from the lamp above the door then sprinted towards the side of the house, tripping light sensors along the way. He swerved, trying to track my movements despite the distraction caused by the flash of triggered floodlights. By the time he readied a shot I was safely up against the house and making for the rear. I could hear him cursing as he rushed back to the front porch.

Without stopping, I circled the house—this time not triggering any security lights owing to my closeness to the structure itself. When I peered around the corner of the house towards the front entrance I could see the guy standing there, gun still in hand, watching the opposite corner where he expected me to reappear.

"Freeze!" I shouted in German. "I've a gun aimed directly at your back.

I walked steadily towards him. "Very slowly raise you hands, holding your gun by its barrel."

He complied, exhibiting a professional steadiness one only acquires after numerous confrontations of this sort. This was no ordinary chauffeur, nor any other sort of domestic employee. It seemed Herr Werner and his clients had set up a lethal welcoming for me.

I reached up and removed the gun from the man's hand, noting the quality of the nine-millimeter weapon, and slipped it into my jacket pocket. "That's a good lad, now lead the way into the house." I wasn't too worried he had accomplices since they would have been expected to give assistance once he discharged his weapon. Still, I took the precaution of having him in front as we advanced through the front door and down the hallway.

As I suspected, the walls of the house were filled with valuable paintings but I doubted I'd find the ones I was looking for. "Who else is here?" I demanded once we'd entered the large living room where the television was playing—obviously the room he had been in when I came on the scene. He just smiled grimly, not making any effort to reply. I smashed him across the face with my thirty-eight. As he fingered his bloody right cheek I stepped back, directing the aim of my weapon at his legs.

"I'll ask you one more time, who else is here? This time if you fail to answer I'll shoot out your left kneecap, you understand?"

"No one," he croaked, spitting out blood.

"No house servants?"

"All sent away for the night."

"And the owner of this house, where is he?"

"He is out of the country…at his other home."

"When did he leave here?"

"Earlier today."

"Where is this other home?" I asked.

"I don't know…honest to God I don't know. I was brought here just today to provide security for the place. I don't know the man or anything about him."

"Well, let's see what we can learn by a tour of the house," I said, grabbing the man and pushing him forward. We marched through the rooms on the ground floor, my gaze directed at the artwork, looking for signs that some wall pieces were missing. I struck pay dirt in the study: the white plaster surface of the wall directly opposite the man's desk was without artwork, and there were tell-tail signs that picture-hanging hardware had been hurriedly removed: gouged plaster, pencil marks to guide positioning and unswept plaster on the floor.

"Take a seat over there," I said, pointing to a leather love seat under the window. Once he was in the grip of the soft cushions I was pretty sure he'd have some difficulty springing up with enough momentum to take me off guard. I moved behind the desk and sat down. There were several photos on the desk—all depicting Mediterranean-like scenes of coastline, boating, various persons in bathing suits. I rifled through the contents of the desk drawers, looking for anything that would give me a clue as to where his second home might be.

It was in a pile of correspondence that I found what I was looking for: a letter still in its envelope. The correspondent was thanking her host for the splendid weeklong stay at his villa. The letter had been mailed to an address on the island of Sardinia— probably brought back here as a memento of the affair. I slipped the letter back into its envelope and placed the envelope carefully in my back pocket.

I got up from the desk chair and walked over to where the security man was sitting. "Get up!" I commanded.

"Yes, do get up Hans. And you, Church, very carefully hand your weapon to Hans."

I glanced over to the doorway and saw Beatrice standing there, a thirty-two semi-automatic held steadily in her hand.

"You know this gentleman?" I asked.

"Yes, and he's no one to fool around with so please hand him your gun without any tricks."

"I'd say we have a kind of Mexican standoff here," I said, continuing to point my weapon at Hans who now stood less than three feet from me, "but I have something of an advantage: my target is close whereas your target is all the way across the room."

"An advantage that can easily be neutralized by multiple shots wouldn't you say?"

"Perhaps, but before we continue down this line why don't you tell me what you're doing here?"

"All will be explained once you surrender you weapon. Do it now!"

I hesitated and she fired. The shot entered one of the love seat cushions—inches from me.

"The next shot will not be a warning so move!"

And move I did, throwing my thirty-eight onto the couch to free both hands then grabbing Hans, shoving him in front of me just as Beatrice triggered a second shot. She wasn't kidding, the shot was aimed squarely at my torso but hit Hans instead. As she tried to line up a third shot I reached into my jacket pocket, removed Han's nine-millimeter semi-automatic and shot her. Both Hans and Beatrice crumpled to the floor. I knelt down and checked Hans for a pulse but came up with nothing; the bullet seemed to have entered his heart. I approached Beatrice with care, not sure whether her injuries prevented her from firing her weapon. When I made it over to where she lay I could see that her shoulder was pretty torn up. She was grimacing from the pain but no artery seemed to have been severed.

"Why'd you do it?" I asked after kneeling down and pushing her weapon out of reach.

"Werner is my boss, Church. I was tasked to monitor your activity."

"No, I don't mean why you hooked up with me but why you'd get yourself involved in a possible homicide?"

"I didn't have a choice. That call I received during dinner was from him, ordering me to make sure Hans took care of things…I was just to report back."

"That doesn't explain the use of a gun…Christ! You would have killed me with that second shot!"

"I don't know," she sobbed, "I was desperate to have you subdued so Hans could take over and I could leave…I panicked."

"Well, don't move if you can help it…it'll just cause added bleeding. I'm going to call for an ambulance."

I went over to the desk, picked up the landline and dialed the emergency operator. "Yes, operator, please dispatch an ambulance and police to my home. There's been a shooting…one of the victims is badly wounded." I put down the phone before she could answer any more questions, moved quickly over to where Hans lay and slipped the gun I'd used to shoot Beatrice with into his dead hand—the cops would think Hans had done the shooting. After recovering my thirty-eight I returned to where

Beatrice lay and reassured myself she was still exhibiting a healthy pulse despite having lost consciousness.

I fled the house—confident I'd left no traces of my own presence—and hurried over to where I'd left the rental car. I started it up, put it in gear and pulled back onto the road, taking care not to hit Beatrice's sports car parked nearby. Using my high beams, I raced through the narrow streets—anxious to get back on the main highway before the emergency vehicles showed up. I didn't quite make it. I could see emergency lights flashing up ahead so I doused my lights and quickly turned into the next driveway I encountered. Without hesitation, I turned the engine off and exited the car, scrambling for concealment among shrubs growing nearby. I watched as two police cars and an ambulance sped by. After waiting about five minutes—to make sure no additional police cruisers were on patrol in the area—I slipped back into the car and slowly drove off.

Once I was back on the principal road leading to the center of town I began reflecting on the unexpected involvement of Beatrice in the whole syndicate operation. I couldn't say I was totally shocked by the revelation, having had a couple of uneasy moments when I couldn't square her behavior with what should have been called for given the situation, but having her show up with a gun was way off my radar. She must have followed me out there, I reasoned, and was forced to improvise once she observed me taking control of the situation out on the front porch. I probably shouldn't have left the front door open but at the time I was more concerned with having an escape route than in securing my back.

It was close to midnight when I pulled into the valet station at the hotel. I turned the keys over to one of the young guys manning the station and told him to return the car to the rental agency. I pulled my bags out of the trunk and walked over to a parked taxi. Once the bags were stowed and I was comfortably seated I instructed the cabbie to take me to Terminal T3 at Cointrin International Airport.

DAY 11

THE RIDE TO THE airport was too brief to allow for a quick nap so I focused on my next move. I had to believe Beatrice would be in no position to alert Herr Werner of the debacle at the residence here in Geneva given her need for immediate surgery on the shoulder. And with Hans dead and the police treating the residence as a crime scene chances were good no one among the regular domestic staff would have access and thus would be ignorant of what actually transpired. And since I intimated in my phone call that it was the owner of the house who was calling it's likely the authorities would wait some time before extending their search for him beyond the city. That meant I had a fair chance of catching the man before he moved the paintings from the villa in Sardinia—that is if I could get there quickly enough. It was with that thought in mind that I rushed from the taxi, bags in hand, heading for the terminal entrance, once we'd pulled up at the curb.

Terminal T3 was the business terminal where I hoped to meet up with the crew of the executive jet Chelsea had booked for me. I hurried over to the reception desk and asked if the jet chartered for William Church had arrived. I was informed that it had and that I would find the crew in the coffee shop.

At this hour the coffee shop was virtually empty. Several men in mechanic's outfits were sharing a table. At another table sat a young man in a pilot's uniform reading what appeared to be a technical manual. I went over to him.

"I'm looking for the crew of the jet chartered to pick up William Church—that happen to be you?"

"Yes, sir. I'm co-pilot on the flight. Are you Mr. Church?"

"I am. Where's the pilot?"

"He's catching some sleep…we've been taking turns monitoring the reception area so as not to miss you…were told you'd probably want to take off at a moments notice."

"Good thinking…and yeah, that's right, I'll want us to depart just as soon as we can."

"My name's Johnson…Officer Johnson," he said as he stood up, slipping the manual into the soft leather carry-on bag he had with him. "You have any other luggage besides these two pieces?"

"No, that's it. Can we head for the plane now or do you need to check in with the dispatch office first?"

"We can go now, sir. We'll notify dispatch from the cockpit. Here, let me take those."

"No need, I can handle them," I said. "Just lead the way."

We left the coffee shop and walked across the reception area to a double door leading out onto the tarmac. The place was lit up with powerful floodlights, making it almost as bright as daylight. Executive charters of all sizes were parked nearby—most were jets but some were prop-driven.

"We're over here," said Officer Johnson, pointing to a small jet-powered craft off to our left.

I could see interior lighting through the open fuselage door as we came nearer. "Adan, our charter client has arrived," shouted Johnson as he climbed up the

boarding steps.

I stood at the bottom of the steps waiting for the two men to get themselves organized. After a few moments a tall slender man who I reckoned was in his mid-forties leaned out the fuselage door and looked down at me. He was dressed in a pilot's uniform, but unlike that of Officer Johnson this one displayed four bars on the sleeve and sported shoulder epaulettes.

"I'm Captain Jeffries," he said as he climbed down the steps. "Officer Johnson tells me you're our charter, that right?"

"That's right."

"The flight manifest I've got shows us making for Chicago… that you're understanding also?"

"That was the original plan, Captain Jeffries, but we'll need to make a run down to Sardinia for a pickup before heading for the States."

"You authorized to change the flight plan?"

"I'm the principal in this deal…so, yes, I've got the authority."

"This pickup—it entail much weight?"

"No, just a half-dozen framed paintings…probably a total weight far less than if we added another passenger."

"Don't see a problem there. Well, let's get your luggage stowed," he added, taking hold of my two bags and walking to the front of the craft where he unlatched the cover to the forward cargo bay. He hoisted the bags up and shoved them in, pushing the luggage already in the compartment back to make room. Once he was satisfied all items cleared the opening he closed the cover and secured the latch.

I followed him up the boarding stairs and imitated his crouch as I passed through the fuselage opening. The passenger cabin was surprisingly spacious, configured as it was with only four seats, a small galley and washroom. The door to the cockpit was open and I could see Johnson already strapped into the co-pilot's seat talking quietly into his microphone.

"Make yourself comfortable, Mr. Church, it shouldn't be too long before we're ready to depart—just need to go down the pre-flight check list and file a flight plan. Which airport on the island you figure on landing at?"

"The Olbia-Costa Smeralda Airport on the northeastern corner of the island…you know it?"

"Yes sir, flown in there on many an occasion. Should take us no more than about an hour and a half before touch down once we're airborne."

As I selected a seat and sat down I began to get a glimmer of an idea of how to manage the extraction. "Captain Jeffries, I'll need my luggage brought into the cabin."

"You sure?" asked Officer Johnson.

"Yeah. I'll need to change clothes during the flight."

"Okay, I'll get it," he said, unbuckling his lap and shoulder straps and awkwardly climbing out of his cockpit seat. He walked back to the open fuselage door and descended the steps. I could hear the latches on the forward storage bay being opened and my bags being slid out. There was a loud slam as Johnson closed the hatch. He reemerged at the fuselage door and slid the two bags between two of the unused seats. "Can I get you some coffee?" he asked.

"No, thanks. I'll probably try to get some sleep during the flight."

"Fair enough, but if you change your mind we've got a fresh supply in the galley."

Johnson was just about to return to the cockpit when Captain Jeffries called back that we'd received clearance to move the plane into position for takeoff. "Secure the craft for departure," he shouted. Johnson turned around and headed for the fuselage door. He triggered the hydraulics that retract the boarding steps then manually slid the door in place and locked it. I could hear the slow whine as the two jet engines began to turn over. Johnson returned to the cockpit and strapped himself in. They left the cockpit door open, giving me a clear view of flight preparations but I barely looked up, my thoughts focused on the extraction scenario I was cooking up.

"Wake me thirty minutes before we're scheduled to land," I shouted through the open cockpit door.

"Will do, shouted Jeffries as he dimmed the cabin lights and shut the cockpit door.

I was lulled into a state of deep relaxation as the craft slowly began to move out onto the taxiway, and was almost fast asleep by the time Jeffries and Johnson powered up the engines, released the breaks and allowed the craft to hurtle down the runway and into the air.

* * *

"We're just about to begin our approach to the Olbia Airport, Mr. Church," said Officer Johnson as he gently touched my shoulder. "You said you'd like to be awakened at this time."

"Yeah, thanks, Johnson," I replied as I shook the sleep from my eyes and began to unbuckle my seatbelt. "I'll take that coffee now…if it's still drinkable."

"Thought you might so I brewed a fresh pot," he replied with a smile. "There's also fresh Danish and croissant if you're hungry."

"Sounds good, lead the way."

Johnson poured me a cup and pulled out a metal tray from the warming oven filled with bakery goods. I placed two croissants onto a plate, along with strawberry preserve and butter. Johnson did the same. We stood next to the galley bar and ate.

"How'd the flight go?" I asked.

"Traffic was pretty light and the craft is handling well…should be a smooth approach."

"Any chance you can persuade the guys in the Olbia control tower to call me a taxi?"

"Christ, it'll be almost three o'clock in the morning by the time we touch down and roll to a stop. You've got to understand, Mr. Church, these locals take their domestic life real seriously... pulling them out of bed in the middle of the night is not something they're likely to regard favorably...but, hell, if you insist, the least we can do is give it a shot."

"Tell them to tell the driver I'll pay double the going rate."

"Don't think they're much into money...prefer the simple life—with all the government-subsidized trimmings...that'd be my guess."

"Yeah, well let's give it a try."

"Okay," said Johnson as he returned to the cockpit to radio the control tower.

Meanwhile, I pulled out my luggage from where Johnson had stowed it and opened the larger bag where I kept my clothing. I removed the one business suit I always carry—a dark gray single-breasted suit made to order for me by a London tailor. After making sure the suit had no obvious travel wrinkles, I stripped off the clothes I was wearing and put on the suit pants, together with a white dress shirt, conservative monochromatic tie and black dress shoes. Before putting on the suit coat I clipped the holstered semi-automatic to the leather belt at my waist. I check out my appearance in the mirror of the small lavatory. My aim was to resemble as much as possible a conservative northern European banker—the kind of guy Herr Werner would feel comfortable being around. Except for my size and obvious athleticism I thought I'd be able to pull it off, but I'd need to come up with an explanation for the discrepancy.

Before returning to my seat I pulled out the leather gloves from my leather jacket and stuffed them into a back pocket, thinking I'd need to be careful not to leave behind any prints should things get a little crazy.

"I'll need you to refasten you seat belt," said Johnson, who'd come out of the cockpit to tell me we'd begun the final approach to the runway. "You want a refill on your coffee?" he added.

"Thanks, I'd like that," I replied, pulling together the straps of the seat belt.

The lights of Olbia were clearly visible as the plane banked steeply, the pilot trying to line up for a smooth descent. I studied them as I sipped my coffee, wondering whether I'd have a driver waiting for me when I deplaned. Actually, I knew the island fairly well, having spent a couple of months in the region during graduate school studying the archaeological remains of the island's distinctive Nuragic Culture. I'd managed to get over to Olbia on a couple of occasions at that time and came to appreciate the grandeur of her rocky coastline, her emerald green waters and her exquisitely concealed coves and bays.

The runway lights seemed to sparkle as Jeffries brought the craft to a touchdown, then all of a sudden they seemed to flash—each visible for a microsecond as we swiftly taxied down the tarmac. The craft rolled to a stop just outside the General Aviation facility at the Arrivals end of the terminal. Johnson went aft and opened the fuselage door then activated the hydraulics for the boarding steps assembly, causing the steps to deploy.

"How long you think you'll be?" asked Jefferies who'd come into the cabin as I was getting myself ready to deplane.

"Can't tell for certain," I replied, "but figure it'll take me at least a couple of hours and possibly more. Best strategy would be for the two of you to remain on standby...like you did in Geneva."

"Not a problem. We'll refuel the craft and do a maintenance check, then maybe get some sleep. I take it we'll be heading for Chicago on the next leg?"

"That's right. Any other stopover would be at your discretion... for refueling or the like."

"Well, good luck with the pickup," said Jeffries, shaking my hand. "I get the feeling this business you're about to undertake is anything but routine."

"You've got good instincts," I said with a laugh. "Be back as soon as I can." And with that said I stepped out of the airplane.

"Hey, Johnson, see if you can secure some gin, vermouth and a lemon for the next leg—I think I'll be in the mood for a Martini when I get back," I said to him as he stood at the foot of the stairs.

"Will do, Mr. Church...it's a pleasure flying with you."

I waved back at the two of them just before entering the Executive Lounge.

* * *

The Executive Lounge was cheerfully furnished in brightly colored contemporary furniture clearly meant to give the arriving traveler a welcoming sense of what lay before him once he stepped out into the sunshine and ambiance of Sardinia's famous Costa Smeralda. The room was empty except for the presence of a young woman stationed at what appeared to be a reception desk. I went over to her.

"I'm William Church. The crew of my plane radioed ahead for a driver...any chance you people were successful in locating one?"

"It was no problem, Mr. Church, we are accustomed to such requests and have a handful of drivers willing to come out at odd hours. You will find your driver in his vehicle—parked just outside. Is there anything else I can help you with?"

"No thank you, that's all I needed."

"Well, have a pleasant stay, Mr. Church."

"I hope to...although I'm afraid it'll be much too brief."

I walked quickly through the arrivals area and out into the Sardinian night. The air

felt cool—but not uncomfortably so—and was laden with the pleasant scent of flowers and of the nearby seashore. I spotted a dark colored sedan parked in the taxi rank with its parking lights on. As I approached, the driver's side door opened and a short, stocky Sardinian in a rumpled black suit climbed out.

"Is it you who wishes a driver this time of night?" asked the man in slow, accented Italian.

He must be at least sixty, I thought as I stepped closer. "Yes, it is I who wish to make use of your services," I replied in Italian.

He opened the door to the rear seating area and gestured for me to climb in. I did so. After shutting my door he climbed back in behind the wheel then turned around.

"Where is it you wish to go?" he asked.

I pulled out the envelope I'd found at the Geneva residence and read off the address.

"Ah, I know the place," he said, shaking his grizzled head affirmatively, "it's maybe about a half-hour drive from here…at this time of night. I can take you there but it will cost you."

"I understand," I said, handing him Euros in the amount specified. And I'll pay you a bonus if you'll agree to wait until I've completed my business."

"How long the wait?" he asked.

"I don't know, but the bonus will reflect the amount of time you're required to wait…agreed?"

"Agreed!" he said with emphasis as he started up the car and pulled out of the taxi rank.

There wasn't much traffic this time of night: residents would be sound asleep and workers with early morning duties at the various villas and resorts along the coast wouldn't be getting on the road for another hour or two. Still, the roads were often narrow and winding as we traveled north, making it difficult to drive even at the posted speed.

It was a quarter to four in the morning when the elderly Sardinian pulled up to the wrought iron gate at the entrance to the villa. I could hear the surf crashing against the rocks below and knew we must be out on some sort of narrow peninsula between two coves. I climbed out of the car and walked over to an intercom phone mounted on the brick post at the left side of the gate. I pushed the buzzer.

The limo driver remained in the car, his window down, looking at me. I pushed the buzzer again—this time not letting go, just letting it ring so whoever was charged with monitoring it couldn't ignore it and go back to sleep. Finally, a sleepy voice barked out a "Who's there!" in Italian.

"Herr Kirche befindet sich hier!" I said, using German.

A delay of some moments followed, then a new voice rang out of the tiny loudspeaker—this time in German: "Yes, what is it you want!"

"I wish to speak with Herr Falke…a matter of some importance!"

"Impossible, the household is fast asleep! Come back in the morning…but no earlier than ten o'clock."

"This is a matter that cannot wait! You would be wise to awaken him and tell him an associate of Herr Werner is at the gate. Tell him I have come directly from Berlin with urgent news regarding our recent business transaction."

Another delay, then the gates swung open slowly, powered by silent electrical motors. I climbed back in the car and motioned for the driver to proceed. The driveway was narrow and descended sharply as we approached the villa. Lights had been turned on, illuminating both the building and the circular area of pavement out front. We pulled up and parked. As I climbed out of the car the front door of the villa opened and two men emerged who I immediately took to be security. Both appeared to be German. One had a shaved head, the other a closely cropped thatch of blond hair. By the look of their clothes it was clear they had dressed hastily, and a glance at their expressions left no doubt what kind of mood they were in. I needed to assert myself quickly.

"Take me immediately to Herr Falke—there is no time for delay!" I shouted in German, loud enough for the whole household to hear.

"Quiet, please," said the one with a blond crewcut, "you must explain yourself more fully before it will be possible to awaken Herr Falke."

"The information I bring is much too sensitive to share with you or your comrade unless specifically authorized by your employer...do you understand!"

"I'm sorry, we cannot allow you to enter without assurances as to who you are and what your business is...especially why there is such urgency attached to it."

"Very well, tell Herr Falke you have turned away an associate of Herr Werner of Berlin and in consequence both his safety and that of a particular set of his possessions are at terrible risk!" And with that I turned around and stepped towards the car.

"Let him in!" ordered a slightly built man in a robe standing at the open front door.

"Yes, Herr Falke," said the blond as he stepped aside and motioned to the guy with the shaved head to do likewise.

I followed the man into the villa. Lights' had been turned on in what appeared to be a kind of parlor, but one with floor-to-ceiling glass around more than half its circumference. One of the sections of glass had been opened, allowing the sound of the wash of tidal action against rocks below to enter the room.

"So, what is it that requires you to fly all the way from Berlin and awaken me in the middle of the night, eh?"

"Herr Falke, my name is Wilhelm Kirche. I am an associate of Herr Werner and was instructed by him to come directly here. I apologize for the intrusion but those were my orders."

"Well, I must say you have followed them to the letter, Herr Kirche. But now that you are here and you have my attention perhaps you would be good enough to tell me what it is that has brought you here."

"I regret to inform you, sir, that there was an attack on your Geneva residence earlier this evening. The security guard provided by Herr Werner—the man named Hans—has been killed and another of our associates—a woman—was seriously wounded."

"This happened at my residence? Why wasn't I informed immediately! Why didn't someone call?"

"The police have not permitted any of your staff access to the residence and no information of the events has yet been made available to the public. Except for Herr Werner and the police no one knows what has transpired...no one, that is, except for the freelance American agent and his associates...the ones who perpetrated the attack."

"You mean the man who Herr Werner warned me about...the one attempting to recover the paintings?"

"Yes, that one."

"But why didn't Herr Werner simply call me?"

"Herr Werner is unfortunately under tight police surveillance owing to his arrest and release yesterday in connection with a homicide in Berlin. He suspects any phone calls he makes are monitored and did not wish to arouse any curiosity among the authorities regarding you and your dealings with him. I'm sure you understand."

"Yes, yes that makes sense...but why haven't the police contacted me? Surely, they would have ways of learning where I am."

"One would think so, Herr Falke, but it seems you are being looked for in and around the city of Geneva. I suppose at some point they'll realize you've left the country and will take measures to locate you that will eventually prove fruitful."

"I see," he said.

After a pause to allow Falke to give the matter some thought, I added: "Herr Werner felt that it would perhaps be wise to take advantage of the interim to arrange for the further concealment of the paintings before the authorities become involved."

"But what interest would they have in the paintings?" asked Falke, somewhat alarmed.

"Unfortunately, the man killed in Berlin was a well-known art restorer from Chicago...the very man who supplied the syndicate critical information making the acquisition of the Impressionist paintings possible. Herr Werner worries that even the most remote possibility of the authorities connecting you to the events in Berlin and in Chicago must be taken seriously."

"And he believes the presence of the paintings...that is, should they be found in my possession..."

"Precisely, Herr Falke, and there is another danger: there is the very real possibility this American agent somehow learned of your Sardinian villa and has concluded the paintings have been taken there. Given what he and his associates have already done it would seem prudent to anticipate the possibility they would attempt to take the villa by force in their search for the paintings."

"This is outrageous!" exclaimed Falke as he paced the room. "Where am I expected to put them? Does Herr Werner appreciate how much he has compromised me?"

"He does, Herr Falke, and that is precisely why he commissioned me to fly directly here. It is his opinion that the paintings would be less of a problem if he were to assume full responsibility for their safekeeping. With them out of your possession there would be no possible connection between you and the unpleasant events that have recently taken place. Once these matters are settled he would promptly return the paintings."

"That doesn't make sense! It is he who's under surveillance not I!"

"Yes, but I'm not. And as a long time employee of the syndicate there have been other occasions when I've been asked to perform such a service…to protect the interests of a client."

"Where would you take them?"

"That I'm afraid I couldn't divulge, Herr Falke. "But be assured the repository is entirely suitable for art of such caliber and is secure. Herr Werner's reputation would demand no less as I'm sure you would agree."

"But what about that headstrong American? He could barge in here at any time, not realizing the paintings have been taken elsewhere."

"Yes, that is true, and in such an eventuality the important thing is for you not to be endangered. Herr Werner would suggest you secure an invitation on a friend's yacht…perhaps a cruise of a week or so. If the American shows up your security staff can deal with him—together of course with the assistance of the Italian police. It would be fitting if he ends up in custody."

Falke continued pacing, trying to think through his alternatives. Neither he nor his two security men seemed to focus on me directly—preoccupied as they were with the distressing news I'd conveyed. I stood attentively, my hands clasped together at my waist, my expression earnest and concerned. Finally, Falke seemed to make up his mind.

"Very well, Herr Kirche, we'll do as Herr Werner recommends. You are ready, yes, to take possession of the paintings at this time?"

"I am, sir. I have a private jet on standby at the airport and my driver is just outside. If your assistants would be so kind as to place the paintings in the back seat I can promise you they will be off the island in less than an hour."

"What documentation will be provided to assure me the paintings are in Herr Werner's possession and will be returned when requested?"

"You must understand, Herr Falke, such a document should it be discovered would be just as dangerous to you as the paintings themselves. But Herr Werner has anticipated your concern and instructed me to assure you that he will at the very earliest opportunity communicate with you personally and assure you of his commitment to safeguard the paintings as well as to protect your good name."

Falke nodded, accepting the merit of this line of reasoning, then he turned to me and said: "Please wait here, Herr Kirche, it will only be a moment." With that, he signaled his two security men to follow him out of the room. I hesitated to take a seat, not wanting to undermine my effort at presenting myself as a loyal subordinate who knew his place. Instead, I walked over to the open window and peered out. No lights were on and the night was still dark but I could catch just the barest hints of a sunrise on the horizon. My senses inevitably gravitated to the sounds of the waves lazily rolling up against the rocks below or playing out on the tiny cove beaches that lay on either side of the villa.

A short time later, Herr Falke returned, along with his two security men—both were carrying what appeared to be custom-fitted carrying bags each of which I imagined contained a single framed painting. They appeared to be well padded and to have a zipper along one of the long edges. Each also had strap handles for convenient transport.

"Here are the paintings, Herr Kirche," said Falke, pointing to the carrying bags, "I shall have them placed in your car."

"Yes, thank you, but if it wouldn't be too much trouble perhaps you would allow me to verify the contents of the bags…in your presence of course."

"Yes, of course," he said, motioning to the security men to place the carrying bags gently on the floor.

I knelt down and unzipped the first bag. Holding it wide open I was able to inspect the painting—it was the Renoir portrait from the Chicago collection. I zipped the bag up and turned to the second bag, verifying that it contained another of the Arnold Walker paintings. I repeated the procedure for all six carrying bags and satisfied myself that the six paintings stolen from the

Walker home in Chicago comprised the contents of the bags that lay before me.

"Everything seems to be in order, Herr Falke," I said, standing up. "You may instruct your men to place the bags in my car."

"But how do you know the identity of these paintings, Herr Kirche? Somehow I cannot believe you were a party to their transit through Berlin."

"No, I was not, Herr Falke, but Herr Werner supplied me with photos of the paintings at the time he gave me my instructions… see here," I said, pulling out the envelope Emily Parsons had given me containing the photos of the missing paintings and hoping he would not examine them too closely—not knowing what technical detail might reveal them as having been produced in the United States. Fortunately, he merely glanced at the snapshots as I fanned them out—like a hand of cards—before turning his attention back to his men and signaling them to pick up the bags.

"I won't accompany you out to the car, Herr Kirche, it is rather late and a man of my age needs his rest…you understand."

"Yes, of course, Herr Falke," I said, shaking his hand. "It has been an honor to meet you, and please be assured the paintings will be well looked after." With that said, I followed the two security men out the front door.

The old Sardinian was holding the rear door open as we approached the car. The padding was thick enough it was possible to rest the bags one on top of the other, forming two stacks of three across the back seat. Once this was done, I thanked the two men and climbed in beside the driver.

"Back to the airport?" asked the Sardinian, as he started up the car and put it in gear.

"Yes, and as quickly as possible," I replied as I looked back at the two security men who stood in the driveway watching as our car climbed up the hill towards the electrified entrance gate. I let out a sigh of relief as we passed through the gate, having feared some nagging doubt might have prompted Falke to detain us by shutting the gate. Still, as long as I was on the island there was a danger I'd be intercepted—either by a pursuit vehicle or by agents based in town who would be waiting at the airport. That couldn't be helped, I thought to myself, and I'd just have to deal with it. With that thought in mind I twisted around in my seat and placed a hand on the carrying bag closest to my fingers, reassuring myself the con had actually worked!

* * *

We hadn't gone more than ten miles before the rapidly accelerating headlights of a pursuing vehicle caught my attention. "Pull over… quickly!" I shouted.

"But why, signore?"

"Men with guns are after us…you need to get out of the car and find somewhere to hide."

"But my car?"

"Do it now!"

The old Sardinian did as instructed, pulling off to the side of the narrow road and bringing the car to a halt."

"Now run…quickly!"

"Yes, signore," he said as he opened his door and climbed out. "I will be up there," he added as he began to clamber up the steep slope above where the car had come to a halt.

I watched him as he struggled to advance towards a cluster of small oak trees about sixty meters from the roadway. Satisfied he'd found a place of concealment I turned my attention back onto the road just as a large sedan came to a screeching halt right in front of the taxi, blocking any attempt on our part to make a fast getaway. I was standing at the rear of the taxi, using it as a protective screen as Falke's two security men jumped out of the other car, their guns drawn.

"Come forward—your hands up where we can see them!" shouted the blond-haired guy.

"Can't do that, pal, and I wouldn't advise you to come any closer—I'm armed."

The two security men quickly sought cover by crouching low in front of the taxi. "You have no escape…there are two of us!" shouted the blond-haired guy.

Just then, the guy with the shaved head jumped away from the taxi and fired a shot that angled down—across the trunk of the taxi—clearly hoping to pick me off as I crouched close to the bumper.

I responded quickly, leaning out from the rear of the taxi— one hand holding the bumper for stability—and letting loose one shot that hit him as he scrambled for cover.

"Stop it, all of you!" yelled a third figure just emerging from the large sedan. It was Herr Falke, now dressed and looking quite distinguished. I hadn't paid much attention to him earlier—just an unkempt, slightly built old man with thinning gray hair and closely-trimmed beard. "Herr Kirche...if that is your name...I've just been made aware of the fact that you're an imposter!"

"I suppose you've been in touch with Herr Werner," I said.

"Yes. I thought it advisable to phone him once you'd left... something about you made me a little uneasy—I think it was the rather distinctive American way you held yourself...not at all German."

"Well, it's a pity. I was rather pleased with my performance."

"Enough sarcasm, Herr Kirche, I will have my paintings back...now!"

"Herr Falke, everything I said to you regarding the threats you face—from both me and the police—were absolutely true. Your identity is now known, your possession of six illegally obtained paintings would be of considerable interest to Interpol, your connection—however circumstantial—with the murder of Herr Bettledorf would I'm sure be of interest to the Berlin Stadtpolizei, and I'm sure the Geneva police would like to know the reason a paid assassin—Hans—was in your residence the night he died. All of this will come out should you insist on holding on to the paintings. A prudent man would acknowledge he's lost the advantage and would gracefully retire...perhaps to acquire other art in a less hazardous manner."

"Ah, but all such threats require you to be in a position to make this happen, Herr Kirche. Should you not survive...well then..."

"Don't flatter yourself that your two security men will prevail, Herr Falke, and do take into consideration the very real possibility you yourself might incur serious injury should matters get out of hand."

I watched as Falke bent over to examine the wound of the guy with the shaved head and to converse with the blond-haired one. Eventually, he stood up.

"You seem to have disabled one of my men…that places me at something of a disadvantage."

"Let me make it very easy for you, Herr Falke, consider this simply as a business transaction…one where your supplier failed to deliver the merchandise as promised—the supplier being Herr Werner. I would imagine you're a sufficiently good customer the syndicate will want to reimburse all the money you've put towards this unfortunate acquisition so as to be assured of your future business…and to avoid the unpleasant prospect of having you spread the word regarding their ineptitude in this matter."

"I see your point," replied Falke, "does this mean you'll refrain from alerting the authorities should I leave the paintings with you?"

"What would there be to alert them about?" I countered. "The paintings would have been safely returned to their proper owners…I imagine the police would simply regard you as someone naively duped into believing Herr Werner and his associates when they claimed to be able to legally secure paintings that were patently not available. No, I think your worries would be over, Herr Falke. My only concern is to return the paintings—that's what I'm paid to do."

"Very well," said Falke, "we'll be on our way…but I must say, Herr Kirche, you've proved to be a most persistent adversary. I do hope there won't be another occasion where our paths cross."

"The solution is rather simple, Herr Falke, in the future try to acquire artworks using the wealth you so obviously possess…and stop dealing with people like the notorious Herr Werner."

He waved dismissively and signaled for his two security men to return to the car. The uninjured one climbed behind the wheel while the guy with the shaved head limped over and climbed in beside him. Falke settled into the rear.

Once Falke's car sped off the old Sardinian made his way back to the road.

"Did they shoot my car?" he asked as I took his hand and helped him down the steep earthen bank.

"No, the shots were not meant for the car…you'll find everything's all right. Now, can we resume our journey or do you insist on inspecting the car's body for bullet holes?"

He just grunted and shuffled over to the door on the driver's side, opened it and climbed in. I followed suit.

"What did they want?" he asked as he pulled the car back onto the road and slowly began to accelerate.

"A misunderstanding…that's all—nothing to worry about," I said, trying to allay his fears and get him to focus on the business at hand.

"Crazy people…these rich ones," he growled.

"How soon will we reach the airport?" I asked, making another stab at getting his mind off the shooting.

"Soon, signore…and not a minute too soon—I tell you!"

I ignored his outburst and thought about the incident. Was Falke's acquiescence too precipitous? Was he planning on a more successful interception at the airport? It would make sense, especially if he could mobilize a larger team. I pulled out my cell phone and punched in Johnson's cell number—the one he gave me just before I left the plane.

"Johnson? Church here. My ETA is about ten minutes from now. Have Captain Jeffries get the plane ready for an instant takeoff—engines warmed up, flight plan filed, the whole works."

"Will do, Mr. Church. Ah…is anything wrong?"

"Yeah, I've got an angry client whose temper may lead him to do something real foolish…it wouldn't hurt to alert the police… maybe get them to be real visible at the airport."

"Roger that!" said Johnson just before I disconnected.

* * *

Sure enough, as we approached the taxi rank at the airport I could see a group of about five men being rousted by two uniformed members of the Polizi de Stato.

"Don't park here!" I shouted in Italian. "Drive onto the tarmac…where the planes are parked!"

"It is against the law, signore, they will fine me!"

"I'll make it worth your while…just do it!"

Grumbling to himself, the old Sardinian swerved away from the taxi rank and jumped a curb as he headed for the side of the terminal. The group of men seemed to sense what was happening and pulled out their guns. As four of the men began to run after us, one remained behind—his gun leveled at the two disarmed policemen whose hands were held above their heads.

"Hurry!" I shouted.

"Yes, signore!" he replied—his eyes fixed on the image in his rearview mirror of the four men with guns in pursuit.

We made it around the building and out onto the tarmac.

"Head for that plane with its engines and lights on!" I shouted, pointing to the jet—now no more than about seventy-five yards away. I could see Johnson at the foot of the steps. The old Sardinian closed the distance fast and pulled to a screeching stop right in front of Johnson.

"Keep the motor running," I shouted as I leaped from the car and flung open the back door. "Johnson, get these bags into the cabin!"

I lifted two of the bags out from the back seat and handed them to Johnson. "Handle them carefully, but hurry!"

"Will do, Mr. Church," he said, taking a good grip on the bags and starting up the stairs.

The four men were closing in on us, their guns clearly visible. I unholstered my semi-automatic, assumed a precision shooting stance and began to fire. I dropped two of them before they had time to react. The remaining two let off a couple of wild shots then scattered—anxious to find cover among the other parked planes. I continued to lay down a field of fire as Johnson hurried to unload the rest of the paintings.

The gunshots brought out other police from the terminal building. As they approached, the two unhurt attackers ran for the side of the terminal, hoping to make it back to their car before being apprehended. The two wounded men pushed their weapons away, signaling their willingness to give up. I holstered my weapon and walked over to the open driver's side window of the taxi.

"Here," I said, handing the old Sardinian a thick wad of Euros, "this should more than make up for the excitement I caused you this night. Now, get out of here before the police haul you in for trespassing on airport grounds."

"Yes, signore, and thank you," he said, pocketing the money. "But call someone else next time you come to the island!" With that said, he put the old taxi in gear and backed the vehicle away from the approaching police, turned, then sped off towards the side of the terminal building.

"What's going on?" demanded the first policeman to reach me.

"A kidnapping attempt, officer. These men and their companions chased my driver and me in their car, forcing us to drive right up to my plane in hopes we could escape. I should hurry, officer, these men have disarmed two of your policemen and are holding them out near the taxi rank. They are in great danger!"

Without another word to me, the policeman and several others ran towards the side of the building in pursuit, shouting to each other to hurry.

"All six bags are safely stowed in the cabin, Mr. Church," said Johnson from the open fuselage door. You ready to take off?"

"Yeah, let's get out of here before those cops get back," I said, running up the boarding steps.

Johnson retracted the stairs, secured the fuselage door and headed for his seat in the cockpit. Jeffries released the brakes and began to taxi the plane out onto the apron. I plopped down in the closest seat, fastened the seat belt and kept my fingers crossed the control tower wouldn't order Jeffries to stand down.

Apparently, the traffic controller had not been apprised of the gun battle and gave Jeffries the green light to take off. With no planes in the queue besides ours, Jeffries was able to swing into position, ramp up speed, barrel down the runway and lift off without any further need for communication with the control tower. Minutes later, the craft was out over the Mediterranean, heading for home.

While still high on adrenaline I pulled out the satellite phone Johnson had placed in the seat pocket and punched in Sanderson's home number, realizing that on the East Coast it would be late at night and the office would be closed.

"Yeah? Who is this?" said a sleepy voice.

"It's Church…you up to receiving a brief progress report?"

"No. Jesus Christ, Church, send me an email. Why the hell call up in the middle of the night to give me a progress report?"

"Even if the report ends with 'Mission Accomplished'."

"You're kidding! You got the paintings?"

"They're stacked up right behind me in nice custom-made carrying bags, compliments of our European adversaries."

"And where the hell are you?"

"On that executive jet you're paying big bucks for—high over the Med and heading home."

"Goddamn, that's great!"

"So, old buddy, get yourself dressed and hop on a plane. I'll need you at Chicago's Midway Airport no later than eight-thirty tomorrow morning Chicago time…you got that? Oh, and roust Emily out of bed and get her over there as well—I promised her I'd let her take the credit for personally handing the paintings back to the Walkers."

"Ah, you're such a generous soul!

"Remember that when I send you my bill."

"Any complications I should know about?"

"Nothing I can't handle, but just remember I'm counting on you to grease the way through customs when I declare these paintings."

"Yeah, I get you…so I suppose I'll have to wait until Chicago to hear all the gory details."

It'll be better for your digestion…I promise you."

"So you say."

I broke the connection and this time punched in Inspector Bleibtreu's number. All I had was his office number and at this hour all I'd get is his voicemail but that's really all I wanted—not anxious to have him press for details. As soon as I was connected to his voicemail I started in: "Inspector Bleibtreu, this is William Church. I'm happy to report I was able to take possession of the six paintings at about four-thirty this morning, Berlin time. They all appear to be undamaged and are currently en route to the United States. Thanks for your many courtesies during my stay in Berlin." I hung up and returned the phone to the seat pocket. He'd probably like a whole lot more information but was savvy enough to realize I'd be reluctant to supply it.

The plane was still on an upward trajectory so I settled back and waited.

Once we reached cruising altitude I unbuckled my seatbelt, stood up and moved over to the small galley. Sure enough, Johnson had stocked the bar with a bottle of high quality gin, good Italian vermouth and a fresh lemon. I made myself a large, ice-cold martini and returned to my seat. As I sat there enjoying the chilled beverage I tried to puzzle out how Falke had sufficient time to arrange the airport take down after the failed attempt on the road. Ten minutes simply wasn't enough time. Then it came to me: Falke had planned the airport encounter while still at the villa. He wasn't counting on the high speed pursuit to do any more than recover the paintings—my death, presumably in the context of a kidnapping gone awry, was the actual objective of those five guys at the airport. Hell, they may not have even known about the paintings. I smiled as I realized my story to the police at the airport—about my being the victim of an attempted kidnapping—would unwittingly probably be corroborated by the guys the cops apprehended.

Relieved that there didn't seem to be any loose ends in my romp through Europe I settled back and let the martini do its work. The sun was now well above the horizon and bright rays of light poured through the windows of the cabin. I reached up and pulled down the window shade next to my seat. In no time at all I was fast asleep.

DAY 12

"WAKE UP, MR. CHURCH," said Officer Johnson as he gently shook my shoulder, "we're about an hour out from Midway...thought you'd like some time to freshen up and maybe eat something."

"Yeah, good idea," I said, shielding my eyes from the glare of sunlight. It seems Johnson had taken it upon himself to raise all the shades in the cabin, letting in an abundance of early morning sunlight. "What time is it...stateside?" I asked.

"It's eight-thirty in the morning East Coast time," said Johnson. "While you freshen up I'll put together a breakfast tray."

"Make sure it's got something I can get my teeth into—I'm starved!"

"How about steak and scrambled eggs?"

"Just what the doctor ordered," I said as I rose from my seat and stretched.

I stripped off my shirt, tie and suit pants, pulled my toiletry kit from out of the smaller of my two bags and headed for the small cabin lavatory. Twenty minutes later, freshly shaved and hand washed, I pulled out from my larger bag a pair of jeans and a fresh shirt. By the time I'd dressed and stowed the old clothing Johnson had my tray ready.

I sat down, slid the tray table over my legs and leaned back, giving him plenty of room to place the tray down, together with a carafe of black coffee and a tall glass of freshly squeezed orange juice.

"Looks like Chelsea spilled the beans on my mania for fresh juice," I said, looking up at him.

"Yes, sir, she did make that point rather energetically."

I dug into the eight-ounce filet and scrambled eggs with relish.

* * *

We touched down at Midway Airport close to nine o'clock in the morning Chicago time. Jeffries taxied the plane over to the General Aviation Terminal and shut down the engines. Both he and Johnson emerged from the cockpit and joined me in the cabin.

"We're to wait here for customs and passport control," said Jeffries as he headed over to the galley and poured himself a cup of coffee.

Johnson went over to the fuselage door, unlocked it and slid it out of the way. He then hit the button activating the hydraulics that extended the boarding stairs. "You plan on getting off here?" he asked me once he'd returned to where Jeffries and I were standing.

"Why, do I have an alternative?" I asked.

"Well, we've got a charter originating out of Los Angeles later today," said Jeffries, "Johnson and I thought maybe you'd like to hitch a ride out West with us seeing as you're based in San Francisco."

"Any chance you can route yourselves through SFO?" I asked.

"Don't see why not," said Jeffries, "especially if your corporate sponsor is willing to pick up the extra cost…shouldn't be much I don't imagine."

"Let me touch base with the company rep…but hell yes I'd like a lift—no doubt about it," I said, taking another sip of coffee.

Moments later, a team from the International Arrivals concourse boarded the plane to inspect documents and whatever items we were declaring. Guy Sanderson was with them.

"Hey, Church, good to have you back!" he said, shaking my hand. "The flight okay?"

"Yeah. Listen, Guy, this here is Captain Jeffries and this other fellow is Officer Johnson. They've taken real good care of me… thought you'd like to meet them."

"It's my pleasure, gentlemen," said Guy, shaking hands with each of them. "Thanks for helping out. You can tell your supervisor we'll definitely keep your outfit in mind next time we need to secure a charter."

"They've also offered to let me hitch a ride out West providing the insurance company agrees to pick up the tab for dropping me off at the airport in San Francisco."

"That right, Captain Jeffries?" asked Sanderson.

"Yes, sir," replied Jeffries.

"Well, I'll certainly authorize it if that's what you want, Church, but I thought you'd want to accompany Emily when she delivers the paintings back to the Walkers."

"No, I'm thinking my job ends with the handover to you and Emily. Anyway, she's the lead operative here in Chicago and I'd just as soon let her get full visibility."

"Suit yourself," said Sanderson, "Okay, Captain Jeffries, you're hereby authorized to drop off our friend here at SFO."

"Glad to hear it, sir, he's kind of grown on us…don't have too many charters that involve the kind of excitement that Mr. Church seems to generate in the course of his work."

"Tell me about it," said Guy, "I swear, he'll drive a guy to drink with all his close calls. You're just lucky to have avoided being in the line of fire."

"Well, actually, sir, we were in the line of fire…at the airport in Sardinia—but Mr. Church handled the situation before it really turned ugly."

"Jesus, Church, what the hell were you doing in Sardinia?"

"I'll give you a rundown over coffee while these guys get the plane serviced."

"You've probably got a good hour, Mr. Church," said Jeffries. "I'll send Johnson to get you when we're ready to depart."

"Thanks, Jeffries," I said, turning my attention towards the rear of the cabin where I could see the boarding team talking with Johnson.

"Will there be any difficulty in getting the paintings through customs?" I asked, looking over at the customs officer who was inspecting each of the paintings.

"I've already explained the special circumstances of the paintings," said Guy. "They're okay with it, and once they've verified these are the paintings stolen from the Walker home they'll give us the green light to take them into the terminal."

A short time later, Sanderson, Johnson and I carried the paintings from the plane to the terminal. As we walked through the door Emily walked over. She was wearing one of the outfits she'd purchased during our earlier trip to Chicago—the one consisting of a black sleeve-jacket, white knit top and gray pencil skirt. I placed the two paintings I was carrying onto a nearby seat and gave her a quick embrace.

"So, Church, You pulled it off...and you're still in one piece I see, looking him over carefully.

"Yep, still good as new, and you're looking just as gorgeous as ever." I said with a smile. Johnson and Sanderson stood nearby, a little impatient to move things along.

"Okay, Emily, they're all yours," said Sanderson, pointing to the six carrying bags containing the paintings.

"What? Oh, yes," she said, absentmindedly—trying to regain her professional pose.

"Let's get them into your rental car so you can be on your way," said Guy, trying to deflect the awkwardness of the situation.

"Yes...yes, of course," she replied as she busily reached for one of the carrying bags I'd place on the chair. "Will you be accompanying me?" she asked.

"No, Emily," I replied, "I'm catching a ride to the West Coast with the charter jet. Anyway, I thought it best if you handled it alone...you know, as principal company rep in this case."

"What about you, Guy?"

"Church is right, Emily, you can handle it. This way you'll have a good customer singing your praises—can't hurt from a career standpoint…am I right?"

"Very well, I can see I'm not going to get anywhere trying to change your minds," she said as she turned around and headed for the terminal's street exit. Sanderson, Johnson and I followed along behind.

Emily had parked her rental in the drop off area just outside the exit. It wasn't legal to leave the car unattended but she'd charmed the cop on duty, persuading him to cut her some slack given the importance of the pickup. We stowed all six paintings on the rear seat—two piles of three, just as in the taxi back in Sardinia. Emily watched carefully, trying to reassure herself the paintings would ride safely despite the potholes and erratic driving sometimes encountered on the city's streets.

"I'll meet you in the coffee shop," said Sanderson, sensing that I wanted a few moments to talk with Emily alone.

As Sanderson and Johnson headed towards the terminal I held the car door open for Emily.

"It's unfair," she complained, "I don't even have a chance to find out what happened in Europe. I'd hoped you would come with me so we could talk on the way."

"The plane is leaving in about an hour, Emily, there's no way I could help make the delivery and be back in time. Anyway, Guy will have all the gory details and can fill you in."

"But what about us? This doesn't give us any time to explore our feelings for one another…and I was counting on having an opportunity to wear that pretty evening dress I bought when we were here."

"I know, Emily, and I regret it, but the fact is I've been on the road for almost a week and really need to crash for a while. Listen, why don't you plan on coming to San Francisco when you've got a break in work …it'll give us an opportunity to spend lots of quality time together—some sailing, an escape to the wine country, lots of intimate dining…what do you say?"

"I'm not stupid, Church, I can recognize a brush-off when I hear it," she said with a smile as she turned the ignition key and started up the engine. "

"Don't take it that way," I said, "just rack it up to the fact we're two persons with complicated and busy lives. There's no one else in the picture so your feelings rank way up there in my estimation, but we can't always act on those feelings."

"Don't kid yourself, Church, you more than anyone else I know controls the circumstances of his life. If you wanted to brush everything else aside to spend time with me you would!"

There wasn't anything I could say to challenge her—she was right. All I could do is shrug my shoulders and back away from the car. She gave me a final look then hit the accelerator. I watched her drive away, wondering whether I'd just made a big mistake and hoping she'd let me make it up to her next time we were teamed together.

I walked back to the terminal and headed for the coffee shop.

* * *

Guy shoved a cup of coffee over to me as I sat down across from him. "So give me the scoop," he said, fixing me with a penetrating stare.

I gave him a rundown of the events beginning with my encounter with Herr Werner's two thugs on the way to Herr Reichwein's flat in Charlottenburg and ending with the shootout at the Olbia Airport in Sardinia. He listened intently, not interrupting, but once I'd finished he began to ask questions. Most were probing, trying to elicit details I'd chosen to suppress—like my full involvement with Beatrice or my role in the gunfire at the Swiss home of Herr Falke—but a few were the kind that remained unanswered even in my own mind. Probably the most perplexing was how Falke thought he could manage to recover the paintings at the airport after the shooting.

"He must have had a plan," said Guy, "or he wouldn't have let you drive away with the paintings."

"Not necessarily," I countered, "he knew with only one shooter available he stood a real risk of getting killed if the shooting continued. Even the paintings weren't worth taking that level of risk."

"You think he was able to get a call through to the gang at the airport once you'd driven off?" asked Guy.

"Possibly, but I think the most likely tactic on his part was to turn around and follow us at some distance as we made out way to the airport. If he timed it right he could pull up once I was subdued or shot and remove the paintings from the taxi without anyone noticing given all the attention being directed to the violence nearby."

"I sure in hell would have liked to have seen his reaction to the swarm of cops over the kidnap gang and the sight of your jet taking off with all the paintings," said Guy, leaning back in his chair with a big smile on his face.

"Would have been satisfying, I agree," I said, taking another sip of coffee.

Just then, Johnson came into the coffee shop and gave me a thumbs up. I nodded, letting him know I caught the signal. "Looks like the jet's ready to leave," I said, standing up.

"Well, you've sure earned whatever you'll be billing, Church, this recovery has saved the firm millions of dollars."

"Let's keep in touch," I said, shaking his hand, "I doubt this will be the last of the claims you'll need me to handle."

"Let's just hope they don't involve our notorious Herr Werner," said Guy more soberly.

"I kind of think my friend, Bleibtreu, will have him somewhat boxed in now that he's tied to the Betteldorf murder."

"Have a good flight," said Guy as I walked towards the exit.

I waved and pushed through the door.

* * *

As I walked to the plane I pulled out my cell phone and hit the fast dial for Chelsea. I figured she'd be on duty at the concierge desk right about now.

"Hey, Chelsea, it's me, Church.

"Church? What's up…you all right?"

"Fit as a fiddle…thought I'd give you a head's up—plan to be arriving at SFO later today."

"You get the paintings?"

"Yeah, they're being returned to the owners as we speak."

"Wow! Nice going! Anything I need to do?"

"Yeah, stock the fridge with a week's worth of oranges and give Jack a call…tell him I'd like to get out on the Bay tomorrow afternoon—when the winds pick up—and hope he can break free to join me."

"Will do…and while I've got you on the phone I need you to know I'll be expecting you at the performance tonight."

"What performance?"

"Jesus, Church, you've got a memory like a sieve—the premiere of the dance performance I'm in…you know, the one I've been rehearsing for weeks now."

"Yeah, of course, Chelsea…sorry—sure I'll be there."

"I'll have a ticket in your name set aside…just ask Julie for it, she'll be handling admission."

"Give me a hint, where's it going to be performed?"

"At that little theatre in the Mission where you attended the last dance concert…you remember."

"Oh, yeah, the one with the old movie theatre seats."

"That's the one."

"Well, I'd tell you to break a leg but considering the nature of the performance I'd guess that would be in real bad taste."

"Goodbye, Church."

"Yeah, see you tonight, Chelsea."

I broke the connection and climbed the boarding stairs. Jeffries had already warmed up the engines and Johnson was standing by to secure the craft for takeoff. I settled into the forward seat on the port side and looked out. The sky was clear—nothing like the overcast weather that had greeted Emily and me during our earlier visit. I could feel the craft moving as Jeffries began to taxi onto the apron.

"Our ETA once we're airborne should be around two o'clock California time," shouted Johnson through the open cockpit door...you okay?"

"Yeah, thanks," I replied, thinking of the two foot swells I'd be cutting through just east of the Golden Gate Bridge come that time tomorrow.

The End